INTO THE HIGH RANGES

INTO THE HIGH RANGES

THE PENGUIN BOOK OF

MOUNTAIN WRITINGS

EDITED BY RAVINA AGGARWAL

PENGUIN BOOKS

Penguin Books India (P) Ltd., 11 Community Centre, Panchsheel Park, New Delhi 110 017, India
Penguin Books Ltd., 80 Strand, London WC2R 0RL, UK
Penguin Putnam Inc., 375 Hudson Street, New York, NY 10014, USA
Penguin Books Australia Ltd., 250 Camberwell Road, Camberwell, Victoria 3124, Australia
Penguin Books Canada Ltd., 10 Alcorn Avenue, Suite 300, Toronto, Ontario M4V 3B2, Canada
Penguin Books (NZ) Ltd., Cnr Rosedale and Airborne Roads, Albany, Auckland, New Zealand
Penguin Books (South Africa) (Pty) Ltd., 24 Sturdee Avenue, Rosebank 2196, South Africa

First published by Penguin Books India 2002

This anthology copyright © Penguin Books India 2002
Introduction © Ravina Aggarwal 2002
The copyright for individual pieces vests with the authors or their estates.

Page 240 is an extension of the copyright page. While every effort has been made to trace copyright holders and obtain permission, this has not been possible in all cases; any omissions brought to our attention will be remedied in future editions.

Typeset in Sabon by Mantra Virtual Services, New Delhi
Printed at Thomson Press, Noida

CONTENTS

INTRODUCTION

This is not *that* kind of mountain book: the kind where globe-trotters pause to pose with simple natives and dharma junkies rhapsodize about glimpses of Shangri-La, where heroic mountaineers stand alone on Himalayan peaks and daring generals ambush enemies to save the country's crown, where trekkers moan about their incompetent guides and Sahibs lament that everything went downhill when the Raj ended. Those stories have their own following, I suppose; the essays and creative works in this anthology dislocate familiar routes to take an intimate detour through the high ranges. They are selected from a range of writings in the last decade that delve into the literature, history, culture and politics of India's varied mountainscapes.

The book opens with a series of journeys spanning the tropical jungles of the Western Ghats, the sandy deserts of the ancient Aravallis, and the icy ridges of the Himalayas, meditative passages through which the sojourner, setting out for the mountain's edge, gains a new perspective on life in the plains. The quest for such transforming experiences has beckoned travellers to mountains time and time again. During the colonial period, for instance, visitors from the West favoured mountains as spaces of seclusion and mystique waiting to be uncovered. Driven by a killing curiosity to the heights of exploration, some became prey, others masters in dangerous games of espionage and conquest. Some travellers arrived, their souls war-weary, scouring the hills to hunt down creatures of the wild, the bigger the game the better. For others, the mountains were for killing time, a retreat away from the heat of the plains, an escape from the shackles of their humdrum lives.

The narratives included here both acknowledge the legacy of such colonial longings and offer critical insights into their projects of discovery. They lead us to elusive trails along which the pilgrim retraces the sensual and literary landscapes of poets and thinkers whose imprints have radically altered the present. Predictable destinations have unusual travellers. There are sons, raised in the shadow of Everest, who cannot resist its call but recognize that reaching the summit, once deemed the ultimate act of masculine glory, is an obsession that demands a lofty price from families and communities bearing the burden of travel. And there are girls, restricted by gender and class from travelling for pleasure, whose forbidden fantasies of freedom beckon them to snowy mountains, which are often linked with romance, with scandal points, honeymoon spots, and love scenes in movies. Distant mountains hold the promise of realization, even if it is fleeting.

In addition to travel literature, this collection also contains reflections by several authors who view the mountains and hills as home. They describe homes that are built from the intricate labours of everyday life, herding pashmina goats in the Changthang plateau, delivering milk in the Mussoorie hills, cultivating tea on the terraced slopes of the Bhutan Dooars, preparing for school in the Ladakh ranges, organizing uprisings to support conservation in Tehri-Garhwal. Homes become realms of solace and healing, relived through the sounds and scents of Garhwali deodars, Nilgiri cliff goats, rock and roll tunes, and Pahari folk-songs.

Memories of home are not untainted, however; for some writers, they are tinged with the ache of innocence lost, a loss that is felt when one revisits the past and learns that cultural and historical barriers have rendered some groups invisible to the mainstream. Mountain communities continue to be dismissed as backward and uncivilized and local means of self-sufficiency are drastically affected by modern practices of development. In the name of development, forested lands are converted into plantations and factories, mountainsides are blasted for railways and highways, flowing rivers blocked for accommodating dams and tourist resorts, and systems of education introduced that make no room for ethnic and religious differences. Now, instead of quaint, winding memory lanes, the homebound trip is likely to occur on tarmac roads with snow-capped mountains painted on wayside markers that read, 'India is a Bouquet of Flowers, and Your Hometown a Rose in It.'

Perceptions of home are further complicated by characterizations of mountains as sturdy and impenetrable frontiers, defending the homeland from external intruders. This is an image that dates from maps made by the British, in which mountains were made to stand for lines of separation, and is all the more prevalent in contemporary conceptions, in which mountains have become symbols of India's boundary wars with Pakistan and China. While the national media celebrates the accomplishment of armies in strife-torn zones, the cost of protecting the frontiers has taken a heavy toll on border environments. And although contributions from non-Indian locales are beyond the scope of this volume, these words of Eqbal Ahmed, written after the 1998 nuclear tests in Pakistan, resonate closely with the Indian situation: 'I saw on television a picture more awesome than the familiar mushroom cloud of nuclear explosion. The mountain had turned white. I wondered how much pain had been felt by nature, God's most wondrous creation. The great mountain in Chagai will turn in time to solid ash! And we, who are so proud of our mountains?'

Today, due to feelings of alienation and dissatisfaction with the central government's programmes of assimilation, movements of resistance and insurgency are features of virtually every mountainous state on the border: Jammu and Kashmir, Nagaland, Manipur, Mizoram and Assam. Accordingly, the last segment of this anthology dwells on the violence and havoc wrought in regions where mountainsides are sprayed with blood and bullets. But authors also express the hope that peace and humanity will triumph despite the current discord. Writing of a place designated as the highest battlefield in the world, the mountaineer, Harish Kapadia, makes a wish that 'someday soon, there will be peace on the Siachen glacier. Roses (*sias*) will grow wild, ibexes will roam and mountaineers will explore and climb freely.'

As sites of conflict and displacement or domains of desire and belonging, as homes or locations away from home, mountains have invariably inspired writers. My own thoughts for this book benefited from discussions with Christopher Wheeler, Suzanne Zhang-Gottschang, Srirupa Roy, Mahesh Rangarajan, Vijay Prashad and Banu Subramaniam. I thank Kai Friese for getting me involved in this project, Kamini Mahadevan for her enthusiastic and persistent editorial support, and friends in Ladakh who taught me most of what I know about mountains.

Ravina Aggarwal

PART I

NEW JOURNEYS, OLD ROUTES

SABA DEWAN

IN SEARCH OF SNOW

New Delhi, 3 May 1996. On a hot summer evening, in a quiet
suburb of Delhi, twenty-five young voices rise again and yet
again to pay lusty homage to the sultry Paro—'*Kyaa adaa kyaa
jalwe tere Paro! Dil ke tukde ho gaye hazaaron*!' (Your style
and grace oh Paro, have shattered my heart into a thousand
pieces). Our bus is more than two hours late. The girls have
been waiting since afternoon when they trooped into the Action
India office, escorted by protective mothers and fathers and
brothers and uncles. After issuing last-minute instructions, the
relatives have finally left. The girls sing songs, eat peanuts and
'pass time'. '*Zara sa jhoom loon mein . . .*' (let me sway just a
bit . . .). Just how many film songs do they know? Enough, it
seems, to keep in good stead until finally the bus swerves in,
swirling vast amounts of dust, and a wild scramble begins to
get in first. Everyone wants to sit next to the window. Everyone
wants to sit with friends and at the last minute everyone feels
the need to use the lavatory, to wash up and to fill water bottles.
'Why didn't you think of this before the bus came?' we ask
them. 'What were you doing all this time? We are already late!'

SABA DEWAN did her masters in TV and Film Production from the Mass
Communication Research Centre, Jamia Millia Islamia, New Delhi in 1987
and since then has been making independent documentaries. Her work has
focused on communalism, gender and sexuality. She is also a visiting faculty
member at the Mass Communication Research Centre, Jamia Millia Islamia,
New Delhi.

'Please, please, please Didi, just wait a moment,' they beg. Hurry, hurry! Giggling, squealing, fighting, shouting, protesting, complaining, laughing and singing (that always), the bus finally begins its journey through the night to the distant snow-topped mountains in the Garhwal region of the Himalayas.

Kamlesh, sixteen years old, with a naughty face and twinkling eyes, gives a contented sigh and gazes out of the bus window as we speed through the night. Throughout the afternoon, she led the girls' singing and burst into spontaneous dance at the sight of the much-awaited bus. Kamlesh had wanted to come so very desperately and had been unsure until the last moment whether she would be allowed. In another three months, she will be engaged to the boy chosen by her parents and then no school, no stepping out of the house. Their community is very strict about these rules. The boy's parents have made this a condition of accepting her as a future daughter-in-law. It is a wonder that her parents have allowed Kamlesh to come for this trip at all, but then her mother always does find it difficult to say no to her.

In many respects, Kamlesh considers herself much luckier than most girls in her community who are married off when they are still children. Her parents braved community criticism and let her attend school till Class nine. But ever since her father got laid off from his factory job and had to make ends meet by selling vegetables, the pressure on the family to marry off the three daughters as soon as possible increased considerably. This is Kamlesh's last chance to have fun with friends and she is determined to make the most of it.

There are eight adults accompanying the twenty-five young travellers. Two women volunteers from Action India and six of us, the film crew, who will shoot a documentary on the girls' journey in search of snow over the next ten days. Six months ago, I had been invited by Action India to make a documentary around their project with adolescent girls from the 'resettlement colonies' of Delhi. These sprawling areas of political and civic neglect, inhabited almost exclusively by the poor, are a creation of the government's long-term drive to 'cleanse' the capital's centres of unseemly squalor through periodic demolitions of squatter slums by removing the poor to far-flung areas earmarked for 'resettlement'. During the Emergency period in 1975–77, about 15 per cent of the population of Delhi was displaced to the edges of the metropolis within fifteen months.

Since the late 1970s, Action India, a Delhi-based voluntary organization, has been mobilizing women from resettlement areas around issues related to gender equity, urban poverty, domestic violence, reproductive health, social justice and communalism. Over the years, the organization increasingly felt the need to address the needs of adolescent girls and young women of the area. Living in the shadow of much loved brothers, girls learn to make do with less from early on—with less food, less health care and much less with educational opportunity. Most of them transit from infancy to adulthood as apprentices to their hard-working mothers.

Action India began working with groups of adolescent girls around issues of their status, education, health, sexuality and opportunities. It was these different groups of girls, aged between twelve and twenty, whom I met over a period of six months. Through workshops, one-to-one interactions and mutual observation, we forged a relationship based on sharing our experiences of life, our hopes and dreams. They had rainbow dreams. They dreamed of finishing school, of attending college, pursuing careers, of boys and romance. Strange new yearnings and desires shimmered in these dreams. They dreamed of fun and laughter away from closed-in homes and restricting rules. They dreamed of lands far away, of new people, new customs. Most of all they dreamed of the mountains, and high peaks and snow: white, soft snow which they had seen only in popular Hindi films. In their dreams, they wore diaphanous chiffon saris and romanced brazenly in the snow; taboo dreams not meant for girls like them.

Action India was receptive to my proposal that we take the girls for a trek to the mountains, an activity usually the preserve of middle-class school children during their summer vacations. The organization garnered additional funds, made the necessary arrangements with trekking clubs, bought woollens and shoes and rucksacks and water bottles for the young travellers. Its most challenging task, however, was to convince anxious mothers and hesitant fathers to let their daughters go off for ten days to distant mountains unescorted by family members.

'But you must understand that our girl stays at home, she has never been out. We may be poor but we are respectable people. We don't let our daughters loiter outside.'

Vimla, fourteen years old, stares unblinking at the television that is always switched on in her one-room house. She does not once allow herself to look at either her parents or me as we try and negotiate permission for her to come for the trek. She had sent me several frantic messages to come and speak with her parents on her behalf. 'When adults speak, what is the need for the children to say anything!' asks her mother rhetorically. Both she and her husband work twelve hours a day on construction sites as skilled labour. Vimla, the eldest, had to leave school in Class six to take care of the house and her two younger brothers who go to school. Only on rare occasions does she find the time to attend the Action India meetings with the other girls. Her day begins at 5 a.m. when she helps her mother to quickly prepare the food that her parents take with them to work. Then she gets her brothers ready for school and feeds them breakfast. Once everyone has left, Vimla does the dishes, washes clothes and cleans the house. The television is her constant companion. By late afternoon, her brothers get back and she gives them their lunch. Then it is time to buy vegetables for the evening dinner. It is Vimla's only outing for the day and she cherishes it.

She is careful not to take more than half an hour over her shopping lest her brothers report it to her parents. Then back to getting dinner done, boiling tea for her exhausted parents and more television. Her parents say they cannot let her go on this trek and that is final. As I step out, Vimla whispers in my ear, 'Didi, I want to come too. I really want to see snow.'

Kalyani, Uttarkashi, 4 May. The roar of a mountain river, clear, fast-moving, and young, echoes through the narrow valley, dense with conifers and ringed with distant snow-capped peaks. The song of a hundred birds rises and falls and merges with the chittering of thousands upon thousands of invisible grasshoppers. And silence. Silence so profound that it hurts the ear. It is afternoon. The sun is a mellow gold tempered; the cool breeze laden with pine resins. After a hot, dusty and bumpy bus ride through the plains and up the foothills and across the mountains and down the valleys we have finally arrived at Kalyani, a small hamlet fifteen kilometres from the town of Uttarkashi and our base camp for the trek to Dhodi Taal. Since none of the girls has any experience of the mountains, we will spend two initial days here, go for walks and climbs and get prepared for the longer trek ahead.

The girls are absorbed in painstakingly trying to count all the visible snow-capped peaks and identify the one they will reach at the end of the journey. 'It is too far, Didi, we will never manage to reach it. How will we ever climb such high mountains? What will the view be like from up there?' Some others in the group are busy inspecting their camping tents, collecting sleeping bags and letting out whoops of excitement at the sheer novelty of everything. 'Didi, look, just look how cosy the tent feels with all the flaps down! And, Didi, look at this bedding—it zips up like a bag and it's so soft!' I marvel at their energy. All of us, the adults, are exhausted by the long bus journey and just want to sit and drink our tea and rest. The girls have other plans for themselves. To their delight, they are invited to use the cricket kits that are kept for trekkers at the base camp.

Where did they learn to play cricket? During all my visits, I have not once seen the girls play outside their houses. Their only access to the outside is strictly regulated. Home to school and back. Home to the Action India centre and back. 'Didi, we are children! My mother says that I have grown up but I tell her I am a child.' I remember the girls' repeated attempts to claim childhood during my meetings with them. It had been in sharp contrast to my own memory of adolescence when there had been a great need to be identified as an adult and not as a child. Being grown-up had been full of exciting possibilities, anything could happen, be made to happen. For the teenage girls that I was interviewing, puberty had signalled the opposite: the closure of all possibilities. 'My mother does not allow me to wear skirts any more. I am not allowed to step outside the house alone, nor allowed to run around and play. There is work to be completed all the time. Didi, I was so much happier as a child. I wish I had never grown up!'

So when did they learn cricket? Braids are tucked under jaunty caps. Pads are tied on and ththuck! swings the bat against the ball. It rolls and tumbles down the sloping mountainside, chased by girls desperate to save a boundary. They have picked up the basics from countless television matches watched avidly by their brothers, and as for the rest, they are imaginative and enthusiastic. Victorious yells from the winners. Brave attempts at booing from the other side. The 'old boys' game' is reinvented by a group of working-class girls, out to make and break rules!

The gentle mountain breeze has now turned wild. It whistles aggressively down the narrow valley and whips the spiky conifers to break out in a frenzied dance. The scarves and towels that the girls had laid out on the grassy slope become restless and take off on their own in different directions. The sun deserts us and cricket is finally abandoned. Tired, the girls settle inside the snugness of their tents over sweet milky tea and hot pakoras. In the flickering candlelight with the wind raging outside, they share small rebellions that had profound consequences.

Neeraj, one of the oldest girls in the group, nineteen, savvy and sophisticated, talks of how she blackmailed her family into allowing her to come for the trek by threatening to electrocute herself. 'I love life. Of course, I was planning to do no such thing but my mother got very scared and convinced my brothers to let me go. I always do what I feel like. At the most people will say that I am a "bad" girl. Big deal! I don't bother with such talk. I just go ahead and have fun.' The other girls look at Neeraj with awe and fully aware of her heroine status, she tosses her hair and delicately nibbles at her pakora.

Puari, 6 May. The morning at Kalyani had brought heartbreak. Just before we were to start off for Puari, our instructor, an earnest young man, had firmly announced that each girl could take only two sets of clothes on the trek. Gauzy scarves, flimsy kurtas, billowing shalwars, sequined shararas, clothes borrowed and begged of sisters, cousins, neighbours, to be worn when the girls would play in the snow (film stars dressed like this in films, didn't they) would have to be left behind at the store in Kalyani. Were they here to go on a trek or take part in a fashion show? They have a long tough trek ahead and their rucksacks ought to be as light as possible.

Tears, protests, mutiny. They would wear what they pleased. Who was this fellow to say anything? They had come for a holiday not to look like frightful frumps. More heartbreak when no support was forthcoming from the accompanying adults. The girls sighed and unpacked and looked pained. Not all dreams were put away so easily, however. Deep inside the

rucksacks were kept hidden lipstick and kohl, mascara and face
powder, pins and ribbons and combs that would be whipped out
every morning during the trek and put to good use. OK! So they
would wear boring clothes and shoes but at least their faces
would be those of film stars!

Neither was the earnest trek instructor easily forgiven.
Revenge was claimed as soon as we began our climb towards
Puari. Each instruction was greeted with adolescent giggles, some
high-pitched, others full-throated, but all devastating in their
capacity to unnerve. I felt rather sorry for the increasingly
embarrassed young man who walked silently ahead, having
abandoned his earlier attempts to enforce discipline. Not that
his mutinous wards had much energy left to giggle after their
initial display of spirit. The climb from Kalyani to Puari is across
the river and up a thick forest, dark and lovely and steep and
endless. For first-time mountain climbers, from the city
especially, it proves to be exhausting. This is not at all how
they had imagined themselves in the mountains! 'How much
more to go, Didi? Please let's sit down! My legs are giving way!'
Sweat pours down, smudging kohl and lipstick. Red, yellow,
blue ribbons droop and painstakingly creased trousers borrowed
from obliging brothers or cousins look crumpled. But they are
past caring about film-star looks. 'Oh dear sisters, my mother
must be imagining her daughter playing in paradise. She would
never dream that her poor daughter is walking through the fires
of hell! This, I swear, is my first and last journey to the
mountains.'

Shehnaaz does not join in the chorus of complaints. A small
girl, looking even younger than her twelve years, she walks
quietly with determined surefootedness. Nicknamed 'Sharmilee'
(the shy one) by the group, Shehnaaz hardly ever speaks. Even
during my initial meetings with the girls, her instinctive reaction
would be to cover her face whenever she was asked a question.
Therefore, I had been rather surprised when she had softly

murmured that she too wanted to come for the trek. But how would that be possible?

Shehnaaz's father had deserted her mother, grandmother and four other siblings just when the family reached Delhi from their village in Bengal. Her mother, elder sister and Shehnaaz work as domestic labourers to run the family. She washes dishes and sweeps the floors in four middle-class homes. She starts early in the morning and gets done by afternoon. Then she attends the informal classes run by Action India. Going for the trek meant taking an 'off' from work for ten days and she couldn't take the risk of doing that. She would lose her jobs—that was certain. Just when there seemed no way out, Shehnaaz's sister, just two years older, volunteered to take on her work as well, even though she herself worked in five houses. Shehnaaz could make her journey in search of snow.

It is late afternoon when we finally reach Puari. High up in the mountains is a gently undulating meadow, all soft and velvety and green, smudged with hundreds of small mountain flowers, violet and blue and pink and white. After the climb through dark forest paths, it feels as if we have landed on the roof of the world. Snow-topped peaks flank Puari on one side, and on the other are green, dense forests through which we had made our way up. A hush falls on our group. Shehnaaz lets out a long sigh of pleasure and shuts her eyes for a moment. Then she smiles, looks at me, and says, 'Didi, this is the most beautiful place on earth.'

There is cool lemonade waiting for the tired girls, followed by tea and hot bread pakoras. There is a flurry of activity. We are ordered to get our camera ready. The girls really want to be photographed in Puari. Families back home have to be shown the beauty they have witnessed. There is a bonfire at night. Orange and red flames dispel the darkness and the meadow resonates with young voices singing songs of love and hope and dreams. *Isliye raah sangharsh ki hum chune zindagi aansoon*

mein nahaayi na ho (we have to tread the path of struggle so
that our lives do not remain drenched in tears . . .).

Bhewra, 7 May. Next morning the walk from Puari to Bhewra
is relatively easy and short, without too many steep climbs or
descents. We pass through several villages on the way and the
group falls into easy conversation with curious local girls their
age, many of whom accompany us over quite a long distance.
Despite the language barrier, they are able to communicate with
each other and discover that they have much in common. Their
new friends too look after the home and their younger siblings
while their mothers go to work in the fields or walk long
distances in search of fuel and water. The fathers of many of
the girls have to work in faraway cities like Delhi. Most of
these girls have studied till primary levels in the local
government-run schools but then had to stop because middle-
and higher-level school education is available only in distant
Uttarkashi, where their brothers are sent, but not they.

I notice that Kamlesh, who all this while had been chattering
happily with her new friends, starts looking increasingly
troubled. Her usually cheerful face is drawn, her lips tremble.
'Didi, I don't want to go back to Delhi.' She clutches urgently
at my hand. 'I don't want to get married.' And she starts sobbing.
Over the past few months, Kamlesh has talked about the fun
she has in school and her desire to do well in studies. But she
has never in my presence questioned her parents' decision to
marry her off. What choice does she have if she refuses to get
married? 'I could finish school and get a job. I would like to do
that. Even on television they show that girls should be
independent. In our meetings too we talk about it—then how
can I just trot off like a docile cow and let myself be tied to the
nearest peg?' Hot words. And some colour comes back to her
face. What can she do to change her parents' decision, I ask

again. Kamlesh does not reply. It is a difficult question to answer immediately, especially for a sixteen-year-old girl. Loyalty towards parents is being weighed against new, heady ideas about freedom and independence. Kamlesh, I can see from her expression, is thinking, and for the moment our conversation ends.

We reach Bhewra by noon. Almost the entire area is terraced farmland with few forests in sight. Our campsite is almost completely surrounded by fields on all sides. There is no space to play or to wander around as in Kalyani and Puari. Understandably, the girls are quite disappointed. But only for a little while. Soon, I see them busy playing cards or carom or experimenting on each other's faces with make-up. Some others are using the spare time to mend their own and their friends' clothes. Many of the girls are busy warming water for much-needed baths. Hours slip by gently and quietly and, yes, happily.

Dinner, however, begins on a distinctly chaotic note. The camp volunteers are perhaps new to their work and take ages in getting the meal ready. When it is finally served, I face a near mutiny from my crew who declare the dal and vegetables to be unfit for human consumption and demand better fare after a hard day's labour. Some of the girls also join in the protest and there is an angry exchange between the guests and the camp staff. In the midst of the dinner, I see fourteen-year-old Sangeeta sobbing quietly in a corner. 'Didi, I am thinking of my baby brother back home. This is much better food than he must be getting in my absence.'

Sangeeta has lost both her parents over the last four years. Her mother died of tuberculosis and her father followed a few years later due to some undiagnosed illness, leaving behind Sangeeta and her seven-year-old brother. All that the children had to their names was their parents' small grocery shop that everyone assumed would be impossible for children to run. Sangeeta proved everyone wrong. With the help of some start-up capital from Action India, she runs the shop, looks after the accounts, makes monthly purchases and manages to continue her studies. She ensures that her young brother attends school regularly as well.

Sangeeta was persuaded by Action India volunteers to come for the trek and leave her brother in the care of their old grandmother, who lives with the children. The volunteers have promised to check on them regularly during her absence. Nevertheless, Sangeeta frets. Several times during the journey, I have seen her quietly tuck away the biscuits and sweets served to her to take back for her little brother. At fourteen, Sangeeta is already an adult.

Dhoditaal, 8 May. We start early next morning for Dhoditaal, our final destination in this trek. It is a long walk. From barren hillsides we walk into thick forests. The sky above is covered with a canopy of tall trees and the ground underneath is slippery with pine-needles and cones and leaves. Small but fast-flowing rivulets are crossed with shrieks of fear and excitement. Except for the birds, we hear nothing. An occasional cry, probably from a startled cow or horse, is immediately understood as the roar of a wild tiger or lion or bear and the girls shiver and hold hands and enjoy their fearful anticipation. We climb down mysterious valleys, miles upon miles of delicate bamboo maze, and then make our way up exhilarating hilltops scented with pine. The snow peaks now seem to be coming much closer.

Somewhere on the journey, the girls get separated from each other and a group loses its way. Since we always walk in batches of six or seven people, we are close to Dhoditaal when we realize that some of the girls are missing. Shehnaaz, Neeraj and Sangeeta are part of this group. We wait a while and then quickly decide that some girls should accompany Action India volunteers to Dhoditaal and inform the people at the camp about the mishap. Meanwhile, a few of the film crew start walking back in search of the missing girls with the trekking guide. The next two hours are difficult for all of us. What if there has been an accident? I am filled with nervous apprehension and imagine the worst. Finally, when we find the girls sitting by a crossroad, I burst into relieved tears.

The girls are remarkably calm. Somewhere, during the walk, they had stopped to eat their packed lunches and had discovered a pond with clear cool waters close by. Amidst half-believed jokes of it being magical, they had all decided at (predictably) Neeraj's suggestion to take a quick bath in it! I am shocked. How could they do this when they had repeatedly been told never to fall behind from the rest? And then I see their faces and remember the thrill of being on one's own, of breaking rules, of having fun, the thrill of being young. Hours had passed happily at the magic pond. It was only when shadows started lengthening and the air turned chilly that the girls had realized the time. Except for their own nervous footfalls, there was no sign of human presence in the forest. The girls had been quite frightened but realized that they had little choice but to walk on. Somewhere along the way, Sangeeta had taken the responsibility of finding the destination.

We finally reach Dhoditaal by late evening to an emotional welcome. Everyone crowds around us with questions. The girls who were missing do not appear to be the least bit repentant or embarrassed by their misadventure. The evening belongs to them, and they regale their friends with stories of near-missed encounters with wild beasts, heroic courage and enviable presence of mind. Even the biting cold of Dhoditaal, situated at 10,000 feet, loses its sting in the face of such feverish excitement. But as darkness falls, it becomes even colder. The thin sweaters and cotton walking shoes of the girls provide little protection from the chill, and soon numb hands and chattering teeth need to be warmed by the blaze of the bonfire.

Dhodital, 9 May. Next morning, we awaken to the beauty of Dhoditaal, that derives its name from its small and crystal-clear lake, an intense sapphire set within a ring of emerald mountains. On the higher reaches of these slopes, on the Bakariya Top glacier, lies snow—white, soft, and so far, out of reach. Not today though. Serious preparations are being made for the brief one-hour climb to the glacier. Hair is combed and styled. Dexterous strokes of mascara are applied with the help of small pocket-sized mirrors. Lipsticks are passed around and flaming red, burnished brown and toffee coffee are painstakingly outlined and filled in. Today is finally the day of the snow. Everything is possible today. The girls will play and dance and sing songs and throw snowballs at each other. Just like in the movies.

Bakariya Top. Sometimes, dreams need to be reworked when translated into reality. The glacier, when we reach it, is just one small patch of slightly muddy snow. It usually is much larger, even in May, but this year the snow has melted faster than usual. I feel upset for the girls. Through their young lives, these girls have had to make do with little, or much less. What will happen to their desire to run across vast fields of snow? I look at them and try to gauge their level of disappointment. For a brief moment, their faces do look surprised and crestfallen. Is this what snow is all about? Perhaps white, endless snow exists only within the frame of the film image?

But this too is snow and they have finally reached it! So much effort went into making this journey possible. They cannot now waste this moment fretting about the snow that has melted. Laughing, shrieking and singing, the girls are staking claim over their patch of snow. A few immediately start pouting and smiling and posing for posterity. Others instinctively do what countless girls their age have always done in snow. 'Please, sisters, don't hit so hard. I want to make snowballs too!' 'So why don't you?' 'Didi, look out!' I duck and escape the snowball Neeraj had thrown at me. 'Didi, come and see our snow "girl".' For a first attempt, the snow girl is most impressive. She is short and round. A red scarf is tied jauntily around her head and black sunglasses are perched on a pert twig of a nose. Standing proud, she accepts as her natural due the lusty homage of groups of girls hurtling down the snowy slopes singing, '*Kyaa adaa kyaa jalwe tere Paro! Dil ke tukde ho gaye hazaaron*!'

New Delhi, 2001. Five years have passed since our journey in search of snow. Meanwhile, I completed my film, *Snow*. On its first public screening, the entire group was present and answered audience queries with the poise of veterans. Since then though, we have not been able to meet as a group regularly. I have been able to keep in touch with many of the girls individually and have followed their journey towards becoming women.

On her return from the trek, Kamlesh refused to get married. She got support for her decision from the other girls in her area. For some time, she even left home and stayed with one of the older girls in the group. Finally, her parents relented and today, her schooling completed, she has joined Action India as a full-time volunteer in its adolescent girl programme. Shehnaaz returned home to a happy surprise. During her absence, her elder sister decided that she would continue with Shehnaaz's jobs permanently so that the latter could go back to full-time school. Neeraj, the rebel of the group, got pregnant by a boy she was in love with a few years back. He backed out of a commitment, however, and much against her will Neeraj was forced by her family to marry the boy of their choice, as a punishment for bringing dishonour to their name. I know though that Neeraj is too much of a free spirit to be quelled for long. There is still the wanderer's look in her eyes and the desire to journey to faraway lands. Sangeeta, however, was forced to abandon her journey very early in life. At the age of seventeen, exhausted with adult responsibilities, she swallowed pesticide and committed suicide.

JAMLING TENZING NORGAY

AN OMINOUS FORECAST

Rimpoche bunched his *mala* rosary into his cupped hands and blew on it sharply. He withdrew the string of beads slowly and inspected it, turning his head slightly and squinting, as if trying to peer inside each individual bead. He looked up at me.

'Conditions do not look favourable. There is something malevolent about the mountain this coming season.'

I felt as if I had been punched in the stomach—a feeling that surprised me considering that I was nothing of a devout Buddhist.

Rimpoche sat on a wide, flat cushion, and he adjusted his robe and began to rock back and forth as if he, too, had been surprised by the divination. He clapped his hand loudly to call the attendant monk. His clap broke the silence the way a guru's clap in a Buddhist teaching is meant to trigger awakening to the nature of emptiness, sparking a flash of recognition that all life is impermanent, containing no inherent existence. I

JAMLING TENZING NORGAY was born on 23 April 1965 in Darjeeling. In 1996, he summitted Mount Everest, just two weeks after nine people died in the mountain's most deadly storm ever recorded. He is the star of the film *Everest* which, with his help, captures for the first time on large format film the breathtaking view from Everest's summit. For his bravery, Norgay received His Holiness, The Dalai Lama's Award, as well as the National Citizen's Award from the President of India. He is the tenth person in the Norgay family to stand at the top of the world. 'An Ominous Forecast' has been excerpted from *Touching My Father's Soul: A Sherpa's Journey to the Top of Everest*, HarperSanFrancisco, 2001.

experienced a narrow, momentary space of calmness, a millisecond of emptiness, then felt my stomach again.

A monk padded in quietly and served us tea, gently lifting the filigree silver cover from Rimpoche's jade teacup, which sat on a silver stand. The monk then offered me some fried breads from a woven bamboo tray. I declined, then accepted after the third offer. Such trays are always kept heaped full, and I had to concentrate to avoid knocking off the other pieces. My hand was shaking.

IN EARLY JANUARY 1996, I had travelled here to Siliguri, West Bengal, for an audience with Chatral Rimpoche, a respected but reclusive lama of the Nyingma, or 'ancient lineage', of Tibetan Buddhism. His principal monastery was located in Darjeeling, where I lived with my wife, but Rimpoche's patrons and supporters had built him a small monastic centre in the northern plains of India, several hours away by jeep. The West Bengal landscape is relentlessly flat, far from the remote monasteries that the Nyingmapas established, beginning a millennium ago, across the Himalaya. I felt fortunate to have been born on the south side of the Himalaya, safe from the Chinese invasion of Tibet. Since the late 1950s, Tibetans have been crossing their border into India, Sikkim, and Nepal seeking refuge. Partly as a result of their unerring devotion, Tibetan Buddhism continues to flourish along the south side of the Himalaya, including among my people, the Sherpa.

Rimpoche's chapel and quarters are painted in the bright primary and earthen colours of Himalayan monasteries. Accented by the tall prayer flags on the roof, the compound looked invitingly familiar across a landscape of banana trees, Tata trucks, and blowing dust. It hardly seemed like a place to get a technical reading on the advisability of attempting to climb the world's tallest peak, Mount Everest.

I told Rimpoche that I was there to request a divination, then cautiously asked him about the coming season on the mountain.

I wondered how accurate such divinations really are, statistically speaking. The ability of some lamas to see into the future is remarkable, my parents always said, and their words can be frightening for some. Indeed, fear of prior knowledge of events is one reason why many Sherpas are careful about requesting divinations—and one reason why lamas often shroud their counsel in generalities and aphorisms. The truth, especially when presented in advance, can be too much for some people to accept graciously. They tend to become angry or to deny it, only further exhibiting the 'afflictive emotions' of anger and ignorance. Many lamas feel that lay-people don't use knowledge of the future properly. Seldom do people apply it to further their self-understanding or to aid noble causes. Again and again, people hope vainly to control events that have yet to occur, events that never seem to play out in the way they imagined.

Raised in a religious family, I was aware of the danger of asking questions of lamas. 'When you request a divination, you must always be prepared to abide by the answer', my father, Tenzing Norgay Sherpa, had cautioned me. Fine, as long as it was a positive answer or even neutral. But this divination was unequivocally bad.

I was already firmly—inextricably—committed to climbing Mount Everest. Should I tell my teammates on the Everest IMAX Filming Expedition about Rimpoche's ominous forecast?

How could I? I was the Climbing Leader. Were I to drop out, and only three months before the start of the climb, it would cast a long shadow over the expedition and, I felt, over my father's name and my family legacy. My wife, Soyang, was the reason I was here. She is a young and educated Tibetan woman, yet traditional and reserved. She was against my plan to climb Everest unless a lama pronounced it safe.

A week earlier the veteran Himalayan mountaineer David Breashears had phoned me from the United States. He said that a modified IMAX movie camera had been successfully field-tested and that funding had been secured for an expedition that would try to haul the cumbersome forty-two-pound device to the summit. An extraordinarily ambitious goal. 'I need you, Jamling', he told me. 'Your story, your father's story, and the story of the Sherpas will be important to the film. But I first wanted to make sure you haven't committed to another climb for this spring. If not, then welcome to the team. Let's talk details soon.'

Soyang overheard the phone call. She had been uneasily quiet all afternoon. That night, lying in our bed at home in Darjeeling, she sat up and looked at me sternly. In a determined voice, she said that we had better talk about my Everest plans.

'You don't simply say you're going to climb Everest in the manner that you say you're going to see a movie.' Her tone was imploring, but not entirely dissuasive. She knew that I'd been dreaming of Everest for years and that if I didn't go I would regret it for the rest of my life. Ever since I was a boy I had heard stories of my father's historic climb of Everest with Edmund Hillary in 1953. I had always wanted to join my father on the summit. When I became an adult, and after my father's death, my desire to climb Everest only intensified. I wanted to preserve the family name, which was being eclipsed by a new era of climbing. My father and Hillary's first ascent was approaching the limits of living people's memories.

But other forces were also driving me. I had to learn what it was that had driven my father and what he had found on the mountain. Our relationship had been old-fashioned—he was strict and disciplined—and when he died, much had been left unsaid. I was twenty-one years old at the time, and I knew that there was so much more for him to teach me and so much more for me to learn.

Soyang rolled over and was quiet again, then got up to nurse our young daughter. When she returned, she said that if I first had a *mo*, a divination, done by a high lama, and if his forecast was favourable, she would relent. As I lay in bed, I thought of the effort it had taken me to get this far, and I knew the timing would never be perfect. I had already missed two chances, and I felt that this, the lucky third time, had been prescribed by fate, or karma.

While I was growing up in Darjeeling, my father directed the Himalayan Mountaineering Institute, India's foremost mountaineering school, which provided training for the citizens and armed forces of several South Asian countries, and for Sherpas and Tibetans. In 1983, during my last year of high school, I heard that an Indian expedition was planning to attempt Everest. I desperately wanted to join them and knew that getting selected for the team at my young age would require my father's influence. I wanted to be the youngest person to climb Everest.

I cut classes one day to meet him at our family home and found him in the sitting room with his secretary, Mr Dewan. He dispatched Mr Dewan so we could speak. I put on my most assertive, adult face, secure in the knowledge that, for Sherpa families in Darjeeling, it was understood and expected that children would follow in their father's footsteps. For me this was no problem, because I loved climbing. And I felt a duty to make my father proud by upholding his reputation. But my trepidation was clearly showing.

I asked him.

'You aren't ready,' he answered abruptly—too abruptly, I felt.

Had he thought about it? Might he want some time to consider?

'I can't help you with it,' he continued. 'I'd like for you to finish school and go to college.'

I groped for a response, for words that would casually deflect his reply, but his fatherly conviction told me he had made a decision.

As I picked up my rucksack and headed for the door, I noticed that my hands were trembling. My body felt stiff and awkward. I could see blown snow drifting into and filling the footsteps he had made for me up the mountain, leaving only a powdery, seamless expanse of white.

'I climbed Everest so that you wouldn't have to,' he said as I stood near the doorway. 'You can't see the entire world from the top of Everest, Jamling. The view from there only reminds you how big the world is and how much more there is to see and learn.'

Instead of returning to school, I walked up the street to the house of my uncle, Tenzing Lotay, to ask him what I should do.

Uncle Tenzing was equally abrupt. 'You have no experience, Jamling, and you need it to join that team. Those guys are very proficient climbers.'

'But it's not a matter of experience,' I countered. 'It's a matter of desire and motivation and strength.' I was Jamling, derived from *Jambuling Nyandrak*, the full name given to me by a high Buddhist lama. It means 'world renowned.'

My logical mind, trying vainly to speak over the din of my emotions, told me that my father and uncle were right. I would need age and experience.

It wasn't until 1995 that I came close, for the second time, to getting a shot at the mountain. An American had invited me to join his team if I could raise $20,000, my share of the costs. I was working in New Jersey at the time, and America was a more likely place to find sponsors than India, so I stayed there to work and raise funds.

I sent out hundreds of requests but got nothing. No money, no sponsors. As consolation, the leader invited me to trek to Base Camp with them anyway. He even asked me to guide part of the expedition: the group of volunteers who had signed on to clean up litter along the approach route. It was a ticket to Everest, and I took it, though I was disappointed—humiliated, in fact—to be a simple trekker on an expedition to Everest and a garbage collector, Asia's lowliest occupation. I bore no ill will towards the American team, but it was then that I vowed to redeem my family's name and my father's legacy.

BOWING TOWARDS CHATRAL RIMPOCHE, hands together, I respectfully backed out of his reception room and stepped into the claustrophobic heat of the Indian plains. I felt I was walking through a dungeon, chewing on the distasteful words that Rimpoche had thrown me. He was said to be able to divine the intentions of those who came to him for blessings. Half-hearted Buddhist that I was, I wondered if my motivation was entirely pure. My mother had told me that the poorest of people would dress like nobility in borrowed clothes, and approach him with offerings of whatever paltry sums of money they had saved. He could easily spot them, and always sent them away with their offerings.

I returned to Darjeeling with troubled thoughts, which began to invade my dreams. Soyang slept poorly, too. I told her that Chatral Rimpoche didn't have much to say about the mountain this season, but she saw right through me, just as I felt Rimpoche had.

Not only would I be defying my wife if I chose to climb, but in disregarding the lama's words I'd be going against my family and religious heritage. I knew what my mother would have thought had she been alive. The last time she defied the cautious directive of a divination, she died.

Like many traditional Sherpas, my mother, Daku, became more religious and devout as she aged. In the years before her death, she grew single-mindedly attentive to Chatral Rimpoche, donating grains, sugar, and other staples to his monasteries in Darjeeling and Siliguri. She commissioned the painting of *thangkas* (religious scroll paintings) for the assembly halls, and paid for the construction of monks' quarters.

Daku was outgoing and social. She often travelled with my father when he was invited overseas to give lectures, and she never suffered culture shock. Typically, they were VIP guests of local dignitaries, but she always took her Himalayan trinkets along with her and spread them out on a blanket on the steps of their hotels to sell to passersby. From that beginning, she built a small trading business, expanded into the travel trade, and opened an office in the Darjeeling bazaar.

Her sole motivation was to send her three sons to Saint Paul's, one of India's most expensive and elite private schools, located on a ridge just fifteen minutes' walk from our home, and to send her daughter to the Loretto Convent. When my youngest brother, Dhamey, began attending Saint Paul's as a boarding student, my mother had largely completed what we regard as the second stage of life. She had fulfilled her obligations and duties as a householder. She remained as busy as always, but her face and body movements told me she was anticipating the final phase of life, the religious phase, when she could devote herself to spiritual matters and preparation for death. She was only in her late forties, but one cannot begin spiritual practice too soon. Years before at the stupa of Boudhanath in Kathmandu, it had surprised me to see her prostrate by body lengths around the stupa. Wearing a heavy apron over her street clothes, she would stretch out on the stone walkway, reach out with her hands as far as she could, place her forehead on the pavement, then rise and step forward to begin her next prostration at the furthest point her fingers had touched.

After my father died in 1986, she began to dream of going on pilgrimage to Pema Cave, in the remote region of Pema-kö, high in the hills of southern Tibet and the Indian states of

Arunachal Pradesh and Assam. She knew that pilgrimage is an excellent way to gain merit. And if the pilgrimage site is holy and powerful enough, one can gain direct transmission of wisdom simply by appearing before the deities present there and bathing in their sacred blessings.

Pema-kö, however, is legendary for its unfriendly hill tribes that are believed to poison strangers, and the area is restricted even to Indians from outside the region. It took a year for my mother to gain permission to visit this site. Before departing, she sought Chatral Rimpoche's blessings, and then she set out from Darjeeling with two of his monks. The trail was long and torturous, and the journey took them over a month.

At the time, my brother Norbu was living in California, and when he phoned me in New Jersey, he was disturbed and frightened. He had received a call from Darjeeling saying that Mom was in Siliguri, after having been evacuated from a remote part of Arunachal, and that she was very sick. Little else was known about her condition.

She had reached Pema Cave, at which point the more devout pilgrims must circumambulate three sacred mountains. While circling the nearest mountain, she took ill with undefined internal problems and decided to retreat to the town of Tuting to recover. She remained there for eight days, yet her sickness worsened. The doctors were unable to identify her ailment, so they put her on a plane to Guwahati and then Bagdogra, and from there the monks took her by car to a hospital in Siliguri. Medical staff in underequipped rural hospitals sometimes prefer to send difficult cases to larger hospitals to sidestep blame if the patient dies on their watch. Indeed, for many on the subcontinent, hospitals are known as places where people go to die.

At the hospital, my mother lost her appetite entirely and grew weaker. She asked continually about her family. My brother Dhamey and sister Deki were also in the United States, and just before we caught flights to India, I received another phone call. The barely audible voice on the phone informed me that she had died. It was 22 September 1992. She was fifty-two years old.

We returned to Darjeeling with her body for the cremation. I was distraught, but the monk who had accompanied my mother reminded me that most people are born with a time of death already prescribed by their karma and astrological alignment, and that whatever time they die is the right time. I'm not sure I believed that; it sounded like a rationalization. Then he told me that it was remarkable that her body gave off no odour, which Buddhists claim is a very good omen and a sign of a great practitioner. For me, it was little consolation.

At her memorial service, another monk from Chatral Rimpoche's monastery approached me, saddened that the community had lost 'Neela', as they referred to her, the familiar but respectful term for 'aunt'.

'Ever since her death, it's as if our hands have been bound,' he said. 'When she visited our *gompa*, she brought with her an aura of serenity and compassion. We all felt it. Once, after a long absence, she viewed the statues in the assembly hall and said to us. "These deities are crying, they are sweating and writhing, due to your negligence in cleaning them!" She sponsored many repaintings and regilding of the statues, but many times the painter, witnessing the sincerity and depth of her devotion, refused to accept payment from her.'

The day after her funeral, I saw the monk again, and he told me that Neela had turned down an offer to be evacuated by helicopter from Tuting; he also suggested that she may have been poisoned by the Pema-kö people or that she could have sustained the bite of a poisonous spider or inadvertently eaten a poisonous plant. For countless events that transpire in India, it seems it is difficult to identify causes or assign blame.

He then told me that Rimpoche had done a divination for Neela, and he foresaw that this particular journey to Pema-kö looked extremely unfavourable. He advised her not to go. 'Stay here in Siliguri. I will give you some land, and you can build a house on it and practise *dharma*,' Rimpoche had offered.

I was shocked to hear this, but somehow I could understand my mother's reasoning. She was torn between her devotion to Rimpoche and her desire for merit and blessings from this holy site. She knew that it was not Rimpoche she would defy by going on pilgrimage. It was her own planetary alignment, her own fate she was tempting—a risk she was willing to take for the sake of additional merit. That her motive was a spiritual one did little to assuage my grief. It seemed unusual, and perhaps prescient, that she had already bought many of the wedding gifts and other items for her children, though only Norbu was planning to marry at the time she died.

My mother had not heeded Chatral Rimpoche's premonition. I was beginning to think that I should. For one thing, I was still firmly planted in the householder stage of life, with a wife, young daughter, and thoughts of more children. Because I had an obligation to care for them, I had an obligation to care for myself. As the Buddhists say, I had been granted a 'precious human rebirth', which should not be squandered.

I was unsure of my belief in Buddhism, however—skeptical, in fact. Nonetheless, it would have been as excruciating to defy our family's religion as to abandon my hopes for climbing. Fortunately, there was still one other possibility. We were going to Kathmandu, Nepal, shortly, where I would be able to seek a second opinion about the coming season on Everest. It would have to be favourable.

Soyang urged me to visit Geshé Rimpoche, her family's guru, a learned lama I had met some years before. He was living in Kathmandu and was known for his accurate divinations. Even foreigners posted at some of the embassies sought him out for advice.

We had planned to spend the spring of 1996 with Soyang's

parents, who lived in a Tibetan community just south of Kathmandu. They were refugees, wealthy by local standards, and their house would be a good place to prepare for the Everest IMAX Filming Expedition. And to prepare for another divination.

The day before we left Darjeeling for Nepal, I stepped out of the back door and hiked through the trees above our house. Intersecting the ridge, I followed it to the top of Tiger Hill, Darjeeling's highest point, a good place to string prayer flags. *Lungta* they are called—windhorses. With each flap of the flag, my mother would say, the horse depicted on the cotton print gallops off into the wind with prayers, circling the globe, benefiting all sentient beings. I tried several lengths of them together, climbed two nearby pine trees, and hung them in a smiling arc across the clearing at the top of Tiger Hill.

In fact, my mother had explained to me, the lungta horse bears a deity carrying wish-fulfilling gems, which we need in order to thrive. But lungta also represents the degree of positive spiritual energy and awareness that propels people—their level of divine inner support. Sherpas say that if their lungta is high, they can survive almost any difficult situation, and if it is low, they can die even while resting on a grassy slope like Tiger Hill. One's lungta can be cultivated through meditation and through awareness and right actions. Indeed, for those with a high lungta, the lamas say, only the karma generated in previous lifetimes that has 'ripened' can bring misfortune.

But at the time, I felt that stringing prayer flags was little more than a superstitious gesture, done only out of respect for my parents. Buddhism hadn't fully captured my heart. It wasn't a subject taught at Saint Paul's, and my father was off climbing and travelling too much to teach me. Perhaps I needed to learn more about it.

From Tiger Hill I looked north across the green valleys of Sikkim and followed the line where the dark blue sky encounters a jagged horizon of black and white—the eastern Himalaya.

Kanchenjunga, the 'Five Treasures of the Great Snows', stood above the others at the intersecting borders of Sikkim, Nepal, and Tibet. Kanchenjunga, the world's third-highest peak at 28,146 feet, wasn't climbed until 1955, well after Everest's successful ascent—though not for lack of trying. Climbers were killed on virtually all of the early attempts on this peak, beginning with the first try in 1905.

From Tiger Hill, the Himalaya seem to bow upwards in the middle, dipping slightly at the far ends, as if spanning a visible arc of the earth's curvature. Jhomolhari and other peaks in Bhutan capture the north-east skyline. Panning back to Nepal in the north-west, I could see the massive giant of Makalu, over 8,000 metres (26,250 feet) tall, and behind it Lhotse and Nuptse. And behind them all stood an incongruous peak, its solid black triangular pyramid seeming to anchor and support the others. A narrow plume of clouds streaked from its summit like a *kata* blessing scarf. It was named Chomolungma, 'Unshakable Good Elephant Woman', abode of the beneficent and protective goddess Miyolangsangma. Mount Everest. I wondered why anyone would want to rename a mountain as sacred and majestic as Chomolungma after a human.

From the moment he arrived in Darjeeling as a young man, my father remained homesick for Khumbu, the homeland of the Sherpas, where he grew up in the shadow of Chomolungma. But the view of the mountain from Tiger Hill reminded him that he had not moved far. It continued to uplift him, then it came to dominate his imagination. He had come to Darjeeling partly in search of work, but mainly to consummate his destiny with this peak.

Far below me lay the hamlet of Alu Bari, or 'Potato Field', where my father first found lodging. In 1932, after sneaking away from his home in the Khumbu village of Thame, he trekked two weeks over high ridges and into deep valleys to Nepal's western border with India. There, a Tibetan trader gave him work for several weeks cutting firewood, then eventually took him to Darjeeling on the steam-powered 'Toy Train', where he found him a job tending cows.

Before 1951, when Nepal opened to the outside world for the first time, Everest expeditions were staged out of Darjeeling, a town that was created in the mid-1800s by the British raj as a hill station. Beginning in the 1920s, the British approached Everest from the Tibet side. On their way northward through Darjeeling, they picked up Sherpas who had moved there from Nepal looking for work.

Many of the early Darjeeling Sherpas, or *Bhotias* (Tibetans), as they were first referred to, settled in the poor hamlet of Toong Soong Busti, just beyond the bazaar at the backside of the ridge. They lived semi-communally in clusters of shacks braced against one another on the steep hillside as if in defiance of gravity. In the mid-1930s my father moved into a tin-roofed structure owned by Ang Tharkay, a prominent Sherpa *sirdar*, or expedition foreman, who had been awarded a 'Tiger of the Snows' medal by the Himalayan Club for his climbing prowess. He would go on to be sirdar for the French on Annapurna in 1950. Even today many Sherpas, including some of my relatives, continue to live in Toong Soong.

My father was a simple boy from the hills, and the upper, wealthy part of Darjeeling town fascinated him. Here were the houses built by the British, modelled on English country homes with high ceilings and spiral, red-carpeted staircases graced by smooth, polished banisters. After he climbed Everest, a prominent Indian newspaper offered him the house we now live in, though he paid for most of it, he said, so they wouldn't someday find an excuse to take it away. During the winters now, we close off much of the house to conserve heat. Only the British colonials could have afforded the labour to cut the wood required to keep its seven fireplaces fully stoked.

After Independence in 1947, wealthy Indians bought most

of these luxurious homes. Some have been converted into guest lodges that house the waves of Indian tourists who ascend the seven-thousand-foot rise to Darjeeling, like thermal convection, to beat the summer heat. After 1953, Indians from West Bengal especially were on a pilgrimage to our door, hoping for a glimpse of the famous 'Sherpa Tenzing'. Hindus believe—or used to, anyway—that any human who could stand on the summit of Everest must be an incarnation of Shiva, the wrathful destroyer deity of the Hindu trinity. My father made no such claims, of course, and he quickly grew tired of the obsessive adoration.

The Planters' Club—until 1947 a social venue for the British only—still presides over the middle of town. Sitting in the shade on Tiger Hill, I pictured the early days of the Sherpas. Ragtag groups of them in long braided hair would line up on the terrace below the club's veranda, shoulders tensed, hands stiff at their sides, to be scrutinized by the British in pith helmets and puttees, busy consulting their expedition conscription lists. Working for the obsessed and often eccentric foreign climbers was sometimes difficult, but the pay was respectable considering that the Sherpas were coming from a subsistence, barter economy. And, especially for my father, climbing was an adventure.

In the early thirties my father carried milk from his landlord's cows past the Planters' Club to sell in the bazaar. One of his customers was my late stepmother, his second wife, Ang Lhamu. She later came to visit him when he worked as a labourer on the reconstruction of the Saint Paul's School chapel, following the Great Bihar Earthquake of 1934. She brought milk for him to drink, the first of many generous deeds that culminated, I learned from a respected lama, in her contribution to his success on Chomolungma.

THE FOLLOWING MORNING, Soyang and our daughter and I departed Darjeeling for Nepal. Riding in a succession of cars and rickshaws and a small commercial plane, we arrived in Kathmandu that evening.

A FEW DAYS before our departure for the mountains, I visited Geshé Rimpoche again. He placed in my hand a packet of sacred relics, in the form of brown, spherical pills containing minute quantities of the hair and fingernails of high lamas, mixed with hundreds of herbs. He told me to place them on the summit if I reached it. He also handed me some *sungdis*, blessing strings made of thin braided nylon to wear around my neck and to tie on to the key climbing equipment, such as my harness, ice axe, and crampons, for protection. He also gave me a small pouch of what looked like sand, and indeed it had been collected from intricate sand mandalas created during lengthy rituals in his monastery. This was mixed with blessed grains of rice to make a protective mixture called *chaane*. He told me to sprinkle this on dangerous stretches, or wherever I felt scared, such as in avalanche-prone areas and the Khumbu Icefall.

Rimpoche also presented me with a protective *sungwa* amulet, a piece of handmade paper inscribed with astrological designs and religious symbols and mantras. As I watched, he folded it precisely and bound it in a crosshatch pattern of coloured threads. He told me to wrap the amulet in plastic, to protect it from sweat and dirt. I made a mental note to have it sewn into a silk brocade bag, too.

Geshé Rimpoche then turned on his cushion and reached behind him into a stack of texts wrapped in saffron-coloured cloth. 'I was waiting for your return visit,' he said as he opened the texts and began flipping over folios on the prayer table in front of him. 'I wanted to read something to you from a text by the eighteenth-century scholar Jigme Lingpa, *Treasury of Precious Qualities*':

When the eagle soars up, high above the earth,
Its shadow for the while is nowhere to be seen;
Yet bird and shadow still are linked. So too our actions:
When conditions come together, their effects are clearly
seen.[1]

He read on, selecting passages that seemed to have been written especially for me, addressing my own personal dilemma. I marvelled at the depth of memory it took to simply remember all these references and where to find them. My Western education seemed a jumble, a misguided detour from such simple yet detailed thought.

Rimpoche then pulled me towards him and whispered some mantras in my ear. He told me to repeat them in audible tones while on the mountain, especially in hazardous places.

I left Geshé Rimpoche's feeling protected and prepared but mildly anxious. Whether the butter lamps at the stupa and blessed threads and mantras would work or not, I didn't know. But I was beginning to feel that the healthy scepticism I learned in America would have its useful limits. I was headed for a dangerous mountain and would need all the help I could find.

1.   Requoted from Patrul Rinpoche, *The Words of My Perfect Teacher* (Boston: Shambhala, 1998), p. 119.

INDIRA VISWANATHAN PETERSON

IN SEARCH OF THE FORTUNE-TELLER FROM THE HILLS

As a Tamil brought up in the Shaiva tradition, I have long heard of Kurralam as a site of pilgrimage. Famed for its Shiva temple, the Tirikutam ('Three Peaks') hill and the great Tenaruvi ('Honey') and Vadavaruvi ('Northern') waterfalls, Kurralam was already praised as an ancient sacred place in the *Tevaram* hymns of the seventh-century saints Appar and Sambandar, poems that I have spent many years studying and translating. From 1977 to 1980, I made pilgrimages to most of the temples that the saints had visited and sung about in the *Tevaram*. Somehow, I never managed to include Kurralam in my journeys. On this trip, though, Kurralam is my sole destination.

I engage a car and driver to drive me from Tirunelveli, fifty-eight kilometres east of Kurralam. Accompanying me are Rajan, a student from St. Xavier's College, Palaiyankottai, and T.V. James, a professional photographer who I have hired for taking photographs for a book I am writing on an eighteenth-century Tamil dance-drama about the temple, landscape and

INDIRA VISWANATHAN PETERSON, Professor and Chair of Asian Studies at Mount Holyoke College, specializes in Sanskrit and Tamil literature, Hinduism, and South Indian music. She is the author of *Poems to Siva: The Hymns of the Tamil Saints* (1989) and *Design and Rhetoric in a Sanskrit Court Epic: The Kirātārjunīya of Bhāravi* (2002), and editor of Indian literature, *The Norton Anthology of World Masterpieces* (1995). She is currently writing a book on the *Kuṟavañci* dramas of Tamil Nadu.

lore of Kurralam.

Driving west along the banks of the Tamraparni river under a cloudless January sky, we pass verdant rice-fields criss-crossed by irrigation canals. I soon realize that the slender white shapes that dot the emerald-green fields are waterbirds—egrets, herons and terns—preying for fish in the canals. We pass farmers and bullock carts. Every few miles, as we drive through small villages, the *gopuram* towers of temples dedicated to Shiva and Vishnu rise above the coconut palms and palmyra trees. The soaring, intricately carved gopuram of the Kasi Viswanatha temple at Tenkasi testifies to the wealth and power of the warrior and peasant elite of the Tamraparni Valley from the fifteenth to the seventeenth centuries. At the edges of every village we see shrines and small, brightly-painted temples dedicated to Icakkiyamman, Karuppacami and Cudalai Madan, fierce guardian deities who dwell in the margins of settlements, and who require animal sacrifice from their devotees.

Just as I get used to this pattern of hamlets, temples and fields on a riverine plain, the landscape changes abruptly. Tall blue shapes loom ahead of us, wrapped in mist. Within minutes, the blurred shapes resolve themselves into the outlines of hills that seem to climb straight up and out of the flat land around them. Another minute, and we see the low, sculpted towers and other buildings of a temple complex rising alongside the hill. We have arrived at Kurralam and its temple dedicated to Shiva, nestled against the Western Ghats, at the western edge of the province of Tirunelveli in the South Indian peninsula.

It was to this sacred site, with its ancient temple, sacred Tirikutam hill and the waterfalls famed for their healing qualities, that the poet Tirikuta Racappa Kavirayar had devoted his celebrated dance-drama *Kurralak Kuravanci, The Drama of the Wandering Fortune-teller of Kurralam*. Kavirayar wrote the drama for his patron Cinnanancattevan, a member of the Maravar warrior community and ruler of Cokkampatti

Palaiyam. The work was premiered at Kurralam temple in 1718 in the presence of the Nayaka king of Madurai. A copper-plate inscription at the temple tells us that Kavirayar was rewarded with a gift of land and the office of the 'poet of Kurralam temple'. In January 1995, I have at last arrived at the sacred site connected with the *Kurralak Kuravanci*, the most famous of the Kuravanci ('fortune-teller') dramas, the subject of my study.

I had been introduced to Kuravanci dramas through two avenues—my study of Tamil literature, and the revival of these dramas on the Bharata Natyam dance stage in the 1960s and 70s. In the dramatic plot of the *Kurralak Kuravanci*, presented in songs that are meant to be enacted in dance, Vasantavalli, a high-born young woman, sees Shiva Kurumpala-natar, the god of Kurralam temple, riding in procession on the main street of Kurralam, and falls hopelessly in love with him. As Vasantavalli pines for Shiva and wastes away in her longing, Singi, a Kuravanci or Kuratti, a fortune-teller from the nomadic hill tribe known as Kuravar, comes to her. She praises the temple and the mountain landscapes of Kurralam, describes her travels and the ways of her tribe, and performs divinatory rituals to predict the lady's success in marrying the Lord of Kurralam. Vasantavalli handsomely rewards the fortune-teller. The scene shifts to the rice fields of Kurralam, where the Kuravanci's husband, the bird-catcher Singan, is setting up nets and snares for waterbirds. Soon, the jealous bird-catcher sets out to search for Singi, and finds her on the town's main street. The play ends with a comic dialogue between the bird-catcher and the fortune-teller, and a song of praise for Kurralam's god.

The *Kurralak Kuravanci* is only one among more than one hundred Tamil fortune-teller dramas with identical plots written during the eighteenth and nineteenth centuries. Set in various sacred places in Tamilnadu, the plays were patronized by the numerous Palaiyakkarars, Zamindars and other rulers of small principalities in the region, and were regularly performed in the courts and temples to which they were dedicated. Studying the literature of this period, I had been struck by the popularity of these plays, both in the provinces and at the court of the Maratha kings in Tanjavur, the centre of Karnatak music and Bharata Natyam dance in the eighteenth and nineteenth centuries. What was the fascination of a wandering fortune-teller and her bird-catcher husband, their mountain homeland, and the ways of the hill Kuravar, for eighteenth- and nineteenth-century audiences?

Seeing performances of Kuravanci dramas on stage had already given me a sense of the allure of the Kuravanci fortune-teller and her mountain lore. In 1944, Rukmini Devi of Kalakshetra had presented *Kurralak Kuravanci* as the first drama to be enacted in the Bharata Natyam dance style after the art form had moved from courts and temples to the public stage in the twentieth century. Throughout the 1960s, I saw performances of Kuravanci dance-dramas dedicated to famous hills in Tamilnadu, presented by celebrated dancers and their troupes. Kamala staged *Tyagesar Kuravanji*, dedicated to Shiva of Tiruvarur temple, Vaijayanthimala performed *Alakar Kuravanci*, on Vishnu of the Alakarkoyil temple near Madurai, and Padma Subrahmanyam staged the *Viralimalaik Kuravanci*, dedicated to Murukan of Viralimalai. The Kuravanci fortune-teller was the nerve-centre of these dramas. Indeed, the Kuratti dance and fortune-telling scenes from the Kuravanci dramas were so popular that the 'Gypsy' or 'Kuratti' dance had become a standard item in Bharata Natyam dance performances in general. Clearly, not just eighteenth-century audiences, but modern Tamil spectators such as myself, found the fortune-teller from the hills irresistible.

The entire atmosphere of the play changed, quickened, when the Kuravanci entered, dressed in her unique costume—a checked sari tied up in a particular style, or a gathered, brightly coloured, chequered skirt paired with a colourful blouse and upper cloth. Her hair was tied up on one side, and decked with

flowers. Among the characteristic features of her appearance
and attire were the tattoo designs (*paccai*) on her face and arms,
the multicoloured strings of beads, *kunrimani* seeds and coral
around her neck, the basket perched on her hip, brimming with
bead necklaces, combs and herbs, and the divining wand or rod
that she carried in her hand. Striking as her appearance was, it
was her jaunty manner and lively songs and dances that
captivated the audience. She arrived, singing songs about the
mountain (*malai*); her songs were in folk tunes and snappy folk
rhythms, and their language had the flavour of spoken dialects—
'*paccaimalai pavala malai enkal malai amme*' ('we come from
the green mountain and the coral mountain, lady!').

The celebrated entrance songs of the fortune-teller in the
Kurralak Kuravanci paint a vivid portrait of this wise, mysterious
and alluring woman, the wandering soothsayer from the hills:

> *She wears necklaces of coral and red kunri seeds*
> *and a white sari.*
> *She carries a basket on her hip*
> *and the wand of divination in her right hand.*
> *She walks with a bounce of her breasts,*
> *a flutter of eyelashes, a coquettish gesture at every step.*
> *She wears a mark of musk on her curved brow*
> *and vetci flowers in her fragrant hair.*
> *Her proud, keen eyes are dark with kohl.*
> *Here she comes, the Kuravanci Fortune-teller,*
> *the golden vine of Kurralam's Tirikutam hill,*
> *the coquette, the lovely girl.*
> *Here comes the Kuravanci, the Kuravanci from the hills!*
> *With swelling breasts and tapered waist,*
> *brow curved like a bow, teeth like jasmine buds,*
> *beauty more enchanting than*
> *the slender spirit-woman of Kolli hill,*
> *girl whose soothsaying skill has swiftly spread her fame*

as far as great Delhi city in the north,
the Kuravanci from the hill where learning flourishes,
the hill of the Lord (Shiva of Kurralam), husband of the
goddess Kulalmoli,
daughter of the great abode of the snows (Parvati).
Here comes the Kuravanci, the Kuravanci from the hills!
(*Kurralak Kuravanci* 49-51)

Kavirayar's description points at the many components of the Kuravanci's mystique—her association with mountains, her nomadic background, her expertise in the occult, her sexual allure, and her air of total self-confidence. The fortune-teller's songs in the Kuravanci dramas evoke for me the ancient and compelling meanings of hills and the sacred in Tamil culture. They remind me that in the scheme of the five physical and emotional landscapes of Tamil Sangam poetry, written more than two thousand years ago, Kurinci, the hill landscape, is associated with the power of the wilderness, the union of lovers, the immanent sacred forces, the great mysteries of the universe. In the *aham* love poems, heroes from the hills traverse difficult mountain slopes to meet their lovers in the dead of night. A young woman's love is as rare and precious as the mountain *kurinci* flower that blooms only every twelve years. In his *puram* poems (poems on public life), the poet Kapilar traces the hill chieftain Pari's magnificence in peace and war to the greatness of his hill, Parambu, which abounds with wild rice, jackfruit, bamboo, sweet potatoes, and beehives full of honey, wild bounty that has no need for cultivators and ploughs. And these Tamil hills are peopled by the Kuravar and other hill tribes who earn their livelihood by hunting and dealing in the produce of the mountains—sandalwood, honey, ivory (from elephant tusks), birds and game.

I remember, too, that Murukan, that most Tamil of the Tamil gods, is a hill god. Dwelling on the sacred Palani,

Tirupparankunram, and other hills, he marries Valli, a girl from the hill Kuravar tribe. If Murukan's Palani hill is one of Tamilnadu's great places of pilgrimage, the hill of Venkatam (Tirupathi), abode of Vishnu as Venkatacalapati, today located in the state of Andhra Pradesh, and arguably the greatest mountain-site of pilgrimage in South India, has always been the northern boundary of the 'good world where Tamil is spoken' (*Tamil kurum nallulakam*). Closest to my heart, though, are the mountain abodes of Shiva in the Tamil land, the hills sung in the *Tevaram*—Kurralam, Tiruvannamalai (Arunacalam), Mutukunru (Viruttacalam). On this cool January day, I have journeyed to Kurralam in order to experience the enduring mystery and power of a sacred mountain abode of Shiva and its physical and emotional landscapes, in the particular ways in which Kavirayar's great drama and the intriguing figure of the Kuratti fortune-teller have made them come alive for me and many other Tamils.

On approaching the temple complex, I find my gaze being drawn, not to the modest temple and its tower (this gopuram is no match for the massive towers of the great temples of the Tamraparni valley, Tirunelveli, Srivilliputtur, Alvartirunagari, Tenkasi), but to the craggy peaks of Tirikutam ('Three peaks') hill. The hill soars above the temple, yet does not dwarf it. Gopuram and hill seem to be moulded to one another; indeed, the temple seems to grow out of the rock itself—a reminder that the sacredness of Kurralam, like other temple sites, centres on its inseparable unity with Tirikutam hill and its landscape. I think of the journey along the flat plain, through miles of green rice paddies and canals, and realize that, situated at the edge of a river valley and the craggy mountains of the Western Ghats, Kurralam evokes in a unique and striking manner the continuous dialogue between the wilderness and cultivated land, between nomads and settled peoples in the Tamil region.

Another feature of the complex that draws my attention right away is a large, low, tile-roofed building that stands not far from the main shrine, also nestled against the hillside. This, I know, must be the famed Citrasabha, the hall in which Shiva Nataraja is said to have danced one of his five great dances in the Tamil region. The structure resembles nothing in the Tamil country to the north and east of Kurralam, but looks for all the world like a temple of the neighbouring Malayalam-speaking region of Kerala and of the hybrid region of Kanyakumari to the south of Tirunelveli. Not surprising, I think, considering the fact that, situated at the edge of the Western Ghats, Kurralam is located nearly at the Kerala border and one can indeed cross over to Kerala via the Senkottai pass.

Sunlight glints off the copper-gilded, tiled roof of Citrasabha. The gilding was done, we are told in the *Kurralak Kuravanci*, by Kavirayar's patron Cinnanancattevan, and I see that the outer walls are decorated by great mural paintings depicting Shiva's cosmic myths and his deeds in Kurralam. As I circumambulate the hall on the outside, looking at the paintings, my attention is immediately drawn to two small figures flanking a large painting of Manmatha the Love-god, mounted on his vehicle, a swan, ready to shoot a flower-arrow from his sugar-cane bow. Could they be . . . yes, they are, a Kuravan bird-catcher and a Kuratti fortune-teller, he with the tools of his trade, and she with her basket and wand of divination, painted in a pleasing nineteenth-century style. The painters were clearly aware of Kurralam's associations with the hill Kuravar. The paintings remind me of the many life-size sculptural depictions of Kuravars and Kurattis I have viewed in the front halls of other temples in the Tirunelveli region—Krishnapuram, Tenkasi, Tirunelveli, testifying to the respect with which these folk figures must have been viewed in the pre-modern era, as people who bring the mystery, power and fecundity of the wilderness to the settled world.

There are more paintings to admire inside the Citrasabha. On coming out of the cool, dark hall into the light of day, however, my attention is quickly captured by the most impressive sight at Kurralam, the great Vadavaruvi (North) waterfall of the Cittaru river crashing down in cleft streams from Tirikutam hill, and the multitude of devotees, men, women and children bathing at the foot of the falls. They have come to bathe in the healing waters of this ancient *tirtha*, place of sacred water, a crossing beyond mundane existence.

Looking up, I see the uppermost part of the waterfall vanishing into dark, densely vegetated cliffs. Monkeys leap about the branches of jackfruit trees on the heights. The *kurumpala* is, after all, the sacred tree around which the shrine of Kurralam was built. A fine mist covers the lower reaches of the waterfall. I am drawn to the falls as if by a magnet, and soon I am one of the crowd of exhilarated bathers. As I stand drenched by cool streams of water, through the roar of the falling waters and the delighted shrieks of the children frolicking in the falls, my ears ring with the Kuravanci fortune-teller's songs of Tirikutam mountain, perhaps the most famous of the Kuravanci drama's songs, which vividly describe Kurralam's mountain and waterfalls in an evocative mix of poetic, mythic, and landscape images:

Vasantavalli:
Slim girl with the bright smile, coral lips,
and breasts scented with sandal-paste,
tell me about the hill that you call your home,
describe its splendours to me!
Singi, the Kuravanci fortune-teller:
On Kurralam's hill
the great waterfall
is a girl playing a game of jacks
with the pearls it sweeps up in its current,

as it smashes the sand-houses
little girls have built in their yards.
On that hill we dig for roots and tubers
and gather honey
and dance our hill-dances.
On that hill we pound roasted millet
into flour with elephant tusks.
On that hill young monkeys
play ball with sweet mango fruit,
and the heavy scent of the champak blossom
drifts up to heaven.
The fertile Tirikutam hill
ruled by the bounteous Lord of Kurralam
is our hill.
There, monkeys court their mates with fruit,
apes beg for the fruit the female monkey lets fall.
Hunters shoot arrows to propitiate the gods,
flying Cittar adepts grow herbs of immortality.
There, the mist from the waterfall called 'Honey'
strikes the sky and comes down as rain,
and the sun-god's charioteer and horses
slip in their tracks!
Such is the hill from which I come,
Kurralam's Tirikutam hill,
hill of the god whose hair is adorned
by the young crescent moon!
(Kurralak Kuravanci 52-53)

I have come to Kurralam to feel something of the spirit of the place and the hill that are the abode of Shiva as well as of the charismatic Kuravanci fortune-teller. I could hardly have suspected that my journey would entail an actual encounter with a woman fortune-teller. After the refreshing bath in the falls, my companions and I visit Shiva's temple. We have missed the hour of *taricanam*, seeing the god in the sanctum, but we circumambulate the temple and its inner corridors, and listen to the priest's retellings of the important myths of the place (*tala-puranam*). After resting for a while, we decide to walk to the foot of the mountain, where we see hawkers selling herbs and spices, especially fragrant cardamom and cloves, grown in estates on the slopes here and on nearby hills. As we bargain for spices, a young woman accosts me, pleading with me to let her read my palm. She is dressed in an everyday sari and blouse, and she carries a plastic basket from which she produces a small wand. Nothing in her appearance or attire indicates that she is a tribal fortune-teller—no gathered skirts, no tattoos, no bead necklaces, no reed basket. But she insists that she is a genuine fortune-teller, a woman who gets possessed and reads palms. A small crowd is beginning to form around us. I decide to let the woman read my palm.

The fortune-teller taps my palm with her wand, reads the lines on it, and states with a fair degree of accuracy salient facts about my marital status, family, children and work. She then begins her divinatory ritual with prayers addressed to the gods and goddesses, chanted in a high-pitched voice. I recognize the names of Murukan, Shiva, and Minakshi, Shiva's goddess-consort in Madurai, but the litany quickly shifts its focus to folk gods—Karuppannacami, Munnati Rayan, Aiyanar, Kali, gods of the wayside shrines, of field and forest, grove and hill, guardian deities and goddesses who can take as well as give life. The fortune-teller goes into a trance and tells my fortune in a keening chant. The deity speaks through her: 'You have travelled a long way to come to Kurralam,' it says, 'and you have a long journey ahead.' I press the deity for details, and am rewarded with oblique statements that I must ponder. Slowly, the fortune-teller comes out of her trance and I pay her for her labours. The crowd disperses. Rajan, my guide, is a bit sceptical of the worth of the fortune-telling session. 'She is not a *real*

Kuratti,' he says, 'but when we stop at the Narikkuravar tribal settlement in Pettai near Tirunelveli, you will have a chance to have your fortune told by some real Kuravancis!' I reply that I look forward to meeting the Narikkuravar ('jackal' Kuravar). Meanwhile, however, I am musing on the enigmatic and confident persona of the fortune-teller of the *Kurralak Kuravanci* and her rituals of divination.

In her song about Tirikutam hill, the Kuratti Singi describes the activities of the Kuravar tribe in their mountain habitat, in images that fully resonate with the descriptions of the hill Kuravar in older Tamil poems:

> *On that hill we dig for roots and tubers*
> *and gather honey,*
> *and dance our hill-dances.*
> *On that hill we pound roasted millet*
> *into flour with elephant tusks. . . .*

Unlike the Kuravar of the classical poems, however, the Kuravanci of the dance-drama is a wandering tribeswoman who has travelled to far-away places.

> *Look at the prizes I have won*
> *for my outstanding fortune-telling,*
> *which has earned me fame far and wide,*
> *for I have told fortunes*
> *in Vanci, in the Malayalam country.*
> *in Kocci and in Konku.*
> *In Mecca and Maharashtra, and the land of the Turks,*
> *people have praised my soothsaying.*
> *I have travelled to Gingee and Benares in the north,*
> *to Sinhala, Colombo and Bengal,*
> *to Tanjavur, Mankalappettai, and the fort-city of Trichy.*
> *(Kurralak Kuravanci 62)*

Surely, I think, the fascination of settled populations with the fortune-teller must derive from her nomadic background as well as from her connection with the sacred hills. I know, for instance, that in an early nineteenth-century drama written in honour of Serfoji II, the Maratha king of Tanjavur, the Kuravanci tells the fortunes of her women clients with polyglot verve, saying 'Show me your palm!' in five languages, including English. However, I am also aware that the fortune-telling techniques of the Kuravanci of the eighteenth-century dance-dramas are close to those of the shamanesses and soothsayers of the older literature.

Urged to divine the outcome of Vasantavalli's love affair, the Kuratti of the *Kurralak Kuravanci* begins her ritual by reading omens. She reads the lady's palm ('Show me your braceleted hand, my lady, show me your hand!'), and predicts general good luck for her. She then invokes gods and goddesses in a long chant set in the *akaval* metre, the metre of classical Tamil poetry and a rhythm connected with the chants of *Akavunar* soothsayers in the ancient poems. Beginning, like my own fortune-teller, with invocations to the 'high gods' of Kurralam and elsewhere, the Kuravanci calls on a large number of village deities.

> . . . *Virgin goddesses on the golden hill!*
> *Aiyanar of the Ariyanka grove, gracious pearl!*
> *Viran in good Kulattur!*
> *Beautiful Makali! Guardian-goddess of Kurralam!*
> *Eternal Bhairava! Ferocious Karuppan!*
> *Munnati Murukan! Vanniyarayan!*
> *'Boar' Matan who springs like the fierce tiger!*
> *Goddess Ekkaladevi! Durga! Goddess Pitari!*
> *I invoke your blessing, give me the gift*
> *of a good divination! Appear before me!*
> *Tell me the object of Vasantamokini's thoughts!*
> *Is it a living being, or an inanimate thing?*

Is it a cotton sari, or a silk cloth? Is it paddy or grain?
. . . . Is it the sign of the garland and marriage in the future?
Of these many signs, show me the one that is the girl's!
(Kurralak Kuravanci 72)

Many of the gods invoked here are local to Kurralam, but the deity who possesses the Kuravanci is Jakkamma, goddess of the Telugu-speaking Andhra region, who appears to have travelled south with warrior-settler communities, and also with nomadic tribes such as the Narikkuravar, between the sixteenth and eighteenth centuries. In other dramas, the Kuratti fortune-tellers invoke and get possessed by Kollapuriyamma, the goddess Mahalakshmi of Kolhapur in Maharashtra, the tutelary deity of nomads who migrated from western and northern India to the peninsula.

I come out of my reverie, grateful to the eighteenth-century poets who have created this image of a wise, strong, graceful, independent woman from the folk stratum of Tamil society, a woman who represents ideals, learning and practices deeply rooted in Tamil culture, and who at the same time brings the languages, gods and lore of places as far as Mecca, Delhi and Maharashtra to the Tamil region.

On the way back to Tirunelveli, we stop, as planned, at the Narikkuravar tribal settlement in Pettai. I know that the Narikkuravar, sometimes simply called Kuravar, are a nomadic community who must have come to Tamilnadu from locations in central and northern India, via Andhra and Karnataka, between the sixteenth and eighteenth century. Narikkuravar groups dwell in temporary settlements in the Tamil countryside, earning their livelihood through the kinds of activities Kuravanci dramas portray for Singan and Singi.

I have seen Narikkuravar families sitting next to their pitched tents at bus-stations and roadsides in the city of Madras (now called by its ancient name, Chennai), and noted how closely their manners and appearance correspond to descriptions of Singi, Singan and the Kuravar in the *Kurralak Kuravanci*. Narikkuravar women wear western Indian (Rajasthani or Gujarati) style skirts with breast-cloths and tribal bodices. The beads and necklaces they wear resemble the jewellery of some nomadic communities of the north. Carrying baskets and wands of divination, they hawk beads and herbs, and tattoo customers. They tell their fortunes, sometimes reading palms, sometimes divining outcomes from counting grain spread out in a winnowing fan. The men wear red turbans, like those of tribal communities in Rajasthan and Gujarat, and deck themselves with beads and feathers. They hawk herbal medicine, aphrodisiac powders and potions, 'jackal horns' (fertility talismans made from the shaven skulls of jackals), small stuffed animals, and birds—both birds in cages, and stuffed birds. Like their nomadic counterparts in the north, and like Singan of the Kuravanci drama, these Narikkuravar are indeed bird-catchers, jackal hunters, and hawkers of jungle produce. Although they have transactions with people in the plains and valleys, their ultimate connection is to the hills and their products. Here in Tamilnadu, these people speak Tamil, but also Vagriboli ('Birdcatcher-language'), a mixed north Indian, Indo-Aryan language that is also spoken by the Vagri communities of Gujarat and Rajasthan. It is clear that the nomadic Narikkuravar are ultimately related both to the north Indian migrant groups and to the gypsies of Europe, although the migrations of the latter had taken place several centuries earlier. The nineteenth- and twentieth-century British ethnographic and administrative reports I have read classify the Narikkuravar and related wandering communities as 'Criminal tribes', a far cry from the respectful treatment these folk groups receive in the Kuravanci dramas.

Here, in Pettai, I am at last able to meet a large community of Narikkuravar, semi-settled (through the efforts of the state government) in an area not far from Tirunelveli town. From a distance, the settlement looks like a tent settlement of nomads anywhere in the world. These tents are made of black cloth or hide, and covered with a layer of white material. They are small, and serve mainly as sleeping quarters. As soon as we arrive at the settlement, there is a rush of men, women and children towards the car. Voices call out in Tamil: 'Buy some beads, lady?' 'Want a tattoo, lady?' 'Shall I tell your fortune, lady?' Rajan explains to the Narikkuravar that the lady would like to speak with them about their customs, for a book that she is writing. They are delighted, and take me around the tents, showing me their crafts, tools and wares, and obligingly posing for photographs. Suddenly I hear one of the men say something to a woman in a language that I know must be Vagriboli, a language that sounds like a mix of Gujarati, Marathi and Hindi, languages that I happen to know because of my education in Bombay. I try addressing the man in a similar mix of languages, showing him that I have understood what he said. Cries of surprise all round: 'How do you know our language?' 'Outsiders around here do not speak Vagriboli!' 'I am from Bombay,' I reply, 'and I understand Gujarati and Marathi.' The bond of a common mixed language breaks the ice, and I am warmly welcomed at every tent.

I get a fortune-telling demonstration, not only with palm reading, but also with numerical divining, using grain in a winnowing fan. I am shown all kinds of beads and herbal remedies, but they quickly see that my real fascination is for the bird-catching equipment placed near some of the tents. One bird-catcher shows me an array of elaborate traps, slingshots, nets and snares, and explains to me how each one works. Another shows me decoys, and demonstrates the crouching and hiding positions that Narikkuravar bird-catchers employ when they go hunting, sometimes in the hills, sometimes in the waterways and fields. I am transported to the second segment of the *Kurralak Kuravanci*, the part devoted to the exploits of the birdcatcher Singan:

> *Wearing a necklace of cockle-shells,*
> *with a heron-feather bound in his hair,*
> *a tiger-skin tied neatly into*
> *a sash around his waist,*
> *scaring tigers away with his ferocity,*
> *a quiver slung over his shoulder,*
> *a bamboo-staff in his hand,*
> *carrying various weapons and snares for birds,*
> *here comes Singan, the famed bird-catcher,*
> *Singan, the Kuluvan hunter of Kurralam's Tirikutam hill!*
> *(Kurralak Kuravanci 81)*

In another song (84), Singan introduces himself:

> *I am Singan the Bird-catcher!*
> *I set snares all day long.*
> *Springing like a lion, I catch birds*
> *in the sacred fields in the land of the Lord*
> *of Tirikutam hill, loud with the hum of bees!*
> *I track them like a hound, I stalk them like a cat,*
> *I crouch like the jackal, follow like a ghost,*
> *and kill them!*
> *I am Singan the Birdcatcher!*

Once again, I am struck by the symbiotic relationship between the hunter and the fields, the wilderness tribes and the settled communities. The egrets and other waterbirds that wait for prey in the canals of rice fields teeming with fish—I had seen these white birds only this morning, in the fields along our route—are the Kuravan bird-catcher's prime target, and both

Singan and Singi come from Tirikutam hill to the temple and town of Kurralam to sell their wares and ply their trades with the men and women of this prosperous settlement.

The sun is setting. I thank the Narikkuravar of Pettai and we leave for Tirunelveli. I say goodbye to my companions and dismiss the driver. The journey to Kurralam has deepened my understanding, not only of the *Kurralak Kuravanci* and mountains in the Tamil imagination, but also of a tribal community in today's Tamilnadu, a people who continue to strive with dignity to maintain their links with the wandering life, the sacred arts and powers of the mountains, and the bounty of the wilderness. As I go to my hotel room, I clutch in my hand small packets of cardamom, cloves and cinnamon bark, fragrant souvenirs to store in little jars in my kitchen in Massachusetts. I know that whenever I open the jars, the scent of the spices will transport me to Kurralam, its sacred hill, and the great waterfalls, and conjure up for me the songs of the *Kurrakkuravanci* as well as the voices of the woman who told my fortune, and the Narikkuravars of Pettai.

GEETA PATEL

JOURNEY TO MIRAJI'S MOUNTAIN

'This is a story from the time in my life when I had first begun to feel flickers of physical desire,' writes the Urdu poet, Miraji (1912-1949), in an essay that begins in Halol, a tiny railway colony outside Baroda city.[1] Fragmented into short, lively and evocative sections, the essay is a record of Miraji's life that ferries readers through his explorations into the roots of his own desires. Like the stories that circulated in his lifetime and continued after his death, Miraji's own story about himself seems to take shape in the short explanatory hiatuses out of which hagiographies are composed. Halol is the beginning of these stories, and the mountain that seems to give Halol its reason

---

GEETA PATEL is a professor of women's studies at Wellesley College. She works on Urdu poetry, aesthetics and politics, Hindi and Sanskrit translations, and is currently engaged in a project addressing risk, temporality and insurance. She is the author of *Lyrical Movements, Historical Hauntings: Colonialism, Gender and Desire in Miraji's Urdu Poetry*, published by Stanford University Press.

1. All the translations of prose are from *Miiraajii: Shaxsiyat aur Fann*, ed. Kumar Pashi (New Delhi: Modern Publishing, 1981). Other texts that inform this piece include: Ghanshyam Joshi, *Pavgadh Darshan* (Ahmedabad: Chirag Printers, 1998); *Shrii Mahaakaalii Maataajii* (Ahmedabad: Gaurav Publication, n.d.); Interviews with Leela Mayor, 10 January 1998; Jayesh Patel, 11 January 1998; David Hardiman, 'Power in the Forest: The Dangs, 1820-1940', *Subaltern Studies VIII* (New Delhi: Oxford University Press, 1996), 89-147.

for being is the organizing metaphor in them.

In 1996, after I had finished my dissertation on Miraji, I began the process of transforming its bareness into a book. What I wanted more of was the thickness of Miraji's life, and I had just begun to follow up cues and clues thrown to me. As a poet, Miraji is considered by many Urdu critics of contemporary lyric to be one of the finest of the twentieth century. Despite this, he seems to have disappeared from the practices of popular cultural remembering in India, unlike his compatriot Faiz Ahmad Faiz. The reasons often proposed for this deliberate forgetting are that Miraji spoke of desires in their simple bareness, and honed the poetry of sensuality and sexuality rather than forging politics through poetry. So I went on a search, a scrounging trip for any information on the poet. I wanted to excavate the details of his life, sedimented into layers of Indian locales to see if I could begin to understand the place of sensuality in Miraji's life and to detect whether the political was indeed divorced from the sensual in his world.

Miraji was born in Lahore, and returned there as a child, but somehow Halol seems to be the origin of the childhood tales that took him along the railways with his father, a bridge engineer. Halol was certainly the first place he describes as a place he remembered. I thought, as one often does when one is in the guise of a researcher, that going to Halol would give me a kernel of memory that I wanted: not just the kinds of abstract narratives that are sometimes offered when memory is sought but memory almost in the Proustian sense, with all my senses alive, that would give me the sensual thickness and pressure of pleasure, grief, and the limits of the worlds from which Miraji came.

Halol is twenty miles from Vadodara, a comfortable distance from what used to be the princely centre of Baroda State. Miraji's father, an assistant engineer in the railways, travelled there with his young family after Miraji was born.

Halol was then a bustling station. Now, in 2001, after a long lingering death, Halol has revived again because a highway has been built alongside it, giving it a reason for fitting in with Gujarat's narratives about state progress. Halol is the seminal place where Miraji learned about his desires, his sexuality, and where he first entered the world of adolescent fantasy. Because of the mountain Miraji saw from Halol—Pavgadh, the tallest mountain in Gujarat—mountains began to inhabit Miraji's literary imagination, and to appear in his poetry. I took a journey to the town of Halol to find out more about what significance this place and the mountain that looms over it had in Miraji's life.

I had initially envisioned myself travelling up the railway line from Vadodara, taking the train to the mountain, but in 1996, Halol station had been shut down and abandoned by the railways. The people I asked in the city of Vadodara, who had moved there recently, seemed to have forgotten that there had once been a station at Halol; it did not live in the historical memory passed down to these newcomers. Locals knew of the station but the railway lines once connecting Halol to the mines and Vadodara had been severed and were only maintained through Champaner and Pani. So I could not travel by train to the station. Instead, I had to arrange for two cars, which I needed to carry my fellow travellers: my brother, Sunil, my parents, Jayesh and Neena, who actually knew where we were going, and of course, two drivers who seemed to want to accompany me on this trip. My brother, who lives in Vadodara, supplied the cars, food and water, and we drove through country ridged by waterways, broken into fields and scrub left over after the British denuded the forests to build the town that was previously appended to the railway colony. Halol, the town, was small and bustling, a typical district headquarters which, though the railway no longer passes near it, still feels like a place thrown up to provide sustenance for a large BBCI railway station.

At the street that cuts the town into two, we asked for directions to the station. It took several tries as we found our way to streets that hugged the sides of the station. Left to turn derelict in the 1940s, Halol station was criss-crossed by lines that angled through a massive, hulking repair shed, a testament to the traffic that once circulated through it, overshadowed by Pavgadh. Even through a summer haze, the starkly sculpted rock-hill rose so unexpectedly from flat checkerboard fields that it was easy to understand why Miraji might have been seduced by its power. He had written:

> Our father was an assistant engineer on a small line there. We lived [in Halol] near the famous ancient historical site of Champaner. The mountain of Pavgadh was four or five miles away. There was a Kali temple at its summit. We could see the mountain from our courtyard. I've written a line: 'Who is responsible for the blue mystery of the mountain?' Though the mountain looked as if it were close by, it held a deep indigo mysteriousness for me—the kind of secret whose allure leaves a profound impression on one's mind.
>
> The monsoons lasted for quite a few months in those areas, and for a large portion of the year the sight of the mountain veiled in the smokiness of the rain held a special enchantment. In my imagination the rivers, draped randomly over the mountain's smoothness, turned into chalk streaks. Their sensual and sexual significance has recently become clear to me. The special characteristic of that region was the profusion of snakes [that appeared] during the monsoons. For a child, the dangerousness of snakes was not as significant as their seductiveness, which, like the story of Adam and Eve, snared men's imaginations. These were the important images [for me]—the mountain's smokiness, flowing streams, and colourful snakes.

Pavgadh's mystery is enhanced by the legends that accrue around its genesis. Each story has it dropping to earth from the skies. One, a local addition to the Ramayana, has it that Pavgadh was created when Hanuman dropped a portion of Mount Kailash as he flew over the region in a rush to get Himalayan

herbs to salve Lakshman's war wounds. Another story attributes
the mountain to Parvati. In this version, Pavgadh is a Shaktipith,
one of the fifty-two places where a part of Parvati's body fell as
Shiva danced destruction in the Tandav. Vishvamitra, the
sagacious friend of the world, is said to have hunkered down
on the mountain to meditate. The mountain's ridge is a site of
pilgrimage. As Miraji said, a tiny Kali (Mahakali) temple,
reached by steps carved into the face of the mountain, nestles at
its top. The temple is an especially auspicious pilgrimage stop
for devotees of many faiths: women travel to it to sing hymns to
Kali for the garbha danced at Navratri; it is one of the twelve
pilgrimage stops for Jains; Mira bhajans are sung there
throughout the year; a Sufi shrine sits close to the Kali temple;
and the Jama Masjid in nearby Champaner is visited by any
pilgrims who want special boons from the Pir buried in one
corner of the once magnificent gardens before the mosque. Miraji
called Champaner a famous ancient historical site (*mashuur
taariixii muqaam*), and in that phrase is secreted the kind of
history, the local tales, both sensual and political, that the poet
alluded to in the late forties in one of his short richly suggestive
prose pieces: 'History says that into every moment from the
distant, secret past is tucked an entire volume of magical tales . . .
and then every fantasy, every thought turns secret itself into
memory or step by step becomes history, or goes onto people a
drop of water.'[2]

Standing at the railway station, its life layered into the
buildings that surround it, I began to see in it the same layers of
sediment that cushioned the rocks of Champaner and Pavgadh,

---

2.   '*Taariix kahatii hai duur o raaz maazii ke har ik lamhe mein ka'ii
      daastaanein hain! Aur phir sab tasavvur aur sab xyall Hafiz:e men jaa
      chupe yaa raftaa raftaa taariix ban gaye ya paanii kii ik buund men
      bas gaye . . .*' 'Miiraajii: Baaten Kitaab-e pareshan' in *Xayaal* May
      1949; the beginning echoes 'Baaten' from *Saaqii* November 1944,
      reprinted in Jamil Jalibi (ed.) Miiraajii: Ek Mut:aalah (Miraji: A Perusal)
      (Lahore: Sang-e-Masil Publications, 1990), 568-70.

which told a long, fractured history of settlement. Seated conveniently on a popular trade route running between the Surat coast and Madhya Pradesh, and between kingdoms, Champaner had variously been reduced to rubble and refortified by the Rajput Chauhans, Patai Rawal, Rajput Muslims and finally, and most famously, by the Muslim king Mahmud Begda, who in the 1400s turned it into the capital of his kingdom. Alfonso de Albuquerque, a Portuguese trader, travelling in Gujarat in the early 1500s described Champaner as 'a great city in very fertile country of abundant provisions'. Even in its now depleted state, the fort hovered, a behemoth, light patterned through the shards of intricately carved *jalis* falling on the ruins of its widely spaced gardens.

In contrast to the fort, the station at Halol, abandoned like the poet who once lived in it, seemed almost ephemeral, a mundane memorial to another history of conquest. This history transformed the land not through ravening armies and large-scale rebuilding, but through contracts: levied on local Bhils and struck with local Rajas. It left its legacy in the crumbling quotidian buildings on the railway line now resettled by labourers and by the occasional descendants of the Bhils and villagers who had been uprooted when the British turned local jungle into 'forests' that could be mined for wood. These are the descendants of the people, 'tribals', whose history of displacement, disenfranchisement and resignification under British auspices, Miraji packed into his attenuated, wry and ironic style that was deeply political nonetheless.

Whenever the English engineer visited [Halol] on his rounds [of railway stations], a hunt was arranged for his entertainment. Children, because they are the tiny descendants of monkeys, ape their parents. So, our childhood games also included hunting. The Railway Dak Bungalow was a short distance from our house. This is a description of a particular incident that occurred when the engineer was visiting [us] on his rounds. His son and daughter strolled with my sister, me, and the two sons of our household servants over to the rambling garden [of the Dak Bungalow] to play. Our other companions, the son and daughter of the Bungalow's watchman, were assembled there. The Bhil tribe lives in that area [Halol]. Having graduated from an agricultural livelihood, they are now skilled at pillaging and stealing, as well as driving or beating for game. In that kind of hunting, people sit high up on a raised platform [*machaan*] and a line of Bhils flushes animals out [of the forest] with many different noises, surrounds them, and drives them towards the platform. We, too, played at driving game in the Dak Bungalow [garden]. We had designated a tree our 'raised platform'. The engineer's son and I, pretending to be the Bhils, had wandered away [to find game]. Just then, the servant's daughter ran towards us, and yelled out that Jamuna was a very bad girl—she was sitting on a tree and peeing. I, well-versed in the set of rules that ordered my family's behaviour, also thought of the act as 'bad'. However, the sensual specialness of that event has since stamped itself on my consciousness. I have just begun to understand the tangled effects of that sensual experience. But at the time, the experience had not only an exotic, provocative seductiveness, but a sense of harmony with nature (as well as carrying a profound moral ambivalence).

The Bhils 'graduated' from a 'respectable' agricultural livelihood into 'criminal vagrancy', Miraji tells us. Pretending to be *shikar* attendants in colonial games people play, children like Miraji aped them. These locals were the props who enabled the game of turning jungle into hunting preserve to come to a successful culmination; they flushed out wild animals for a shoot. Colonial spectacle was the place of Miraji's desire. Under its regimes of propriety, he had been taught the rights and wrongs of public displays, of bodily infraction, 'excess', of the public architecture of class, difference, and gender. The sons of the engineer and the assistant engineer pretended to be Bhils, even as the servant's daughter exposed Jamuna's infraction. Only later, Miraji tells us, could he come to understand the tangled implications of the event: that 'bad' was a family code learned to order, that peeing and the call to its exposure were both provocatively seductive. Like the streaks of white water that lit up Pavgadh in the monsoons, in these seminal stories of Miraji's desire, Jamuna, mountains, streams, *naag, naaginii*, and the snake in the Garden of Eden, all come together. And in these, Miraji's 'origin tales', one begins to see the moments of writing history tightly bound within a sentence or two that he expanded into the enticing, meticulously crafted, political, literary, and historical background offered for the authors whose translations he folded into essays.

In Halol, I saw the faint outlines of the world of the railway colony in which Miraji had lived. Besides the tin-roofed lumbering repair shed, its wooden door still padlocked, one could see at the other end of a length of entangled lines the yellow painted brick station, its waiting courtyard and wrought-iron benches, the blackboard with prices for tickets still scratched on in white, and the huge water tank perched impossibly precariously on the wooden scaffolding, Pavgadh fading into the background. A sadhu clothed in white had laid out his mat and bowl under the wide banyan tree that eclipses the station. The railway lines ran taut curves past the station, disappearing into thick undergrowth and the mountain in the distance, which seemed to be pulled closer in by them, like a kite skittering out from behind trees, tugged by strings no longer seen. The lines, running as they did, appearing suddenly out of one dense horizon and dissolving into another, promised a kind of mystery, the enchantment of beyond, enticing to a dreaming child.

Families squatted in those government tract houses that had been reduced to a few standing indigo white walls, the architecture of their construction exposed: two rooms, one bricked in, one shaded from the sun by a parodic simulacrum of Muslim Gujarati stone *jalis* built from criss-crossed wooden slats. Women hunched in the small yards set in front of each house, husking rice before open-air stoves. In the houses occupied according to railway code by employees, *charpais* were stacked up against walls. On the edges of the colony were queues of electric-blue tube tents, people threshing grain and stretching red saris before setting them to sun-dry, fat round bales of grass, a goat, a cow and a Rabari herding his sheep towards the centre of the station.

Larger houses still huddled close by. One that Miraji might have lived in was long and cool, yellow on the bottom, dusty white on top, nested back behind tall white walls, its slate yard leading to the kitchen, servants' quarters and storage shed a short distance away. Trees, thick mango, long-leaved neem and purple feathery jacaranda, lurched over it. A man, smoking on a charpai hidden in the veranda, said he stayed behind to work on the railways when his family left during Independence. The trees, he said, are a legacy of the British. He still allowed children running in rambunctious groups to play in and out of them. Looming through the trees was Pavgadh.

I gathered my family into the shadows thrown by the tallest mountain in Gujarat, and laid out the makings of a typical picnic lunch, *aloo paranthas*, fruit, *dahi*, and *achaar*. Sitting there, commemorating the mountain, I felt I had ritualized the act of remembering the poet, whose *awaragi—Nagari, nagari phira musafir, ghar ka rasta bhuul gaya, kya hai mera, kya hai tera, apna, paraya, bhuul gaya*—I had come to find by Pavgadh's side. Sharing the pleasure of food, like sharing lyrical sensuality, brought '*Jangal mein Mangal*', Miraji's poem that celebrates poetry, picnics and friendship, home to me. We finished. I packed everyone into cars and we drove slowly by the railway buildings, followed the mountain's edge into the thick brush past the forlorn station and little bustling town on our way back to Vadodara.

PART II

MOUNTAIN MEMOIRS

NAMITA GOKHALE

COMING HOME

I have come to the hills to heal, to hide, to forget. To forgive, to be forgiven. My friends all resisted my decision. My sister even insisted on accompanying me here, but I knew that I needed solitude and soliloquy to come to terms with what had happened. The acid had worked on the bone cartilage, and the surgeon has been cautious in his restorations. I have not looked into a mirror for months now, and my face, that familiar index of my being, has dissolved into absurdity and abstraction. Even my fingers do not recognize the changed contours of my cheeks, of the injured flesh. The avengers of my vanity have broken me, humbled me with these small depredations of skin and bone and tissue, leaving me less than I was.

Where am I? My mother was from these mountains, and I knew this house as a child, spent many happy summers here. It belongs to my mother's brother, my mamaji. He lives in Bangalore now (my parents are both dead) and since he has no children the house will one day probably belong to us, to my sister and to me. I already belong to it. It has taken me in, enveloped my hurt. It soothes my hatred, hushes my sorrow. It

NAMITA GOKHALE was born in 1956 in Lucknow and grew up in Nainital and New Delhi. She began her career publishing a popular film magazine, *Super*. She is the author of two previous novels, *Paro: Dreams of Passion* and *Gods, Graves and Grandmother*. She also writes regularly on literary subjects for various papers and magazines. 'Coming Home' has been excerpted from *The Book of Shadows*, Penguin Books India, New Delhi, 1999.

had been hostile at first, angry that we had forgotten the sanctuary of its love. This old and gentle house, built by a missionary a hundred years ago, was the repository of my youth, the custodian of my dreams. I had been happy here as a child, and I am determined to be that again; to forget Anand's indulgent and wanton act of self-destruction, ignore his stupidity, and restore my life to its own course once again. You see, I have all the right intentions.

After I was discharged from the hospital, Delhi appeared a wilderness of heartbreak and pain. I travelled up to the hills alone, in a rickety clattering deathtrap of a taxi. I covered up my face with a long muslin chunni, Bedouin style, and observed the familiar changes of landscape on the journey up. Every life has its constants: despite all that had happened, as we approached Ranikhet I caught my breath in wonder again. In Delhi I always forget how beautiful our hills are. The Kathgodam road witnesses some incredible changes of scenery, and the last bit before Ranikhet, with its miles and miles of abandoned terraced fields, is almost frightening in its desolation. We took the other road, from Ramnagar. Even though it was late June and the Himalayas were covered in a haze of dust and heat, we had snatches and visitations of their presences all the way through.

The house is set some distance from the main road. There is a deep dip into a small ravine, where a stream flows rapidly through the hillside until it reaches the turn, as though it were running away from somebody, escaping pursuit. The pine and deodar forests suddenly close in, and an outsider might find something menacing about the air. The thick undergrowth and overhanging vines add to the effect. The taxi driver, a tired old Sikh with an air of melancholy resignation, voiced his doubts about our destination. 'This place looks absolutely junglee, memsahib,' he said, a note of concern in his voice. 'There must be wild animals around here, not to speak of thieves and robbers.

Do you really want to go on? We could find a nice hotel in Ranikhet.'

I urged him on, lying about the distance to the house. The exhausted taxi wheezed and coughed towards the hilltop, through the winding kuchha road with its stones and boulders and exposed tree-roots. The splats of cow dung that marked our path seemed almost reassuring, indicating the presence of domestic animals. Two giggling *ghasyarans* in bright blue petticoats, with sickles in their hands and bundles of fodder balanced on their pretty heads, met us as we passed. They stared after us curiously. I'm sure they hadn't seen a car in these parts for years.

As we neared the house a familiar sense of elation overtook me. The very air here is different, it is thinner and purer than city air, its pine-scented effervescence made me feel heady and expectant. The taxi driver was getting more and more alarmed. 'Maybe we should turn back now,' he said timidly, 'I don't think this road leads anywhere.' I knew better. At the next turn of the road we would meet the gates of the house, and the old outhouse where I had played as a child. The hillside was covered with patches of wild narcissus. A Himalayan bird of paradise, a *lampoochha*, made a low swoop across the road, as though in welcome. A pair of marmots, what our hill people call chitrail, swerved before us, panicking at the intrusion of the car. A hoopoe balanced on a clump of bamboo and piped out a tune.

The thickets of bamboo on either side of the road arched and met high in the air. The haze cleared up for a brief moment, and the numinous outline of Nanda Devi, its summer snows gleaming in the afternoon sun, greeted us. Even the driver was disarmed, and a tentative smile played upon his bearded face.

There is a last twist and curve to the road, and then we come to the house. There it stood, in all its loveliness. A gracious veranda encircled its contours. The white blooms of climbing roses clung to the frontage. The windows of the upstairs bedrooms gazed out at the sweep of the Himalayan ranges, now obscured from view. Broken stone steps led down from the garden to the tennis court below, or to what had once been the tennis court but was now an overgrowth of bramble and nettle. The garden was covered with dandelion and forget-me-not, although some clumps of lupin and larkspur struggled against the chaos of weed. The two hydrangea bushes were where they had always been; they had grown to monstrous proportions, the blue flowers streaked and spotted with purple.

The driver extracted my two suitcases from the boot of the car and decided to abandon me. The taxi disappeared in a bustle of groaning and hooting. The smell of diesel hung in the air, offending my nostrils. The muslin chunni and the Bedouin mask had fallen from my face. There was no one here I needed to hide from.

The front door was locked. I would have to call Lohaniju from the servant quarters. I had not bothered to inform him of my arrival. As I stood there, by the solid oak door, I was overtaken by what, for want of a better word, I can only describe as a sense of déjà vu. I had been here before, to this very spot, not in my anterior history as a child or a young girl, but in this very form and this very time. There was an overlay of perception and memory, a mass of recollection that struggled to be set free.

A swarm of yellow butterflies appeared out of nowhere. They settled themselves on the roses and the overgrown hydrangeas; they hovered in mid-air like a celestial garden. Some impress of memory was set loose from my mind. Images fluttered out of nowhere and sprung to life in full form. A procession of people came out from all directions to meet me. They stood there, in the flesh, no phantoms or fantasies but people like you or me. Some I could see clearly, and others evaded recognition. A woman with a bunch of summer flowers in her hand, a woman of surpassing beauty with a sheath of static surrounding her. Two strange figures, cowering in the sunlight, pale personages of undistinguished demeanour. A local Pahari youth, his face hooded in a woollen shawl, a blood-red slash across his pale forehead.

In the distance I could hear the yowling of dogs, their sad insistent barking which dissolved into a sort of collective sigh. The putrid stench of decomposition arose from somewhere around me, followed by the scent of narcissus. The smell was so powerful that it unlocked some secret cache of memory, some hidden intimation of what had been. Snatches of sound filled the air—melody, not lyric.

These were not strangers around me, they were familiar cohabitants of the same space. It was as though we had escaped the confines of our life-scripts, stumbled upon some interstice of experience, some simultaneity of narrative. But who was the narrator?

Just then Lohaniju came loping out of the house. His long legs and lanky, almost adolescent gait filled me with a rush of relief. Lohaniju was there, I was home again.

VIVEK BHANDARI

THE CITY AND THE HILL

When, as a ten-year-old I first read Satyajit Ray's *Sonar Killa*, a short story about the 'golden fortress' of Jaisalmer situated in the desert sands of western Rajasthan, I remember being transported into a place of fantasy and adventure, a world that was a distraction from everyday tyrannies. It was an enjoyable escape, the story of Mukul who is in search of a place he has visited in a previous life, something he knows from his own prolific drawings that depict scenes and places he has never seen. With help from a parapsychologist and a private detective, Mukul's quest for this magical place—where gold and jewels abound—takes him into desert fortresses, as a band of thieves follows along. It was an invigorating narrative, and gave me the kind of rush I used to experience reading Phantom comics, and the adventures of Mandrake the Magician, staples of the childhood imagination for schoolboys in the early 1980s. Now that I look back at those days, this representation of the 'killa' as a magical place seems completely detached from the pedestrian ways in which I connected with the fortress overlooking my hometown, Jaipur.

VIVEK BHANDARI teaches history and South Asian Studies at Hampshire College in Amherst, Massachusetts. His research addresses the diverse ways in which challenges confronting contemporary India are intimately connected to the difficult ways in which the country has negotiated the forces of modernization and nation-building. Although he has lived in the US for the past decade, he retains close ties to Jaipur, a place he visits every year.

Looming high over the city, on a prominent hill of the once-really-high-but-now-eroded Aravalli mountain range, Nahargarh is visible from virtually every corner of the city. Often called the city's sentinel, it is an enduring frame of reference for the people of Jaipur, a reminder of the city's history, a physical marker of its periphery in the north. It also points the way to Delhi, India's locus of power and prestige, or at least that is what most of us Jaipur-walas think. Its imposing qualities— height and grandeur—are offset by the subtle ways in which it is bound-up with our everyday lives. For us, Nahargarh is an avuncular presence that we view with benign favour and a feeling of ownership.

On our drives up the hill to the fortress, my father usually drove the Jeep, with my mother sitting next to him. My sister and I sat in the back, together with driver-*saab*, who was a stoic but friendly presence on these outings. As we drove higher and higher, Jaipur unfolded beneath us, its buildings interwoven like a textured tapestry. The journey from our house in the Civil Lines to the top of the fortress was a Jaipur *darshana*, a tour through the different localities that make up this schizophrenic entity. We went through the old walled city, which, despite being among the most symmetrical and meticulously planned in India, seemed to be succumbing to demographic pressures and automobile congestion, or at least so we thought since we lived in the *new* Jaipur. We then traversed the city's outskirts, went past bazaars, temples, mosques, chhatris, and eventually, the Jal Mahal—a palace in the middle of a lake that was slowly being devoured by water hyacinth. Each one of these areas had distinct personalities, and as the inhabitants of the relatively modern Civil Lines, we felt compelled to comment on them. The old city was dirty and overcrowded, the memorials and temples were in a state of disrepair, because, my teachers sometimes said, we have no sense of history. And as for the water-hyacinth menace that was devouring the lake, well, it was all the municipality's fault! I am not sure if any of us really took these blanket condemnations seriously, but they were the prevailing wisdom on Jaipur's different constituencies at the time. They set the terms on which we related to our city, and if anything, were symptomatic of our sense of entitlement over it.

Once we had passed the urban landscape, the critical commentary that had punctuated our drive through town was replaced by a sense of anticipation and excitement. As the city gave way to the hilly and shrubby terrain of the hills, conversation shifted to questions about how high we were going, whether we'd remembered to bring the camera, water bottle, ball, etc. I was usually quite curious about how high birds could fly, and whether that could give us some sense of the height we were climbing. Someone (usually my sister) spotted a bird rarely seen in the city and ignited debates about the species of the bird, its colouring—and whether somebody in the family was going colour-blind! As my father was an amateur ornithologist, and usually carried Salim Ali's field guide to bird watching, a quick perusal through it usually settled things. My sister and I were usually on the look-out for blue jays as they supposedly brought good luck, a concept that I took quite seriously as a pre-teen. For all of us, visits to Nahargarh were like an escape because they allowed us to spend time on things we couldn't always do at home. What made these trips special was not that we could indulge our little eccentricities, but that we were able to *share* them amongst ourselves; although those of mine that dealt with catapults and rock-climbing were usually nipped in the bud. Around the time I had put the finishing touches on my scheme of hunting evil vultures with a bow and arrow, the main gate of the fortress would come into view, signalling the end of the ascent.

The drive into the heart of Nahargarh, where a palace was located, took us over a flattened hilltop, where ramparts had been constructed for protection. About half a mile wide, unpopulated, quiet and barren, this stretch of land allowed us to feel a sense of freedom from the congestion of the city. The winding road to the palace, traversing roughly the centre of the hill, took us past the Charan Mandir, a temple where worshippers pray to the footprints of Lord Krishna. Right next to it is an odd-looking watchtower, built in the same style as the Jantar Mantar in Jaipur. This is a monument to Maharaja Jai Singh II's lifelong love affair with astronomy. Located adjacent to the temple, this structure has long slopes, small canopies, and little grids painted on its cracking surfaces. These were the maharaja's experiments in geometry and astronomy. Hundredfold magnifications of small astronomical instruments, structures such as these were incredible works of synthesis based on information culled from ancient Indian, Arabic, and Greek texts.

In the preface to his own opus on astronomy, the *Zij-e-Muhammad Shahi*, Jai Singh II revealed that his inspiration for astronomy and the desire to build precise 'architectural instruments' came from a Timurid ruler of mediaeval Afghanistan who had built a similar observatory in Samarkand. Like their illustrious counterparts in New Delhi, these architectural oddities are now crumbling, having weathered the elements, environmental decay and, increasingly, the tourism onslaught. Against the backdrop of Jaipur and the distant Aravallis, they were a symbol of the past for us, conjuring-up supernatural possibilities in my adolescent imagination. As if to dispel such ludicrous imaginings, our drive then took us past All India Radio's modern transmission centre, a flat, angular building which had a tall tower sprouting out of it. It was an official building with absolutely no magical possibilities whatsoever. Quite close to the astronomical curiosities of the founder of Jaipur, this structure was a reminder that the imperatives of modernizing Jaipur far outweighed the pre-modern aesthetic sensibilities of the city dwellers.

From the drive, we could look into the distance at a neighbouring hill where the Indian army had built a large communications facility with a huge dish antenna at its centre, increasingly a common sight on the hills of India. Like the All India Radio tower, this building was indiscriminately planted on the landscape by the state's diktat. Most decisions of this kind came from Delhi, from 'above', usually where most governmental institutions originated. Therefore, it was quite detached from the lives of Jaipur's civilian population, as it was probably meant to be. Because such facilities had little or no contact with the city's inhabitants, they were viewed as unpleasant, sometimes intimidating, but necessary blots on the hilly terrain. The same elitism could not be ascribed to the fortresses. Although they symbolized the same lofty principles as the two transmission centres—state power and military might—they had merged into the cultural landscape of Jaipur over time, and lost their elevated status. In recent times, as the centre of power had shifted to Delhi, the fortresses didn't even symbolize governmental authority any more, only its distant memory. What had not changed over time was the fact that those in power still used high places to mark their presence, and to gaze *down* from positions of dominance. Hills and mountains have always attracted those in authority, and the admiring gaze of those lacking it.

Running parallel to the road was a concrete passage that transported water to the neighbouring fortress of Jaigarh, home of the world's longest, fattest cannon (which had only been fired once, somewhat inaccurately). Considered a masterpiece of engineering, the water passage always invoked comparisons with the Roman aqueducts and a sense of pride among all present, although, as a ten-year-old, I sometimes wondered what all the fuss was about. This aqueduct had become derelict and seemed quite incapable of transporting anything in its current state, let alone water. Age had obviously taken its toll on this drainage mechanism, but this was true of so many things. As for the cannon, it was still there, rusting, wallowing in its corpulence. I loved it as a boy since I could compare it favourably with the 'guns of Navarone', which had terrified the Germans in the Hollywood movie of that name. The movie made fairly regular appearances in Jaipur's only 70 mm theatre at that time, a theatre famous for its *samosas* and tea.

On our short stops during the drive, I explored all possible signs of life in the neighbourhood of the aqueduct and the astronomical structures. Even though I knew that there was little possibility of finding wild animals, there was always the lingering hope that something might emerge from behind the bushes. Snakes were always a risk, but since *nahar* (as in Nahargarh) means 'tiger', I secretly harboured hopes of encountering one. Like most of my imaginary scenarios, this one was based on a misinterpretation about the origins of the name of our fortress. Originally a stronghold of the Mina tribes, the fortress was occupied by the Kacchawaha rulers of Amber in the eleventh century. Legend has it that at the time Nahargarh was being constructed in its present form, a strange occurrence kept upsetting the building process: masons found that their entire work of the day was undone overnight! When the ruler, Sawai Jai Singh, went to investigate, he encountered a *bhomia*, the spirit of a martyred warrior called Nahar Singh who did not want to be disturbed. A *rajapurohit* was then called to appease the spirit, and the fortress subsequently came to be called Nahargarh, not after a tiger, but in memory of the folk hero whose spirit lived there. In retrospect, I might have had better luck looking for lost *bhomias* rather than feline beasts.

During my 'hunting expeditions' I encountered little boys shepherding cows and goats around the shrubs and bushes. Our cryptic introductions usually led to animal patting, candy (and *chooran)* exchanges and, if I had a bat and ball handy, a quick game of cricket. The boys sometimes abandoned their animals and hitched a ride with us to the palace, where we chased the monkeys that ran around the fortress plucking at the trees and shrubs, or scavenging on the litter left behind by the tourist population. At times, the monkeys grabbed at the picnic baskets that we carried into the fortress. We thought of throwing stones (using my brilliant catapult) to ward them off, but my parents discouraged us, pointing out that the monkeys would throw them back, and that they never missed! After that, we just made rude faces at them. Generally, they ignored us as they were quite used to the juvenile antics of brats like us.

From the ramparts of Nahargarh, we gazed over the city. In winter months, especially the period from Diwali to Makar Sakranti, the Jaipur skies were inundated with kites. The arid breeze that blew over Jaipur this time of the year was ideal for kite-flying, strong enough to launch the kites, but gentle enough to allow for control and manoeuvrability. A mild nip in the air and the prospect of the sun's balmy rays sent most Jaipur-walas to their terraces where they spent long afternoons gazing at the sky, 'kite-fighting', and eating *pakoras* while listening to the cricket commentary on the radio. For children returning from school in the afternoon, the journey home was frequently interrupted by short rounds of haggling at the kite-vendor's stall, or minor detours to chase kites falling from the skies. From the ramparts of Nahargarh, the kites merged with the vultures circling over the city. Unlike Japanese kites that have long tails, those in Jaipur were multicoloured squares with a little tail at one end. These kites competed for dominance in the skies. Since they were flown using strings called *manja* (that had been dipped in glue and powdered glass), they had to be guided by the kite-flyer to outwit the other kites. It was a psychedelic spectacle and from high up on our perch, one that unfolded for us on an epic scale. If we stayed until sunset, the skies sparkled with kites that contained small candles that hovered over the city. As the sun went down, all the kites made a final lunge towards each other, and if they succeeded in decapitating the opposition, a loud, victorious exclamation ('kaataaaaaaaaaa!') pierced the sky.

Vultures flew in large numbers over the city. After their long flights over Jaipur's various garbage dumps, cremation grounds and slums, they perched on the jagged rocks of Nahargarh. On our picnics, their menacing presence was never far away. Often, we made eye contact with the birds, something that sent shivers down my spine. As the vultures found their way over the ramparts of the fort, and perched on trees not too far away from where we sat picnicking, the monkeys eyed them suspiciously although they really had nothing to worry about. Some of the vultures perched majestically on the ramparts, as dust-devils conjured up by the winter breeze danced around them. For me, this was usually a time to make a quick dash indoors where there were less menacing things to look forward to.

Within Nahrgarh Fort is the Madhavendra Palace, originally built to house the nine queens of Madho Singh II, Jaipur's devoutly religious and voraciously sexual king, earlier in the twentieth century. Although he had many queens and eighteen official mistresses, the portly Madho Singh remained heirless, a distressing matter for someone in his position. Because of this weakness, it is believed that a concubine by the name of Roop Rai—described as 'that pestilential woman', and the 'female Rasputin' by British officials—exercised considerable influence over the maharaja, and was in fact arrested for siphoning large amounts of money from the royal treasury. Clearly the *zenana* was no picnic, and Madhavendra Palace's complicated, labyrinthine layout was probably not an accident.

As far as we were concerned, the likelihood of getting lost when making our way through the palace's nine chambers gave the palace an air of intrigue. Added to this was the possibility that while gazing upon the city from a window, we could fall over. Part sleazy hotel and part police station, the building had become a truncated travesty of itself, and a bit of an embarrassment for Rajasthan's tourism ministry. It is a testimony to the perversities of modernization and 'development' that as an act of renovation, the palace has acquired faux-windows, painted on walls that were otherwise starkly plain. Worse, it has been repainted from ochre to a gaudy yellow or pink, the latter because Jaipur came to be called the 'Pink City' by a colour-blind monarch. In an effort to make the building, and indeed the whole fortress more appealing to tourists and the consumerist imagination, retainers of the palace have reduced it to a caricature of its former self.

Of course, as children we were never bothered by these things as our priorities were different. Where my father expressed concern over the state of the hotel and police station, we looked forward to the Campa Cola we could buy in the hotel's restaurant, or roasted peanuts from the vendors outside. Where others commented (favourably or critically) on the palace's renovation, the sloppiness of the constabulary, or the growing deforestation, we looked for tales of chivalry and gore spiced with a touch of the supernatural. These came alive in our cryptic conversations with the man guarding the palace gates. Usually middle-aged, with a big, bushy moustache, turban, three-nought-three rifle, and a fading Nehru jacket over a khaki uniform, the guard kept a steely eye on us as I, with my few friends who had temporarily abandoned their cows, planned our entry into the palace. As someone who probably lived in the palace complex, he held a special aura for all of us. His stern gaze usually warmed up after we had bribed him with some peanuts and *chai*. At this point, the stories began, punctuated with words of caution about how we needed to conduct ourselves inside the building.

No, instead of worrying about the forces of modernization, getting lost, or plummeting to our death hundreds of feet below, we went looking for adventure in those parts of the palace that had been closed off, and were now inhabited by various rodents. The fact that there were bats around was apparent from the stink of bat-droppings that wafted through the whole palace. The bats' hiding places were also in the darker, dingier parts of the building, and this meant that we had every opportunity to imagine the worst possible scenarios. Many of these drew upon the tales we had heard from the guard, or the stories of Vikram and Vetala culled from *Amar Chitra Kathas*. Once these fantasies had run their course, we returned to the more illuminated parts of the palace which were populated by pigeons, whose benign presence usually brought us back to the humdrum realities of the picnic.

Munching on *aaloo parathas* and mango pickle, we ended the day intently watching the sun descend over the horizon, painting the sky iridescent hues of red and yellow. Of all the memories of Nahargarh, the one that is most deeply etched on my mind is that of the city at twilight, when the fiery skies served as a backdrop for millions of twinkling lights, glittering all the way to the horizon. From up on our perch behind the highest rampart of the fortress, it was enchanting to imagine that each light was in some way connected to a person going about the mundane tasks of everyday life. Someone down there was having dinner, playing cards, teasing someone, or just, maybe, looking up at us. There was something awesome about the spectacle, one that induced us to listen calmly, silently, to the sounds of the city. Music, cars, conversations and monologues merged with TVs and radios, screeches and bangs, whispers and murmurs to produce a deep, symphonic roar. This was what we had climbed up the hill to reclaim. The fortress was an essential part of Jaipur's identity, serving as a barometer of its ascending, or declining, fortunes. For us, Nahargarh was a retreat that gave us a snapshot into our own lives like nothing else could.

PIYA CHATTERJEE

MYTH, MEMORY, AND OTHER HIMALAYAN LABOURS

Memory, like the mind and time, is unimaginable within physical dimensions; to imagine it as a physical place is to make it into a landscape in which its contents are located, and what has location can be approached.[1]

History is carried in the mind to the remotest places to determine what one's acts mean even there, and who can say how much it weighs for those who carry it?[2]

Starting the gradual ascent up the road from Dehra Dun, past Rajpur, I imagine, in my mind's eye, the hairpin bends getting sharper. The wind is cold against my face, my hands trail in the force of the wind hitting the car. On my left, on top of a hillock, perhaps thirty minutes into the ride, I remember the tree. It is old, I know, denuded of leaves, small; nothing like the lush pines to greet me when I might walk further and further away

---

PIYA CHATTERJEE is a historical anthropologist who teaches in Women's Studies at the University of California–Riverside. She is the author of *A Time for Tea: Women, Labor and Post-Colonial Politics on an Indian Plantation* (Durham, NC: Duke University Press, 2001). She is also Co-Director of the research/activist wing of Women's Studies, Women in Coalition. Sections of this essay are edited from Piya Chatterjee's book, *A Time for Tea: Women, Labor and Post-Colonial Politics on an Indian Plantation*.

1. Rebecca Solnit. *Wanderlust: A History of Walking* (New York: Viking, 2000), p. 77.
2. Ibid. p. 140.

from the town. Up at the top, that is. It doesn't matter, though, that this little tree cannot match the pines; its branching out of dry wood is somehow both sentinel and signal of the high hills and home to come.

I cannot think about the Garhwal Himalayas, where I spent nine years of my childhood, without the miasma of nostalgia and sentiment, aware of memory's capacity to cloud what actual experience I may have had when I first arrived there, leaving my family to enter boarding school. The mountains paint landscapes of an abandoned childhood. I cannot claim them so easily as home. So my approach is littered with loss, with things buried too deep to unearth a road that could lead straight to a tale of mountains. I fear this walk towards such a landscape of memory cannot locate it, fix it into a series of points. The mountains resist, despite all the stories of their conquest, such logical plottings. I cannot fix the pinions, the ropes, the chisel to climb vertically. Memory defies such exacting fortitude.

I remember the hills aimlessly. I circle the paths like a pilgrim walking around Kailash, but with far less purpose. Like so many millions of pilgrims, over so many years, the mountains invoke for me an almost immediate organic, personal connection. I perch on the edge of the hillside, nibbling on grass, watching a white eagle court the sky. My body, ponderous and plodding in such a consideration, is happy to simply sit or simply wander. Myth, desire and loss labour together in this journey back to the forever hills.

It must have been the late 1970s, when I was about ten years old, that I travelled in a school-chaperoned bus from New Delhi to Mussoorie. We were dropped at the bus stop at Picture Palace. From there, our black tin trunks and bedrolls were carried by small, wizened men up the steep hill of Landour Bazaar. These coolies were paid a minute sum to carry our loads. We straggled up on foot, maybe carrying a water bottle and knapsack. As a child of feudal privilege, I never asked why this had to be so. I knew there were hardly any cars plying up that way to the school. I did wonder how such small bodies could carry such weight. They would follow us by foot, gasping for breath. At the top of Landour Hill, before the road became a little more horizontal, we would pause, looking for our batch of trunks. Once, at the top of the hill, a tourist in simple cotton clothes and wind cheater, watched us come up the hill. He then helped one of the men with the trunks to a bench, took off his load, and gave him a hot cup of tea. I remember vividly this act of kindness that we ourselves had been incapable of, in all our naturalised sense of entitlement. I remember the cold mist in the air, the crisp inward flow of breath, the grateful sips of tea.

I remained in that late mountain childhood for nine years. Eight years after I left, I wrote *Song for Himalaya*. I wrote it as if I would write to a lover, a friend: 'So I have come/back to you,/not seeing how/you beckoned before./It was in an/early green light,/this journey of/my return,/a light as transparent/as sun through/a blade of grass:/my fingers/even they were/dappled green/and insubstantial./A fleeting peacock/in a flash of blue/ changed the colour/of startled leaves and/I paused on/the path to breathe in/the brilliant blue air,/the flickers of green./What more to/expect from you,/my Beloved,/but this gasping/green silence?'

In 1991, when I returned to the other end of the Himalayas, the foothills of North Bengal, I never did so with an explicit intention to return to the mountains. I was compelled by more prosaic, academic reasons—to begin research on women and labour in the tea plantations of North Bengal, in the Bhutan Dooars, two hours from Darjeeling. For more than a year, I remained near those foothills and I continue to visit and work in the area. Despite that lack of intention, and through the usual psychic dilemmas of diasporic returns and departures, the Himalayas have become a constant, almost a benediction.

Visiting Darjeeling for the first time that October, I began my work on tea, women and plantation labour. Darjeeling is very different from Mussoorie though both are hillstations where the British would escape the summer heat. The Raj still lives in the names of streets and plantations: the Mall; the Planter's Club; Castleton; Margaret's Hope. I stayed in Mim Tea Estate, a two-hour drive away from the town. We had to get into a jeep at one point because the terrain was so unyielding and steep. I was convinced that the man driving the jeep had the third eye. We careened down unbelievably steep roads. The Mim bungalow was far from the town; all around us were the chest-high bonsai bushes of emerald tea.

From the small arbour of garden around my guestroom, I could see three high peaks. At six in the morning, they glistened, they seemed unreal. One of them was Kanchenjunga, the third highest mountain in the world. I had heard many stories about Kanchenjunga. The Lepchas have one; so do the Tibetans and the Nepalis. The one I heard most often was that Kanchenjunga cannot be climbed. Why? Because the mountain is Lord Shiva resting—see, look at his elbows, see his forehead. That is the summit. How can you put your foot on the forehead of God?

Apparently, for a long time, the Nepali and Indian governments would not give mountaineering permits to outsiders. I haven't bothered to find out whether there was a conquest, and who conquered Her. For some reason, the mountain is transgendered to me. She is both Mother Goddess and Shiva.

One bright morning, when the sky was cerulean, I was preoccupied with a trip I had to make to a neighbouring village. I was looking down at the steep path, watching my step. At one point in that precipitous walk down, I looked up and suddenly She was there. I could almost touch Her: that glorious, silver presence. My breath caught into silence.

I am glad, in retrospect, that I did not search more for the truth of Kanchenjunga's conquest, probably the many ascents. I prefer to think that no one has ever stepped on the forehead of God.

That year, I was driven up to Darjeeling with some planter friends, on the way to Mim and the Darjeeling International Tea Festival. The air became cooler as we wound our way gradually up the road. On the roadside, several young Nepali women with bundles of firewood on their heads watched us impassively. Suddenly, at some distance, I saw a velvet green hillside. I had never seen such a carpet of green. It looked like a thick golf course, completely natural. I looked again and asked my hosts why the hills were so landscaped, so even. Looking amused, they told me that the emerald carpet was actually a huge stretch of tea plantations. Fields of green running into each other. The inclines were so steep, I could not imagine how they were planted. It was strange and beautiful because the layout of bushes was not distinguishable from the general flora. From the distance of the car, the tea bushes formed a soft green carpet cloaking large sections of the hills: nature perfected, curiously unpeopled. Suddenly, banners with names redolent of the Raj interrupted the winding gaze. 'Castleton Tea Estate Welcomes You.' 'The Darjeeling Tea Planters Association is proud to host the President of India.' Then, incongruously, 'Hot air ballooning, Sunday afternoon.' (I imagined this balloon as a floating panopticon looking down upon the viridian landscape.)

The tea festival was a spectacle of the Raj remembered, re-invented, into a post-colonial and national mythos. On the Mall, in this most beautiful of the old British hillstations, the Planters' Club hosted an exquisite banquet, with white-jacketed bearers, their coats frayed at the edges, who circulated through a glittering cosmopolitan crowd. Senior planters, the *burra sahibs*, spoke in the Queen's English.

The presence of the President of India and the Governor of

West Bengal gestured towards the economic importance of this spectacle within the national economy. Japanese and European tea brokers at the tea auction (held for charity) situated the panorama squarely within the global marketplace. This was, after all, Darjeeling tea. Aristocracies of an old world, imbued with the nostalgia of colonial leisures, helped define it as the finest quality of tea.

Today, Darjeeling tea continues to invoke the leisured gentility of an era gone: a memory of colonial life and its powerful images of aristocratic splendour and endless entitled time. Circulating at a high price, tea became a central actor in the iconic rituals of empire re-lived in splendour. Take Castleton's Darjeeling tea, which sold for Rs 6010 per kilo, literally costlier per weight than the going price of gold. Bought by Mitsui Norin Company, a Japanese tea importer that commands 30 per cent of the Japanese market, Castleton's leaf was sold in Taiwan and Japan. Marketed as an exclusive gift item, the tea was packed in bone china containers designed in Italy by porcelain manufacturer Richard Ginori, whose family has been making the finest china since 1735. Ming jars of the seventeenth century were transformed into Italian china of the late twentieth and sold by a Japanese company. Circumnavigating the globe within an imperial collage, Indian tea now weaves another tale of commodified magic. Green Gold!

Even the texts of business and commerce wax eloquent when contemplating the magic of tea. It is, indeed, Nature's strange largesse that offers Castleton's sublime brew whose 'leaves remain wrapped in mystery'. Even Nature appears to have cast a shroud on its secret. From a spur atop Eagle's Crag, 5500 feet above sea-level, the slopes of Castleton hide behind a lace curtain of mist. The mountains offer a gift of magic: fetishism is a sleight of hand that waves away labour into mist. The commodity, leaf and brew, sells not only histories of nostalgia and leisure, but also Nature made as immaculate and eternal as the hills themselves.

What is significant, however, is the manner in which the valorization of Nature is fleshed through the labour of women who, when portrayed plucking tea leaves on the packages of tea, serve to fetishize the product into a landscape both exotic and desirable. Feminized labour on the steep hills of Darjeeling creates the material and bodied histories of their splendour. Labelled as nimble, delicate, and dexterous, women's hands and fingers have long been the iconic justification of dominance in this phase of tea cultivation in the plantations. They are also cheap, devalued in the immediate material practices of plantation labour. Women workers rest at the bottom of the plantation wage structure. Leisure and the capacity to 'taste' are narrative and symbolic acts that must push into shadows the bodied (indeed sweaty and dirty) history that makes the grand rituals of the club a possibility. The tea festival produces an aesthetics of contradiction and pastiche, a post- and neo-colonial commerce predicated on the picturesque and on the invisibility of human toil.

At the tea festival of 1991, against the picturesque beauty of the Darjeeling hills, I saw processions of young girl students from Loreto Convent, dressed as veiled British memsahibs in rickshaws, ironically juxtaposed against 'traditional' Nepali and Lepcha women dancers. And in one photo montage of the tea festival in a Calcutta magazine, I have seen women's dances in the Mall framed beside a small inset photograph of an elderly Nepali woman, in a white shawl, sitting on a chair. She is displayed as 'the oldest living tea plantation worker'. Her mouth is covered partially by a shawl, her features barely discernible, her gaze enigmatic.

The fetishisms of the so-called nimble fingers of plantation workers like this woman create another history of taste, delicacy, and craft in which the mountains are cast as goddesses in one moment and a Shangri-la of women at work in another, covered by ethereal mists weaving 'two leaves and a bud' into nimbly-poised fingers.

Back in the inland empire of Southern California where I live, I imagine again the viridian landscape, that great silver presence of Kanchenjunga. I remember moonlight and pines and the benediction of dark light on the great hills. Gender and labour are now linked to my idiosyncratic mythography of the beloved hills. What I have learned is that the romanticism of nostalgia, and the astonishing visual and visceral effects of silver peaks occasionally glimpsed, elides other histories of the mountains—of labour done to make conquest possible, to redeem the picturesque, to makes bodies of ritual, culture and discovery. I wonder again about the burdens of history, the landscape and its weight of memories.

Now I enter the car, turn on the ignition and, with mounting anxiety, head into the great asphalt arteries of California. I refused, for many years, this entry into speed and a powerful kind of high individualism, because of fear. I preferred to walk the roads forever, to wander aimlessly. For a moment, in this new rush of the world against the metal cocoon of the car, I see the small dry hills of this inland California province. They are familiar and not so familiar. They fade into the dusk and through a skein of nostalgia, desire and sadness, I remember again the Himalaya: magnificent, unconquered, sacred.

I. ALLAN SEALY

A SEASON TO REMEMBER

Bhadon, August-September. Heavy rain. The dark month.
Black nights, lit in flashes so a night-riser has the impression of
lurching from moment to moment. Thunder like the rending
of mountains. Thapa's buffalo calves in the middle of the night.
Thapa dances in his room at the open window, a wild manakin.
Sunrise in a black sky, red in a young crow's throat.
Grey days, moist and cool and heartsweet as water chestnuts.
Perpetua buys a kilo off a passing cart at the gate and Neha
peels them in the kitchen. Pricks a finger on the vicious thorns
while shucking the leathery purple skins. Devil's fruit, she
always calls it, from its baleful horned aspect. But slips a smooth
white heart into her mouth.

Ritu with a bowl of peeled water chestnuts.

Appears in Jed's room a moment sooner than expected and
catches him smiling in the mirror. Her step has changed, too,
he notices, grown lighter.

'Have you seen the mountains?' she says.

'*Can* you see them?'

The high mountains, he means, the snows. His chair is out
there still, facing the gap, though he hasn't sat in it for weeks.
The wood is sodden, but he won't let it be brought in. The cane
is black with mould, the same mould that has begun to appear

I. ALLAN SEALY is the author of two novels, *The Trotter-nama* and *Hero*, and
a travel book, *From Yukon to Yucatán*. He lives in the foothills of the
Himalayas. 'A Season to Remember' has been excerpted from *The Everest
Hotel*, IndiaInk, New Delhi, 1998.

on Neha's onions in the kitchen, under the dry outer skins.

She leads him out there, sets the bowl down on the balustrade beside his dentures, and waves an impresario's arm at the blue range. There is even a cone of white in the gap for him.

'Beautiful,' he agrees, looking across the wretched rain-soaked, moss-blackened rooftops. 'Do you hear that rustling in the undergrowth?'

She cocks an ear at the hills, then smiles. He's teasing.

'Leeches.' He worms a finger at her. 'Marching. You think jackboots are frightening? Not that you would know the sound of those. Well, you haven't heard leeches on the march. One minute the jungle is quiet, not a sound. Then it starts. Like gentle rain. And in a little while the undergrowth is quaking all around you. They've smelt your blood.

'We were coming back from Siloni once . . .'

He leans on the dish pedestal. Already there's a crack in the cement; it wasn't properly wet down after the job. The dish is still not hooked up. He'd like to push it over the edge, preferably as that jackal of a cousin is passing down below.

'It's like a eunuch in a harem,' he grins at her. 'Sees but can't do. They used to tear out the tongue, so he couldn't tell either.'

'You were coming back from somewhere.'

'Yes, from Siloni, when we ran into a storm. One of the coolies said he knew of a cave where we could spend the night. So we ran straight down the scarp into the jungle, following him. The leeches were waiting for us. They drop off the trees onto you, spring from the bushes. On the way down, the coolie who was guiding us twisted his ankle and had to be carried to the cave. When we got there we lit a fire across the mouth of the cave and stripped to pick off the leeches. I must have taken fifty off me: scalp, eyelids, anus. We used enough salt to pickle a man. After dinner we lay in our sacks and told stories. The coolie with the ankle said he couldn't sleep so he'd stay up and tend the fire. He was still sitting there in the morning with his back to the jungle, smiling at the fire. I asked him, 'Didn't you sleep?' He didn't answer, just kept smiling. When I touched him he just rolled over, dead. His back was covered in leeches.'

Ritu, who has been staring at the mountains, shudders and turns aside. She knows about leeches, prefers his collecting stories. But even those are faded. She breathes a deep fresh draught. Here is the real monsoon. Then why is it so flat, unstoried? She feels again the anguish of having woken from the childhood dream, that world of primal colours bathed in light. She can never understand Tsering's dispassion. Her spirit goes trekking across terraces of washed air, longs to be snared by beauty, by some grace it hasn't yet known, but keeps returning to that moment when the kite string breaks.

Jed looks sideways at her. She'll waste her youth. He never learnt to value his till it was gone, vanished into this long dreary decline. He clacks the set of spare teeth on the balustrade. You never learn, no one does; by the time you've mastered life it's time to die. He places a water chestnut between the perfect incisors and guillotines it. And *then* death plays tricks.

'Any news of our friend?' he asks and taps the dish with his cane. The sun has come out.

She shrugs. At first she thought he meant Brij, though he always calls him Nachiketa to her, as if to draw her into the cast. As if there were a role for her there. Heavenly women.

'No TV yet?'

'No.'

'Well,' Jed says, dragging his chair into the shade of the dish, 'it has its uses.' But he decides it's too damp to sit on. He leans on the balustrade and looks the other way, at her hills. 'What about Brij? Did you have a go with the kite?'

Her eyes drift down and she nods a slow preoccupied nod. That irritates him, he can't say why, so he leers at her. 'He didn't tell you the kite joke? This man whose wife can't get enough?'

She takes up the bowl of water chestnuts and crosses the roof, leaving him there.

'*More tail! More tail!*' he calls after her and cackles without pleasure.

She's about to put the bowl down on the bedside table when Brij comes into the room. He looks at her as he did yesterday.

'Where's Yama Raja?'

'By the dish.'

He makes for the roof, then stops and comes back to her. If he doesn't now he never will. He says, 'Ritu,' and puts awkward arms around her. She still has the bowl in her hands. Her eyes bulge at the wrongness of it, but she lets herself be held, returns the clumsy kiss when it comes.

Then breaks away and hurries down the fire escape. Doors banging in her brain as her feet skim the fish-plates. She must leave now, after this. She's gone already. She will tell Cecelia and pack, no staying here now. The iron stair ringing in her ears like conscience. Till her feet touch the ground.

She can't. The shame, the complications, the uncertainty, the wrenching. Better, simpler, to make a pact, avoid him. She goes to the office.

'Jed?' Cecelia says, misreading Ritu's confusion. 'He's an old rogue.'

It's not him, Ritu wants to say, but can't bring her lips to form the words. Unspeakable turmoil.

'I'll talk to him. But he won't let you go.'

'Let Tsering have a turn of the roof.'

Cecelia contemplates the switch; no harm in it. 'Let's see,' she says. 'I'll ask her.'

Tsering doesn't mind. First floor or roof are the same to her, her look indicates. A look that always falls at a point between the eyes.

Jed feels it there and cannot think what it recalls. Then

remembers a night above the snowline, alone. He enters a shelter, one of those huts used by shepherds and climbers, looking for a place to spend the night. Has begun to undo his pack when he feels a prickling in his spine. Turns slowly and sees, hunched in the corner with his hands on his knees, a little man covered in white hair. Head thrown back, eyes focused on nothing. Frozen. Jed sleeps outside, in the snow.

DAVID TOMORY

THE HILLS ARE ALIVE

The Vajra Hammer Band: there's no escaping it tonight, not in
the bar of the Hotel Tibet, where Jamyang and I sit drinking
Old Monk. At one point I am so overwhelmed by memories
that I rush out to buy cigarettes, something I never did before
giving up smoking.

It was twenty-three years ago today that the band began to
play: in Tashi's, just round the corner. Tashi's, replaced now by
a shopping complex, was a dark mountain café made of wood.
In the winter an iron stove simmered in the centre of the room.
We played in the corner by the kitchen door, leaning leftwards
in unison when a waiter came through with a tray. The lead
guitarist played through a Wollensack tape recorder made of
bakelite, I played what used to be called rhythm guitar through
a Playmate amplifier made by the Electric Sardarji in Delhi and
sang through the mike that came with it, and the bassist played
a Fender bass copy with a neck like a banana. His amplifier

DAVID TOMORY was born in London in 1949 and brought up in New Zealand.
He first visited India in 1971. On subsequent visits he has played in a rock and
roll band, travelled extensively, and written for newspapers and magazines.
His first book (published in India by HarperCollins India) was *A Season in
Heaven*, an account of what was called the Road to Kathmandu; his second
was *Hello Goodnight, a Life of Goa*. Currently he is working on a travel book
on the Andaman Islands. 'The Hills Are Alive' has been excerpted from *The
Sound of Music*. With thanks for the original publication to Jamyang Norbu
and the web magazine *High Asia*.

was an antique Macintosh with big glowing valves sticking up: every now and then they caught fire, and then the bassist would have to blow on them.

It was the spring of 1979 in our Himalayan village, and we were broke. But when you want to play, you do play. And if one day you hope to have a drummer and be a proper band, you have to have a name. A name is important for the sake of identity, and also for the sake of public relations. The latter was the bassist's idea. He had an eye for public relations. He pointed out that we were in a special place here, and it would be quite wrong to call ourselves something like Johnny and the Rockers. So in Tashi's we were Subterranean Vajra Hammer, which turned out to be also the name of the bassist's publishing company.

McLeodganj is special because the Dalai Lama lives here. There are any number of prominent Tibetan lamas and several thousand Tibetan monastics and laity living on this little ridge in the Himalayan foothills, and as a result all kinds of visitors have been drawn to the place. The short-stay backpacker throughput is enormously greater now. In the 1970s, however, McLeodganj was more a place where people came to rent houses, to study Buddhism in a serious long-term manner, or simply live. A paragraph ago, I called it 'our' Himalayan village. It wasn't ours, of course, but it could feel that way. You could go away and then come back years later to find most of your friends still there. This made you feel at home in a foreign land. You felt like doing something to enhance this heartening solidarity.

The something we chose was going to need a little luck in the achieving. McLeodganj was not a rock 'n' roll place. It was not rich in band equipment of even the simplest kind. If you broke a guitar string, you tied a knot in it and hoped it held, or you trudged down the hill to Dharamsala to see if the guy in the Hijackers, who ran the little music shop, had a spare one. A few years later there was a major plane hijack, and they had to change their name, but the Hijackers were the original local band. In the beginning, they had the better guitars. Ours were strung with nylon, with monsoon-rusted wire, with only four strings, and had twisted necks, woodworm, and sprung slats in the back. The lead guitarist had been to a posh school in Darjeeling (where he'd learned his blues—note for note—off records eventually so worn as to be inaudible) but even he was stuck with duff guitars.

Today, McLeodganj—McLeod for short, Mecklod in local pronunciation—is modern and burgeoning. But it is still a small place, or perhaps not so much small as compacted. People (monks, shopkeepers, coolies, pilgrims, housewives, trekkers, refugees, shepherds) and their means of transport (buses, taxis, Enfields, scooters, trucks, auto-rickshaws, donkeys) stream out of seven narrow roads into the tiny village square. The square was always congested, and is now completely congested, but the steps at the top have always been a good place to spend an hour with the other loungers and the monkeys watching the passing show.

Sooner or later, the person you were looking for came through the square. If you didn't see that person, you sent a message to their house with the Bun Man. There were no phones in McLeod in the 1970s. The Bun Man travelled the ridge and environs all day with his bun box on his back, doing housecalls like a mediaeval pedlar. His clientele—which survived pretty much intact until the fateful spring of 1984, when Indian visas for Commonwealth and Irish citizens became compulsory—lived above McLeod or below it. If they weren't in the square, there were really only two places a person might be found: Up, or Down.

There were hippies, in the standard-issue drugs-and-flowers sense, but most of the Westerners were more like the Bun Man, eccentric vendors, cooks, fleamarketeers, muttering hermits, instrumentalists, painters, astrologers, seekers and escapers, translators and Theosophists, woodsmen, dialecticians, delvers into Himalayan arcana, Tantriks, knitters and Kabbalists, Poonatics, healers and dealers, modest students of Buddhism in Tibetan sweaters and flagrant charismatics in white caftans. They added another layer of the onion to a bustling township which was mostly Tibetan and partly Indian and was surrounded by villages of farmers and Gaddi shepherds. There was never any communal trouble to speak of: relations were kept steady between these very different communities by equality of income. Pretty much everyone was broke.

In the spring of 1979, there were large numbers of young or youngish people in McLeod with nothing to do. The place shut at nine, and any social activity after that in public places bore the taint of furtiveness and disreputability. Social drinking had to be done in speakeasies, and only in the daytime could people be seen unsteadily emerging from dark shacks at two in the afternoon. McLeod needed a nightlife. It needed a band. After three years away, the first person I ran into, in the depths of a dark shack, was the lead guitarist. In 1976, he and I and others had played in a famous chai shop called the Last Chance— now buried under the bar of the Hotel Tibet—and in the echoing restaurant of the Kokonor Hotel, where we had clustered together around a fat old microphone called The Cosmic Egg.

The lead guitarist was wearing a cowboy hat. We discussed the nightlife problem, called on the bassist and began to rehearse. The lists of tunes we intended to play were written on long pieces of yellow paper intended for the pages of Tibetan prayer books. The tunes themselves were mostly tasteful singer-guitarist songs of the sort we had long been playing sitting crosslegged at firelit parties on hillsides in the moonlight.

There remained the problem of where to play. In a compacted township on a short ridge, it was easy to disturb people. Tashi's seemed the best place on the shortlist: we liked playing there, it was central, the audience soon found us. Within a month, Tashi's was packed every Saturday night and the waiters could not reach the customers. A photograph I had of a typical evening shows several dozen people sitting on the floor, a few trying to dance, two Afghan refugees (the Russians had just invaded Afghanistan) drinking black tea, and the Macintosh amplifier catching fire. And there by the doorway was Tashi, looking worried. Even our sound system was too loud. If you disturbed people at night in McLeod they tended to throw rocks at your roof, and the Tantric College was only half a block away.

Tashi's was where restriction clashed with expectation. We were the only band in McLeod, and tantalisingly close to being a real one; we may not have had a drummer, but we did have a name. This mere taste of rock 'n' roll was making people want more. They wanted a dance band. McLeod was beginning to generate nocturnal energies and an underburn of dance desire. The pressure was on us, the proto-band, to give vent to this desire rather than play tasteful songs in the moonlight. If McLeod was the pressure cooker, then we must have been the valve.

Then the Director of the Drama School (officially the Tibetan Institute of Performing Arts) said we could use their hall. This changed everything. If he hadn't let us play there, there would have been no escape for McLeod's nocturnal energies until the arrival, some years later, of techno, beer bars and video parlours. The hall held about five hundred people. It was made of wood, it stood on the next ridge up from McLeod, just off the promisingly-named Drama Party Road, and was some way removed from residential areas.

The deal was that we were to do benefits for the Drama School, while their staff ran the facilities, which included a stage, a lighting rig, a dance floor, seating, and a backstage room. In the backstage room, someone unearthed, of all things, a drum kit, that someone else had left behind—and this discovery in turn drew out a drummer, a friend of ours. Now fully manned, the band began to expand into a sort of skills co-operative in which our friends turned apple boxes into speaker cabinets, engaged with the lethal mysteries of electricity, unearthed songs from memory, made food for Saturday, carved guitar flatpicks out of plastic box lids, hauled jerrycans of Tibetan chang—much cheaper than beer—from the speakeasies, and offered astrological advice.

The drummer lent us his cabin, down the road from the Drama School, to rehearse in. But he had next-door neighbours. One afternoon, a neighbour came in and asked the lead guitarist, in Tibetan, if we could turn the volume down a bit. There was a sick man next door. Of course, the lead guitarist replied, 'If there's someone sick, we'll stop altogether'—and we did. We sat around fiddling with the Electric Sardarji's patented wah-wah guitar pedal, which, when plugged in and held at a certain angle, picked up with perfect clarity the Tibetan service of All India Radio. An hour later the neighbour was back, saying we might play again now if we wished.

'He's better already?' the lead guitarist asked.

'Not exactly,' the neighbour said. 'He's dead.'

Plenty of people had retreated to this recondite and monastic township in the western Himalaya hoping to escape the late twentieth century that was so onrushing and raucous. And there have always been people convinced that the hells are alive with the sound of music. A French Canadian mystic warned us that electric noises in the forest were upsetting the spirits of the trees. A visiting foreign educationist denounced us for corrupting local youth. What local youth needed, he said, was Shakespeare. Perhaps he was right. Impelled by irresistible forces, the band was to be, or not to be—who knows?—the vanguard of a musical modernity that would culminate in techno.

Notoriety, essential for rock and roll and so soon. In McLeod, a tremor of anticipation was beginning to run through the kind of people found around the music scene there—scholars, mystics, yogis, alchemists—and in the last days of Tashi's it cast up a groupie, a large woman of impregnable chastity who sat on the lid of the equipment trunk and bent it. Soon the first publicity photographs were being taken of the band, exuding leather-jacketed mystique and posing in a fashionably seedy alleyway with, as the photographs revealed, a goat. McLeod had a way of subverting hubris. The plan for teeshirts with Big In McLeod printed on the back never quite happened. At the height of one's stardom one might stroll the streets of McLeod (down the one, up the other) to be adoringly gazed upon only by the mad, matted man who lived in a box by the roadside.

On the night of Halloween in 1981, McLeod shut down at nine o'clock as it always did. Now the needles on the VU metres of the voltage stabilizers in the Drama School began to creep upwards until there was just enough power available to prevent acute speaker distortion. Showtime was nigh. The Kashmiri coolies had carried the gear up the hill to the hall and filled the stage with it. The stage backdrop that night, as every night, would be the Potala palace in Lhasa, painted on a vast white cloth suspended from the ceiling. Likewise painted on cloth, though less expertly, was the breathing skull that decorated the front of the bassist's speaker cabinet. Designed by an architect, the cabinet produced gusts of air that caused the breathing skull's cheeks to bulge out with every note and the cabinet to edge gradually towards the lip of the stage, where it was rescued at the brink, every Saturday night, by one of the Hijackers.

Two sound engineers, one the architect and the other a sitar player, saw to it that the equipment never broke down, though on occasion they looked like doing so themselves. They had to worry about the power supply, for without power the band would be rendered silent and ridiculous before a large audience. The power was generated far away, and it reached Dharamsala safely enough. Every Saturday, the electricity-walas were induced, so to speak, by Drama School negotiators, to grant McLeod an uninterrupted supply. Then the power had to struggle up the hill past the monkeys, the rain, and the landslides, to McLeod. And beyond, up and up a bleak hillside on insecure poles and along sagging wires, to the Drama School, where it emerged into the voltage stabilizers and then into our amplifiers and the Ahuja public address system through one small pink plastic plug.

It didn't bear thinking about. Those days, we needed power for the microphones on the drum kit and the bongos, the Ahuja and its four new twelve-inch speakers, the Macintosh, the Wollensack, the wah-wah pedal, two Vox practice amplifiers wired together, a Roland Cube with reverb, three vocal mikes, and the DJ's tape player. Satisfyingly, fat sheaves of wire ran in all directions—and eventually into the little pink plug. The entertaining of the five hundred, the whole Drama School drama, depended on this one frail junction. I have a sepia photograph from that Halloween night, of the engineers, seated side by side on the technical bench, both wearing headphones and frowning as one at the little pink plug.

Set-up time—the hour of doubtful power before nine o'clock showtime—was always fraught. There was never enough equipment to go round, never enough volume, there were always power struggles, always people trying to corner this slightly louder amp or that slightly bigger speaker. 'You want to hear only yourself,' I heard the architect say to the bassist. 'You want to hear only this macho penis music.' Ah, personality differences, you couldn't be a proper band without personality differences. Not even with the Potala for a backdrop and the Dalai Lama's brother in the audience.

The tickets had been printed on a magnificent old press in Dharamsala. At the top of my own souvenir ticket for Halloween 1981 is a Nativity scene, because the printer didn't have a picture of a pumpkin. On this haunted and moonlit night, people came as spiders (with cobweb), as witches and gremlins, as anything they could improvise the costume for, and even as themselves, for many McLeod people dressed every day in costume. Even the bassist, while insisting on standing tall against effeminacy, consented to wear make-up, because he had been told that without it he would be invisible under the lights.

The bouncers gazed on benignly. The audience was an even mix of Indians, Tibetans and foreigners, with one bouncer per community for equal rights. The foreign bouncer was the Bun Man, imposing in his velvet waistcoat, bowtie, and lungi. The tickets were ten rupees, for the benefit of the Drama School, and only selected members of the utterly broke got in for free. The hall was big and potentially unmanageable—drinks were always there, including the cheap, grey, deceptive chang—but incidents were rare. The bouncers first reminded people of their responsibility to future lives. If that didn't work, they tied them carefully to a post or rolled them up in a carpet.

Over the dancefloor hung a mirrorball constructed by the Director of the Drama School himself. His lighting men had begun to bounce their entire available spectrum off it and off the Potala backdrop. A monk, once a jazz musician and still drawn to the footlights, ceremoniously yanked the curtains open upon an expectant dancefloor and caught the band still tuning up. Showtime. Under a barrage of lighting effects, off we went, the only band in McLeod and the best. Musically, how were we? We were plangent. The bongos, played with a pair of chopsticks and miked up through a giant aluminium horn rented from the bazaar, remained audible in the inner ear for hours.

At the back of the hall stood the caterers and their wares. The tables back there were full of eaters and drinkers and spectators, and the benches to the front of them were full of parents and chaperones and recovering party people. Around the dancefloor at the foot of the stage, were standing and leaning and sitting the observers and wallflowers, the press (our man at the *Tibetan Review*), the Director, genially surveying his fiefdom, and attendant musicians. All of them were watching the dancers, for if the band was the valve, the dancefloor was where the pressure came off.

When I wasn't playing, I would go down there and mingle. It was good to have more than one singer-guitarist when there was only one band and you had to play for something like four hours. By 1981, we had added two more singer-guitarists, one the man from Japan and the other a visiting pathologist at the Delek Hospital who wore silver tights and did heavy metal. I have a photo of the pathologist and myself in red nail polish, eyeshadow and glitter, a pair of late-period Himalayan Bowies, gesticulating furiously. Onstage was our reggae rapper in a dreadlock wig, the man from Japan, the bassist in a silk gown, and our third and last drummer in a glitter shirt. He was indefatigable, and this was just as well. The second drummer had a habit of playing at full speed and then gradually slowing down until he could get offstage, refuel his habit and return. Until we rewrote the song list with all the fast songs at the beginning, there was always a danger of his ending the set by playing heavy metal in waltz time.

The dancefloor would not like that, though its taste was otherwise catholic. Tibetans of all ages seemed to prefer heavy metal, the Gaddi shepherds reggae, Indian tourists rock and roll, and foreign tourists the same—apart from those who preferred to sit outside the hall on a wall, in a meditative cloud of smoke, dreaming of Hendrix. The drunks preferred the back doorway, where they could beam and sway and pause to gaze up at the stars over the snowy mountains above before gratefully toppling over into the soft mud below.

Onstage, the DJ, in the orange costume and *mala* of a Rajneesh *sannyasin*—this was Halloween—was poised like a whippet on one end of the technical bench. His finger was resting on the Play button of his tape player, a sign that the band was coming to the end of a set and his moment had come. He played only the moderns, despite the bassist's appeals for something older and heavier 'because people like it'. In fact, it was he who liked it. The DJ refused. He was rewinding the last tape with a pencil when inevitably a real Rajneesh sannyasin in the audience mistook him for one of his own and called up to him: 'Play that Rajneesh music, Swami!' The DJ refused. The real sannyasin was puzzled.

The DJ was in control. But not really, any more than the band was in control. It was the dancefloor that was in control. The band and the DJ were forever scanning the dancefloor for signs of joy or disaffection. We were all slaves of the dance. The dancers played us. Their waves of energy swept over the stage. You can't beat a monastic mountain village in an earthquake zone for subterranean pressure. You can feel it and see it. You can smell it.

The most cyclonic of all energy waves, of course, being the Night of the Dancing Monks. I was onstage that night, playing something and monitoring the dancefloor as usual, when I noticed an unusual number of Western women with no hair. It did not occur to me that this would become a celebrated scandal for weeks, in the pages of the *Tibetan Review*; at first I thought there must be a lice epidemic. A moment later, two likewise bald people, this time male, both stripped to the waist, one sitting on the shoulders of the other, leapt off the stage into the midst of the dancers. Then I knew they must all be shaven monastics in mufti. A meditation course must have just ended. Energies that had not found expression there were now being expressed.

We didn't play only at the Drama School. We did benefits elsewhere. At the heavy metal guitarist's farewell performance in the Canteen, a soup-scented concrete room with ricocheting echo, we made our most plangent tape. Later, in London, the heavy metal guitarist took it round to a music business manager

who, after some attentive time, said, 'What on earth was that?'
And once, in the Kashag, the Tibetan Parliament building, we
did a benefit for a literary magazine—on the night of the murder
of John Lennon. Bad timing. We didn't do Lennon songs, so
the drummer, who was really a moonlighting singer-guitarist,
went on all by himself, and did one as a tribute.

Then the Disco came up, and we jumped at it. The Disco
was a little concrete bunker in the bowels of the then new Hotel
Tibet, right in McLeod. It had none of the charm or facilities of
the Drama School, but we would no longer have to send the
equipment all the way up the hill on the iron backs of the coolies,
or load it in and out of jeeps. And the Disco held only about a
hundred people at most. For the first time we had enough volume
to fill the space; for the first time we could make a tape on
which you could tell one song from another. Now we could
play tunefully. From time to time people had suggested more
tunefulness, but for the Vajra Hammer Band—as we had become
at some point, possibly because the old name was too long to
go on the tickets—this had been impossible. To play tunefully
you need volume, and there had never been enough of it for the
great big Drama School. But the Disco was minute. Tunefulness
at last, solos you could hear, musical balm; volume, beautiful
volume at last.

We loved that little sweatbox. The lead guitarist had left
by now, and the heavy metal guitarist, so the man from Japan
and the bassist and I and the drummer and the rapper and the
DJ were all that was left. The bassist adored the Disco. Once he
returned from a lightning trip to Delhi—all night on the bus
down, followed by all day on the bus back up—with dengue
fever. For a while he lay wracked and trembling on the stage in
a yellow blanket, only to rise again just in time for the show.
Saturday night fever. The next Saturday, the local police chief
let us know that he intended to come, with his wife, so their
daughter could see the band. The bassist and I met him outside

Tashi's. The bassist, a master of tact, asked him if he'd be so kind as to leave his uniform and gun at home, so he wouldn't panic the hippies. The police chief, a mild man whose nickname was Hitler, agreed, and smilingly fingered his little toothbrush moustache.

The Eighties were a new age, with Reagan-Thatcher looming large, but somehow McLeod kept its old disarming style. It still had hippies. And the Vajra Hammer Band was famous now. Famous in the police lines and the Army base in Forsythganj, and down in Dharamsala, in Nagrota Bhagwan and Pathankot. One night, four scooterists came all the way from Jammu, away to the west. They did the Shuffle and the Funky Chicken—there isn't room in the Disco to really throw yourself about—for an hour or so, in their helmets. This may be for reasons of prestige or for fear that the helmets may be stolen. The scooterists had to leave early to get home before dawn, so, with affecting courtesy, they came up to say thank you and goodbye. Their visors were so steamed up inside that we could not see who they were.

I stepped out of the door to the Disco for some air, only to find a situation going on. Three tourists, hefty, rich—they had a car—and irate, were holding our man from Japan halfway up a wall and shouting, 'We're not paying to get in. This is our country.' In opposition, two Gurkhas from the Army base were blockading the door and shouting back, 'You're not getting in for free. This is our Disco.' This looked like a crisis. But having seen it coming, Hitler, incognito in a striped sweater, had slipped out of the door and gone home. As the bassist and I conferred, he reappeared, transformed, in full uniform, flourishing his pistol in the air. The tourists let fall the man from Japan and hurried off to their car to a heartfelt round of applause from the large crowd that had gathered.

That night was the real McLeod. It had the authentic McLeodish quality of slightly crazed charm that nocturnal energies reliably stirred up at the end of every week. We only played Saturdays. People had families to keep and meditations to do. The bassist worked on translations. The drummer was a student at the School of Dialectics. After the last set we unplugged the gear and stacked it and walked off down the hill, those of us that lived down there, with our guitar cases on our heads, as the moon sank in a dawning blue velvet sky over the jagged purple mountains.

Those were different times. Tonight, I hear the techno beating up the valley from Bhagsunath. Those times ended for me very early one morning when I was staying just above McLeod in one of the Nepali brigadier's little row of rental rooms. It was still dark when the Swiss painter next door knocked on my door and said, 'Come outside. Look.'

Up on the ridge, the Drama School was burning. It was one mass of flame, a big wooden box on fire, lighting up the sky. Later, I heard that human chains had formed and thrown cans of water on the inferno, and I heard that the fire department's tanker had laboured up from Dharamsala—but empty, because with its tank full of water, it couldn't have got up there at all. In an hour, the Drama School was ashes. As I watched it disappear, selfishly, I did not think of the Tibetan Opera people up there who were losing their instruments, costumes and lighting gear, the means of their art. I thought of the Vajra Hammer Band. There would be another hall built, things would be replaced, but not those times. Those times were over.

Though they say that rock and roll will never die. Well, whoever they are, maybe they're right. Things shared in common delight never die—even when, in their fragile earthly form, they go up flaming in the night.

PART III

VIEWS OF THE ENVIRONMENT

RUSKIN BOND

GREAT TREES I HAVE KNOWN

Living for many years in a cottage at 7,000 feet in the Garhwal Himalayas, I was fortunate in having a big window that opened out on the forest, so that the trees were almost within my reach. Had I jumped, I should have landed quite safely in the arms of an oak or chestnut.

The incline of the hill was such that my first-floor window opened on what must, I suppose, have been the second floor. I never made the jump, but the big langurs, silver-red monkeys with long swishing tails, often leapt from the trees onto the corrugated tin roof and made enough noise to disturb the bats sleeping in the space between the roof and ceiling.

Standing on its own was a walnut tree, and truly, this was a tree for all seasons. In winter the branches were bare but they were smooth and straight and round like the arms of a woman

For over forty-five years Ruskin Bond has been writing stories, novellas, essays, poems and children's books. He has written over 500 short stories and articles. Ruskin Bond grew up in Jamnagar, Dehradun, New Delhi and Simla. As a young man, he spent four years in the Channel Islands and London. He returned to India in 1955, and has never left the country since. His first novel *The Room on the Roof* received the John Llewellyn Rhys Prize, awarded to a Commonwealth writer under thirty, for 'a work of outstanding literary merit'. He received the Sahitya Akademi Award in 1993, and the Padma Shri in 1999. He lives in Landour, Mussoorie, with his extended family. 'Great Trees I Have Known' has been excerpted from *Rain in the Mountains: Notes from the Himalayas*, Penguin Books India, New Delhi, 1993.

in a painting by Jamini Roy. In the spring each branch produced a hard bright spear of new leaf. By midsummer the entire tree was in leaf, and towards the end of the monsoon the walnuts, encased in their green jackets, had reached maturity.

Then the jackets began to split, revealing the hard brown shell of the walnuts. Inside the shell was the nut itself. Look closely at the nut and you will notice that it is shaped rather like the human brain. No wonder the ancients prescribed walnuts for headaches!

Every year the tree gave me a basket of walnuts. But last year the walnuts were disappearing one by one, and I was at a loss to know who had been taking them. Could it have been Biju, the milkman's son? He was an inveterate tree-climber. But he was usually to be found on oak trees, gathering fodder for his cows. He told me that his cows liked oak leaves but did not care for walnuts. He admitted that they had relished my dahlias, which they had eaten the previous week, but he denied having fed them walnuts.

It wasn't the woodpecker. He was out there every day, knocking furiously against the bark of the tree, trying to prise an insect out of a narrow crack. He was strictly non-vegetarian and none the worse for it.

One day I found a fat langur sitting in the walnut tree. I watched him for some time to see if he was going to help himself to the nuts, but he was only sunning himself. When he thought I wasn't looking, he came down and ate the geraniums; but he did not take any walnuts.

The walnuts had been disappearing early in the morning while I was still in bed. So one morning I surprised everyone, including myself, by getting up before sunrise. I was just in time to catch the culprit climbing out of the walnut tree.

She was an old woman who sometimes came to cut grass on the hillside. Her face was as wrinkled as the walnuts she had been helping herself to. In spite of her age, her arms and legs were sturdy. When she saw me, she was as swift as a civet-cat in getting out of the tree.

'And how many walnuts did you gather today, Grandmother?' I asked.

'Only two,' she said with a giggle, offering them to me on her open palm. I accepted one of them. Encouraged, she climbed back into the tree and helped herself to the remaining nuts. It was impossible to object. I was taken up in admiration of her agility in the tree. She must have been about sixty, and I was a mere forty-five, but I knew I would never be climbing trees again.

To the victor the spoils!

The horse-chestnuts are inedible, even the monkeys throw them away in disgust. Once, on passing beneath a horse-chestnut tree, a couple of chestnuts bounced off my head. Looking up, I saw that they had been dropped on me by a couple of mischievous rhesus-monkeys.

The tree itself is a friendly one, especially in summer when it is in full leaf. The least breath of wind makes the leaves break into conversation, and their rustle is a cheerful sound, unlike the sad notes of pine trees in the wind. The spring flowers look like candelabra, and when the blossoms fall they carpet the hillside with their pale pink petals.

We pass now to my favourite tree, the deodar. In Garhwal and Kumaon it is called *dujar* or *deodar*, in Jaunsar and in parts of Himachal it is known as the *Kelu kelon*. It is also identified with the cedar of Lebanon (the cones are identical), although the deodar's needles are slightly longer and more bluish. Trees, like humans, change with their environment. Several persons familiar with the deodar at Indian hill-stations, when asked to point it out in London's Kew Gardens, indicated the cedar of Lebanon; and shown a deodar, declared that they had never seen such a tree in the Himalayas!

We shall stick to the name deodar, which comes from the Sanskrit *deva-daru* (divine tree). It is a sacred tree in the

Himalayas; not worshipped, nor protected in the way that a peepul is in the plains, but sacred in that its timber has always been used in temples, for doors, windows, walls and even roofs. Quite frankly, I would just as soon worship the deodar as worship anything, for in the beauty and majesty it represents Creation in its most noble aspect.

No one who has lived amongst deodar would deny that it is the most godlike of Himalayan trees. It stands erect, dignified; and though in a strong wind it may hum and sigh and moan, it does not bend to the wind. The snow slips softly from its resilient branches. In the spring the new leaves are a tender green, while during the monsoon the tiny young cones spread like blossoms in the dark green folds of the branches. The deodar thrives in the rain and enjoys the company of its own kind. Where one deodar grows, there will be others. Isolate a young tree and it will often pine away.

The great deodar forests are found along the upper reaches of the Bhagirathi valley and the Tons in Garhwal; and in Himachal and Kashmir, along the Chenab and the Jhelum, and also on the Kishenganga; it is at its best between 7,000 and 9,000 feet. I had expected to find it on the upper reaches of the Alakananda, but could not find a single deodar along the road to Badrinath. That particular valley seems hostile to trees in general, and deodar in particular.

The average girth of the deodar varies from fifteen to twenty feet, but individual trees often attain a great size. Records show that one great deodar was 250 feet high, twenty feet in girth at the base, and more than 550 years old. The timber of these trees, which is unaffected by extremes of climate, was always highly prized for house-building, and in the villages of Jaunsar Bawar, finely carved doors and windows are a feature of the timbered dwellings. Many of the quaint old bridges over the Jhelum in Kashmir are supported on pillars fashioned from whole deodar trees; some of these bridges are more than 500 years old.

To return to my own trees, I went among them often, acknowledging their presence with a touch of my hand against their trunks—the walnut's smooth and polished; the pine's patterned and whorled; the oak's rough, gnarled, full of experience. The oak had been there the longest, and the wind had bent his upper branches and twisted a few, so that he looked shaggy and undistinguished. It is a good tree for the privacy of birds, its crooked branches spreading out with no particular effect; and sometimes the tree seems uninhabited until there is a whirring sound, as of a helicopter approaching, and a party of long-tailed blue magpies steams across the forest glade.

After the monsoon, when the dark red berries had ripened on the hawthorn, this pretty tree was visited by green pigeons, the kokla-birds of Garhwal, who clambered upside-down among the fruit-laden twigs. And during winter, a white-capped redstart perched on the bare branches of the wild pear tree and whistled cheerfully. He had come down from higher places to winter in the garden.

The pines grow on the next hill—the *chir*, the Himalayan blue pine, and the long-leaved pine—but there is a small blue pine a little way below the cottage, and sometimes I sit beneath it to listen to the wind playing softly in its branches.

Open the window at night, and there is usually something to listen to, the mellow whistle of the pygmy owlet, or the cry of a barking-deer which has scented the proximity of a panther. Sometimes, if you are lucky, you will see the moon coming up, and two distant deodars in perfect silhouette.

Some sounds cannot be recognized. They are strange night sounds, the sounds of the trees themselves, stretching their limbs in the dark, shifting a little, flexing their fingers. Great trees of the mountains, they know me well. They know my face in the window; they see me watching them, watching them grow, listening to their secrets, bowing my head before their outstretched arms and seeking their benediction.

E.R.C. DAVIDAR

CLIFF GOATS

Similar to Sigur, but dissimilar in character and composition, a wilderness is to be found in the upper Nilgiri plateau. This wilderness, or what is left of it, lies due west and south-west of Ooty, beyond habitations, cultivation, government plantations and hydel lakes. It is composed mainly of grasslands. The Nilgiri plateau was originally composed of smooth, rounded, pale-green grass hills that roll away into the distance like ocean waves, broken by dark evergreen *sholas* or stunted forests in the folds and sheltered valleys and black rocky outcrops on the slopes. These together make on outstandingly pretty mosaic. The Kundah range provides the backdrop and the ruggedness essential to a wilderness. This country ends rather abruptly, in fact, dramatically, as it plunges into the valleys below in a serried row of sheer precipices. Silence, which is the sound of this country, is accentuated when an occasional bird call breaks it. In spite of several visits to this country, I never fail to be moved whenever I climb a point of vantage and look upon the soul-stirring sight.

As though this is not provocation enough for me to frequent

E.R.C. DAVIDAR has been a member of various conservation organizations. *Cheetal Walk: Living in the Wilderness* is based on the house he built in 1965 in Sigurhalla, at the foothills of the Nilgiris. Besides this book, he has written *Adventures of a Wildlife Warden*, several stories for children and guidebooks on wildlife sanctuaries. 'Cliff Goats' has been excerpted from *Cheetal Walk: Living in the Wilderness*, Oxford University Press, New Delhi, 1997.

this wilderness (which the British called the Kundhas), there is also the fact that the Nilgiri *tahr*—a fascinating wild goat—has made it its home. To me this region is tahr country. As Honorary Superintendent of the Nilgiri Game Association (NGA), I found a ready excuse to visit the tahr country: I had to supervise the work of the game guards of the Association stationed at its approaches. These trips which started before we set up Cheetal Walk later became interludes between stays at Cheetal Walk.

Mystery surrounds the presence of the tahr in the Nilgiris. Its closest relative, the Himalayan tahr, lives 2500 kilometres away, in the sector between Kashmir and Bhutan in the Himalayas. Many theories have been advanced to explain the presence of their cousin so far south. The one that appears most plausible is the Satpura hypothesis, which postulates that during the Pleistocene, lower temperatures prevailed throughout the subcontinent modifying climate and vegetation to such an extent that it enabled several species of Himalayan fauna and flora to migrate to the south through the Vindhya-Satpura mountains. These Himalayan forms got isolated on the higher altitudes of the Western Ghats during the subsequent warmer climatic periods and have remained there. The Nilgiri tahr and the Nilgiri marten, the laughing thrush and the rhododendron are some of the notable examples.

When I first set out in pursuit of the tahr, it was with the rifle. On our very first outing Joe, my *shikari*, helped me stalk a 'saddle-back' within range and urged, 'Shoot, Sir, shoot'. I took the field-glasses from him and studied the quarry more closely. I was disappointed. It was a saddle-back all right, but not a hoary old male with a distinctive saddle I had set my heart on. Although one saddle-back was permitted on each annual licence, I wanted only one good trophy. Besides, it was early in the season. Upon Joe assuring me in sign language that he would help me get a better trophy, we let the animal go unmolested. A peculiarity of this species is that as the grey-brown males progressively turn darker with age (until they are almost black), the hair on their back, roughly where a saddle would sit, becomes lighter until almost white, forming a saddle-mark; hence the name 'saddle-back'. The maturity of a male tahr is judged by the 'saddle' mark it carries, rather than horn size. Saddle-backs were permitted to be shot and they formed less than ten per cent of the population, of which half were past breeding. I pursued saddle-backs for six years without success and finally, when I lined my sights on the saddle-back of my dreams, my rifle missed fire. That was the last time I drew a bead on one of these magnificent animals whose pursuit was considered the summit of south Indian sport. However, my fascination for this mountain goat of cliffs and precipices did not diminish, as with a camera in hand all tahr became fair sport.

Besides the tahr, the predators that preyed on them attracted me. The open terrain provides ample opportunities for sighting them. On the top of the list are leopards. The majority of them are black, rare elsewhere. I got acquainted with a particular black leopard. Our first meeting nearly turned out to be his last. My friend Charlie Minchin and I saw it simultaneously when driving back from an unsuccessful hunt in the Nilgiri Peak area. In a clearing between two sholas a black leopard was going all out after a barking deer. The streamlined black form of the leopard, the brick-red of the fleeing deer, the green of the emerald turf on which the drama was enacted, set against the bottle-green sholas, all aglow in the rays of the setting sun, was a rare combination of colours and action, a sight I shall never forget. Charlie braked hard and we were out of the car in a moment and stalking the leopard. we climbed a hill and reached the spot where we had seen the hunter and the hunted disappear. There, seventy-five metres below us, lay the black leopard panting, its red mouth open. In our excitement, we bungled the shot and the leopard got away. After I laid my rifle down, I met this leopard a few times. This was because Joe and I knew its ways. But hunters seldom caught sight of the animal, whose velvety pelt was a highly-prized trophy. The black leopard was a highly successful tahr hunter. It would take its position above a feeding herd—tahr are stupid in the sense that they watch out for danger coming from below, forgetting that it could equally come from above—and wait patiently for hours on end for the odd straggler, usually an intrepid juvenile, before stalking it. The last time I saw it, it had grown old, its muzzle almost white. It was never seen afterwards and I guess it had passed on to the happy hunting grounds leaving behind a young black leopard, probably its son, to take its place.

Tahr country is also tiger country. The tigers here are noted for their dark, richly-marked, heavy coats. Resident tigers are few; the rest are migrants. The main bridle path that runs through this country also serves as a tiger trail and I have seen more tiger signs, such as droppings and scratch marks, there than on any other track. The two meetings I have had with tigers, both close encounters, took place on this trail.

When I first got acquainted with this section of the Nilgiri plateau in the mid-1950s, there were no roads within miles of the tahr country, only bridle paths. The longest of them was the Bangitappal trail which, starting at Avalanche, ended in Malabar, through the Sispara Pass. It was the earliest route to the Malabar Coast and was mainly used as a *tappal* (postal) route by spear-wielding *dak* runners. Coming from Ooty, the Koleribetta ridge proved to be the stiffest obstacle. I am not a hill man by birth and as my law practice tied me down to a sedate life during the week, I found the trips to the tahr country strenuous and exhausting. More frustrating was the disappointment of not being able to penetrate the wilderness deeper. The answer lay in camping out. My cub tent came in handy. I pitched camp in the heart of the wilderness and while enjoying the experience, which brought me closer to my men and nature, saved myself a lot of wear and tear. Joe and his men preferred to sleep in the open, around a log fire. One winter, when the weather is usually predictable and days and nights are bright and sparkling, I decided to travel light and sleep in the open, sharing the warmth of the bonfire with my men. The luxury of sleeping bags was unknown then. To keep warm we drank endless mugs of coffee. The spirit of the wilderness seeped into my bones like the cold from the damp earth below and the dew from the heavens above. And I was hooked as never before. I wanted my children—my wife declaring that she was not up to the mark—to share the joys of camping out in the tahr country. In a few years they were ready. There, the rainbow trout, introduced into the Nilgiri plateau after decades of experimentation, sustained us. While the children caught them spinning, I improved my fly-casting. From a hunting ground this wilderness became a place of pilgrimage for us.

The NGA took a special interest in the Nilgiri tahr, having rescued it from the brink of extinction during the latter part of the nineteenth century. In order to keep a watch on their numbers, they were counted periodically. Tahr enumeration was usually left to shikaris registered with the Association. When it was decided to conduct a census in 1963, I decided to direct the operation personally. Recruiting a team of experienced shikaris, I divided the country into sections and starting from Nilgiri peak, covered the entire area systematically. It was a simple count: no classification by age or sex was attempted. However, a note published in the *Journal of the Bombay Natural History Society* attracted worldwide attention and brought me in touch with Dr George B. Schaller who had pioneered studies of the African lion, mountain gorilla, tiger and some Himalayan goat and sheep species, among others. As he wished to do a brief comparative study of the tahr, I invited him to make our home in Coonoor his base. When he arrived I gave him some of the material I had written on the Nilgiris and its wildlife to read. I was particularly proud of a piece I wrote on an all saddle-back associations which I thought would establish my credentials as a scientist. After reading it George passed it back commenting, 'So you enjoyed yourself.' George is a man of few words and he had the remarkable ability to communicate his thoughts with an extreme economy of words. As I wished to make a more meaningful study of my favourite animal besides enjoying myself, I studied George's notes and was struck by the wealth of data he had collected. I realized scientific research is a full-time occupation for which years of specialized study and training would be required. But I could count and had the determination and enthusiasm to pursue this sure-footed goat to the remotest corners of its habitat. And I had Schaller's classification to guide me.

The 1975 count I conducted was a more detailed study. This gave me the confidence to attempt something grand, that is, to census the entire population of the species over the whole of its range. I was fortunate in having the support of the Fauna Preservation Society, London, friends, and managers of plantations in remote areas in this venture. An inventory of tahr locations was the first task. Eighteen disjunct habitats were identified and of these I personally covered fourteen during the next three years, whenever I could snatch a few days off from my onerous job of looking after the interests of plantation managements in Tamil Nadu, one of whose many problems was its work-force of over one hundred thousand and the many labour unions we had to deal with.

The total Nilgiri tahr population was placed at around 2,200. The entry in the *Red Data Book* of the International Union for Conservation of Nature and Natural Resources (IUCN) and conservation plans relating to this species are based on my status report.

The difficulty of the job, not to mention the risks and inconvenience the project involved, such as scaling lung-bursting heights, negotiating slippery slopes and crawling across dizzy precipices in places, were at times a great strain. Besides, we had to contend with leech-infested sholas, elephant herds and solitary bull gaur as well as armed poachers. It was through sheer exercise of will-power that I persisted.

In his book, *Stones of Silence*, Schaller had praised my interest in the tahr and expressed the hope that I would continue to keep an eye on the species. The fact that I managed to live up to his expectation was very satisfying.

Winds of change in the environmental scene in the country have not left the Nilgiri tahr wildernesses unscathed. Tahr habitats, placed as they are on mountain tops, receive rain in abundance. Deep valleys provide storage space for reservoirs, and slopes provide the gradient required to generate electricity. In a power-starved state such as Tamil Nadu, it is natural that power generation should get priority over wildlife. Hydro-electric projects simply bulldoze their way into tahr country, crushing any opposition they might encounter. But it should be possible to stall or stop altogether small unviable adjuncts to projects if opposition is united and vigorous. Planting of exotics poses a more pernicious threat. Eucalyptus, wattle and pine plantations nibble away at the tahr country, reducing the tahr habitat which is now a narrow strip. Persistent and vigorous protests initiated through the Nilgiri Wildlife and Environment Association (NWEA) bore fruit when the Forest Department agreed to reserve a belt of grassland along the cliffline exclusively for tahr.

It is widely recognized that whatever protection the tahr received has been from trophy hunters. A contradiction in terms? Not really, since pursuit was confined to less than ten per cent of the population represented by saddle-backs! For the poacher, however, it makes no difference whether the animal hunted is a pregnant female or a kid. The presence of legal-hunting parties kept poachers out. unfortunately, those in authority, who should have been the first to realize and make use of this ally, refused to accept realities. Following the placing of the Nilgiris tahr in the First Schedule of the Wildlife (Protection) Act, hunting of tahr was banned. It remained a paper ban, however, for a long time, as forest subordinates were unwilling to risk visiting tahr country because of unfamiliarity, the physical exertion involved and poachers. Had alternate legitimate activity such as trekking been planned and introduced in time, the ban would have been more effective. As it turned out, I was one of the few former tahr hunters to have retained an interest in the animal. On a visit to remote Sispara, I came across a poacher hideout (complete with meat-drying racks and evidence of recent slaughter) tucked away in a shola located in a dip. Further investigation revealed that enterprising poachers had been coming from Kerala, scaling the cliffs using cane ladders. My report elicited an immediate response because Raja Singh, the then Conservator of Forests, a former hunter, was a keen conservationist. Guided by Joe, a raiding party visited the area and destroyed the camp and the ladders. Thereafter, I initiated joint patrolling in the area until the Forest Department was able to organize better control and establish its presence there. Tahr country has since been declared a national park—the Mukurthi National Park. But the problem of exercising effective control over this remote area still remains. And tahr are reported to have declined drastically in numbers, according to recent counts.

SUKETU MEHTA

IF A TREE FALLS IN THE FOREST

The rhinoceros was looking at me meditatively. I wasn't in a
zoo, and I wasn't watching the Discovery Channel. I was in
Kaziranga National Park, in Assam. All around me frolicked
hog deer, hornbills, and wild buffalo. One of the rhinos that the
park is famous for was about forty feet away from me, and had
raised its head from placidly eating in the tall grass, several
birds perched on its massive body. It looked prehensile; at forty
million years, a rhino shows its age. The beast, which weighed
up to two tons, looked surreal. It was covered in armour, and it
squinted out at the world through beady little eyes. Then I saw
its horn rise up, that useless piece of matted hair that is worth a
thousand pounds an ounce in the Far East. It could also gore me
to death, if the rhino had a mind to charge at me. Tipu, the
guard accompanying me, told me that just last night two
poachers had come into the park looking for this fabulous prize.
The guards caught them on a boat in the river and shot one
dead; the other fell off the boat and is presumed to have drowned.
'We don't catch the poachers alive,' he said. 'We shoot them,
from a distance or up close. If we hand them alive to the police,

SUKETU MEHTA is a fiction writer and journalist who lives in New York. He
is a winner of the Whiting Writers Award and of an O'Henry Award for his
fiction. His work has appeared in *Granta, Harpers Magazine, Time, Condé
Nast Traveler*, NPR's '*All Things Considered*', *The Village Voice*, and *Indian
Literature*. His non-fiction book on Bombay will be published worldwide in
2002. A longer version of this piece was published in *Condé Nast Traveler*,
November 2000.

they'll just pay Rs 5000 to the police and walk out, and come back. We are all excited by the hunt when we're after the poachers.'

I asked him if he felt any compunction in killing a human being.

'No. It's because of them that we don't know day from night, working out here in the jungle twenty-four hours a day. They are our enemies.' The actual poachers are Nagas, from the neighbouring state of Nagaland, but they use the local villagers as guides around the park. At the park office, I met one such man, an ex-poacher named Soneshwar Nath. He is from an extremely poor family, and the horns command up to Rs 300,000 ($6976) each, a staggering sum in a country where the per capita wage is $310 a year.

A senior forest officer who used to be in Kaziranga, and now works in another Assamese forest, confirmed what the forest guard had told me about the poachers. The wildlife park where this officer works is filled with Bodo rebels, fighting for a separate state, who are armed with AK-47s, against which his .315 rifles are no match. But the poachers only have World War II vintage .303 rifles, good enough to fell a rhino but pretty low on the scale of firepower in the park. When the officer first got to Kaziranga, the rhino kill was enormous—a total of five in just one particularly bad day. But then, he changed his patrolling schedule often, and started killing poachers—thirteen poachers eliminated in just one six-month period, in 'encounters'. He laughs, and then rephrases it: 'So-called encounters.' When he comes upon a poacher, he says, he immediately starts shooting. 'It's better to shoot and kill.'

Besides knowing for a certainty that the poacher will be back after a mere jail term, there is the risk of getting shot himself. 'It's better to be offensive than defensive.' With the press, he manipulates the account of the encounter in such a way that when it appears in the newspaper, the poacher always seems to have fired first. Through such tactics, Kaziranga has been winning the battle against the poachers, at least for the moment. There are now more than 1152 rhinos that wander around the park, up from 1100 in 1988. In 1986, poachers killed forty-one rhinos; by 1997, that figure had declined to twenty-six. For the year 2000, the park achieved a record: only two rhinos killed by poachers till August. And the human count? Eighty poachers shot dead by the park staff in the last ten years.

But in 1998, the rhinos faced an even greater danger: unprecedented floods on the Brahmaputra river, caused largely by deforestation in the mountains where the river springs from. That year, the river flooded its banks and drowned thirty-nine rhinos. Driven by the rising waters, they came out of the forests and on to the highway bordering the park, where many were run over by trucks or shot dead by poachers.

Kaziranga National Park is on the southern bank of the Brahmaputra river; the Himalayas technically begin on the northern bank. But the struggles in this 430-square-kilometre park, a World Heritage Site, between poachers and wardens are replicated throughout the Himalayan parks. That is because it is seen as part of a war. This is one front in the war: the battle against poaching. But all over the hill regions, there are other battles being fought, against deforestation, against dams, against pollution, against the deterioration of the cultural and architectural heritage.

For the past three decades, a mounting crisis has been building in the Himalayas, the world's highest and longest mountain range. Deforestation has triggered most of the degradation. During the past forty years, 40 per cent of the Himalayas' forests have been lost. Nepal has cut down nearly half its trees since the conquest of Everest in 1953. In Himachal Pradesh, timber merchants and subsistence farmers have felled more than two-thirds of the hill forests. The downstream consequence of the Himalayan tragedy is a dramatic increase in floods, leading to hundreds of thousands of deaths in countries like Bangladesh. Then there are the dams: twenty-two large dams built or planned along the 2400-km range, sitting on a seismic hotbed. In addition to flooding whole valleys and displacing multitudes of people during their construction, the very real possibility exists that the next earthquake could cause a catastrophic break in one of these dams.

For several weeks, I travelled right across the arc of the Himalayas, from Arunachal Pradesh in the east to Ladakh in the west, looking at the threats to the mountains and the interdependence of ecology and development. The issues are not simple. Environmental projects that work in one part of the hills may not work in another, because each country has radically different forms of government. Environmental concerns are intimately linked to local political issues, to local ideas about sharing and what a specific culture considers worthy of saving. Still, there are pointers, there are promising experiments which can be replicated elsewhere. I purposely avoided the mega-projects and focused on the smaller organizations, the pinpricks of hope in the larger dark clouds overwhelming the Himalayan region. So I travelled through the battleground, meeting individuals and grass-roots organizations that were working, alone or in small groups, battling mammoth bureaucracies and the currents of history. I went to Kaziranga to look at approaches, legal and otherwise, towards wildlife preservation and to Arunachal Pradesh to see if a blanket ban on logging could work.

A few hours drive west from Kaziranga is Nameri Wildlife Sanctuary, where I drove early one morning on my way to Arunachal Pradesh. Nameri now has an eco-friendly anglers' camp; fishermen are supposed to come here, catch the massive masheer fish in the river, and throw them back into the water once they've photographed their catch. In practice, admits Pankaj Sharma, the range officer, they rarely do so, and there's no way of nabbing them leaving with their catch. Besides, the forest officers are on the look-out for a far more destructive form of fishing by professional fishermen: by dynamiting or poisoning the river. Dynamite is literally thrown into the rivers; when it explodes, the fish die from the shock. This is disastrous for the streams. Another technique is to pour insecticide into the streams; the fish are thus poisoned and float up dead. It is another matter that those unwary buyers in the village markets who buy fish caught this way can get violently sick. Sharma told me that the local tribes used to practise a far more benign form of this technique. They would find the leaves of a certain plant that release a mild intoxicant when beaten. Then they would lay a log across the river, walk on it to the middle of the river, and beat the leaves of the plant into the water. The intoxicant spread through the water, and the drunk fish floated up and allowed themselves to be caught with ease. They died a happy death. And in a few hours, the water was back to normal. The insecticide used today, however, poisons the water and the stream beds for years.

I asked Sharma if he feels depressed about the long-term prospects for conservation in India. 'The future is bleak,' he conceded. The government hasn't paid him for five months. His men haven't been paid either. The previous night, they came in a body to his office and threatened to bring all the elephants they ride on to his office, leave them there, and walk off. Sharma had to plead with them to stay on the job and tend their beasts.

'Conservation money is spent in vain,' he said. Forest reserves don't work. The reason is that the tribals do not harvest the forest as they used to. Previously, they only took from the forest what they needed; and they had an interest in its continued growth, so what they harvested was sustainable. But tribals are no longer content with mere survival. They want a surplus now. Everywhere I travelled in the Himalayas, I saw satellite dishes. I could see how the people of the world ate and dressed, what they wore and what they drove. I was bombarded with advertising urging me to buy the goods of the new world, to be modern. The tribals, now, want much more out of the forest than they used to. They want it to supply not just food and hides, but also a television, a stereo, and a small motorcycle. So they are selling the forest to outsiders, to the timber merchants from the plains. And the Himalayan forests can't support the needs of the timber merchants and their expansive mansions in Calcutta. So the forests die. And the hillsides around the road to Tawang look like a very bad haircut.

Eighty per cent of Arunachal Pradesh, perhaps the most remote area in continental India, is covered by forests. The state supplies 15 per cent of India's timber needs. But in just four years, 1992-1996, the state lost 1417 square kilometres, an area as large as all of Delhi, to the axes and chainsaws of the timber industry. On my way to Arunachal Pradesh, I met a timber merchant in Calcutta who has some of the largest timber interests in Arunachal Pradesh. We were in his car, pulling out of his palatial home, and I was asking him if it would be difficult for me to get a permit to travel to the state, which is restricted even for the rest of India because it borders China. He dismissed my fears. 'Laws are made,' he said, 'for those who abide by them.'

That comment, I later realized, also applied to his attitude towards the forestry laws on the books. Arunachal Pradesh has the greatest biodiversity in the entire subcontinent, boasting 550 species of orchids alone. But it also suffered the most accelerated depredation of its timber, until a vacationing Supreme Court judge in 1996 saw the destruction, came back to Delhi, and made use of two unrelated forestry cases to impose a blanket ban on logging and sawmill operations in the entire northeast. A quarter of a million people lost their jobs. But the trees that were cut won't come back in a hurry.

The smuggling of timber out of the state takes on inventive forms. The forest department inspects trucks leaving the area, to see if they're carrying timber. Sometimes the truck will be empty, and the guards will let it go. But new wood is still reaching the plains. How? The entire truck, a local conservationist told me, is sometimes made out of newly felled wood. In Calcutta, the truck is dismantled, its precious hardwood body broken down, and the tractor sent back up for another life. Each truckload is worth about Rs 300,000 ($6976). The timber gets smuggled out, literally under the forest guards' noses.

For those who successfully obtain a permit to travel to Arunachal Pradesh, the devastation along the road I took in the western part of the state, all the way up to Tawang in the high mountains near the Chinese border, is enough to make you weep.

The first day's drive took me from Tezpur in Assam to Bomdila in Arunachal Pradesh—from the northern bank of the Brahmaputra to the Himalayas proper—and led through scenery that made me alternatively exhilarated and depressed. The road has been built by the army, which is much in evidence everywhere. Every few yards, the army has painted signs along the road: 'Married or Unmarried, Divorce Speed.' 'Drive in Peace, or Reach in Pieces.' Other signs make you realize you are not in Kansas: 'Beware of Elephants.' For most of the road, you see a stunning variety of trees, as it passes through tropical forest to temperate zones with coniferous trees. But there are vast patches where the mountainsides are scabbed from the effects of clear-cutting. A plume of smoke rising up from a black patch of ground betrays the presence of a *jhum*, or shifting, cultivator clearing the ground for his very expensive crops, expensive for the trees that have to be sacrificed for them. In the jhum method, the farmers come to a patch of forest, burn all the trees in it, mix the ash into the ground, plant and harvest their crops for several years, and then move on to burn another patch of forest when the nutrients in the ground are exhausted. Over time, this can seriously affect the health of the forest, although the tribal farmers' defendants point out that this method of cultivation has been going on for millennia. The difference is that whereas in the past the jhum cycles used to be around thirty years, giving the land time to regenerate, now they are as short as four or five years. And the increased demands that the tribals make on the land, coupled with population pressures, means that the cycles get shorter and much more of the forest gets burned than before.

The effects of the tree felling are evident all along the drive, which is usually blocked by landslides in the monsoon. Groups of workers are constantly seen removing boulders which have tumbled on to the roads from mountains eroded when the trees whose roots bind the topsoil were chopped. 'Trees arrest landslides,' as another sign pointed out. On my way back, I encountered several such landslides. At one point, I got out of my car and sank knee-deep in the mud. The road had been half washed away by heavy rains. On the wrong side of such a landslide, you can get stuck for several days until the army comes out and clears the road.

Tapek Riba is a very bored forest officer. He considers his posting an enforced vacation. Riba's activities as District Forest Officer, Tawang, are limited to planting trees in the few hectares of land that the villagers are willing to part with. So he plants fast-growing species, and some exotics like rubina and horse chestnut, that he first tries out in his nursery. Tawang's problems don't come from commercial felling—it costs too much for the timber merchants from Calcutta to send their trucks up this high. Here, the main causes of deforestation are different. Riba showed me.

We drove up into the mountains, half an hour up from Tawang, in the dense fog, past a series of prefabricated army sheds; one of them had a little shrine to Shivaji. The worship of

Shivaji felt wrong for this place; the Maratha regiment had even more clearly demonstrated how out of place they were by imposing this strange god on this alien landscape.

At one point, Riba stopped the car and we got out. At first I couldn't see clearly but then I went closer and I drew in my breath. In front of me were acres of clear-felled stumps, around the remains of an abandoned army camp. The original trees must have been destroyed fifteen years ago, and now even the stumps were being hacked for firewood; they showed red-brown where the bark had been stripped off. In the mist, a solitary bird chirruped, accentuating the quiet. It was the silence of a graveyard.

As we drove along, Riba kept pointing out more and more such sites, where the army or the GREF (General Reserve Engineering Force), the equivalent of the US Army Corps of Engineers, had cleared the trees, for constructing their camps or for fuel for the machines building the mountain roads. We got out again at one spot, where Riba showed me what the mountain had previously looked like. Walking down a little, he pointed out a majestic forest of fir and juniper, tall trees standing undisturbed. 'Why have they been left alone?' I asked Riba. He pointed towards the road. It curved up and away from the forest; it is always easier to cut trees on the upward side of the road, because you can just roll them down on to the road. 'The main destruction of the forest follows the road,' he explained. 'It is . . .' he savoured the word, 'natural.' Where there is a road, poachers and timber fellers have motorized ease of access and exit. Roads kill forests.

The second great cause of the destruction of the forest near Tawang is population. According to the 1991 census, Tawang district had 28,000 people living in it. The current estimate is 40,000. The population has been swelled by outsiders, whom I saw everywhere, owning the shops and tea-stalls: Nepalis, Bengalis, Marwaris. They work harder than the tribals. But they also get colder up in the hills, and so they need more firewood. It takes seven months to get a gas connection, after which you get a cylinder of cooking gas delivered to your house every month. Firewood is cheaper and quicker to obtain. An average family, according to Riba, needs two truckloads of wood annually, eight cubic metres, which currently costs around Rs 10,000 ($232). The state government experimented with giving the tribals permits to harvest trees from the forests around their villages, for their own use. In 1995, 3000 such permits were issued. Riba laughed, remembering the scheme. 'People got permits in the names of dead people, for their pet dog, their pet cat . . .' The permits were resold to the timber merchants, and the permissible quota of trees was vastly exceeded—by about tenfold—and smuggled out by fast night trucks to the sawmills of Assam.

If the authorities subsidized cooking gas still further and made the cylinders readily available, the need for wood as a cooking fuel would be greatly lessened. But the jump in population has meant that all around the hillsides around the hamlets, the trees have been stripped, and the villagers venture further and further inside the forest to chop trees. They are supposed to gather only previously fallen logs, not chop green trees. But the necessity for conservation has not yet impressed itself on the villagers, who see the forest department as their enemy. 'Protection is very difficult,' explains Riba.

Deforestation causes landslides, which threaten the villagers' houses. He needs to impress this fact upon the villagers. But how is he to do this? 'We can't demonstrate a landslide. The effect is felt only by the next generation.' The elders understand, they remember a time when Tawang was under deep forest cover. Now the streams are dry in the summer, and flood in the rains. 'The younger generation wants the forest but they don't want the forest department,' Riba says.

That night, I had first-hand experience of the passions of

this younger generation. I was settling into my room at the tourist lodge in Tawang; I felt I had come to the last place on earth. I might have been the only tourist in town; tourism, both foreign and domestic, is minuscule in Arunachal Pradesh because of tight government controls. Behind me was the majestic seventeenth-century monastery of Tawang, the largest Buddhist monastery in India, through which the Dalai Lama had been smuggled out of China. The impassable Himalayas stretched out all around me; the rudimentary facilities of the tourist lodge confirmed for me that this was off the beaten track, that I was in a far place.

Then I heard a thumping through the wall.

I went outside into the hallway and knocked on the room next to mine. A young man opened the door, and all of a sudden the thumping took on recognizable form: it was the bass part of 'I'm a Barbie Girl.' Inside was a wild scene; the room in near-complete darkness, many couples dancing, dressed, I could see when my eyes adjusted to the darkness, in brand-new sportswear, Fila, Adidas, Nike. Bottles of booze lined tables along the walls. It could have been a club in suburban Detroit. The music was the same, the dress was the same, the poses the young people struck were the same. The young people of Tawang had rented out this room in the tourist lodge; it was the end-of-the-school-year bash, and it went on all night, the music filling the corridors of the lodge—Ricky Martin, the Macarena song, that great international parade of hit songs that last exactly one summer, but are impossible to avoid during it. We are all Americans now.

These kids are not going to be satisfied with the sedate pleasures of yak-herding in a pristine forest. They are going to want more: sneakers, stereos, motorcycles. There is no industry in Arunachal Pradesh. There is only the forest. And there are outsiders who will give them quick money for their forests. While an earlier generation gathered around a tree and propitiated it and asked its forgiveness before cutting it down, this generation, its eyes set firmly westwards, has no use for such superstition. The environment can only be protected if the whole cultural system of the people who live in it is protected.

Back in Bombay, I heard the cellphones of the businessmen go off as soon as the plane landed. Before they got off the plane, they had already begun urgently negotiating deals, making appointments. When I got into the city, it was a hot, steamy night. I drove through man-made canyons, flanked by structures in which humans lived stacked above one another like insect colonies. We are an urban species now; by the end of this century, for the first time in human history, more people will be living in cities than in villages. We have voted with our feet. Through the highways of the city cruise expensive cars drinking the blood of the earth, emitting gases that cause glaciers to melt and flood the places I've just been in. Most of the trees have long since been destroyed here, and yet this is where we all want to be, in cities like this, with one million people per square mile and the one million and first person just getting off the train from Assam. They live in vast shanty-towns, without clean water, without clean air. This is what the young people of the mountains would like to trade their rhinos, their rhododendrons, their traditional houses, their orchids for.

Early the next morning I sat in my study and looked at the rippling Arabian Sea outside, and the white clouds on the horizon were ranged in formation, peaked, massed, in my fancy, just like mountains, abodes of snow. Soon, a monsoon wind picked up, the clouds darkened, gathered, and then the whole sky was just one solid sheet of black.

GITA MEHTA

THE RIVER'S SOURCE

To the great surprise of my colleagues, I applied for the humble position of manager of the Narmada rest house. At first they tried to dissuade me, convinced that grief over my wife's death had led to my aberrant request. Senior bureaucrats, they argued, should apply for higher office. Finding me adamant, they finally recommended me for the post and then forgot me.

For several years now, thanks to the recommendations of my former colleagues, this rest house situated halfway up a hill of the Vindhya Range has been my forest retreat.

It is a double-storeyed building constructed from copper-coloured local stone, the upper floor comprising three spacious and self-contained suites which overlook the gardens, the ground floor occupied by a dining room and drawing room opening onto a wide veranda. Happily, the interiors retain their original mosaic tiles, having escaped the attentions of a British administrator who plastered the outside walls at the turn of the century, giving the exterior of the bungalow with its pillared

GITA MEHTA was born in Delhi in 1943. She was educated in India and also attended Cambridge University. Her books include *Karma Cola: Marketing the Mystic East*, *Raj*, which was her first novel, a collection of essays about India titled *Snakes and Ladders* and *A River Sutra*. In addition to writing, Mehta has also spent time as a journalist and directed several documentaries about India for BBC and NBC. She currently maintains residences in New York, London and Delhi. 'The River's Source' has been excerpted from *A River Sutra*, Penguin Books India, New Delhi, 1993.

portico and balustraded steps an air more Victorian than Moghul.

To one side of the gardens, hidden by mango trees, is a small cottage in which I live. On the other side, the gardens lead to a stone terrace overlooking the Narmada, which flows 700 feet below.

Spanning a mile from bank to bank, the river has become the object of my reflections.

A great aid to my meditations is the beauty of our location. Across the sweep of water, I can see fertile fields stretching for miles and miles into the southern horizon until they meet the gray shadows of the Satpura Hills. On this river bank towering bamboo thickets and trees overgrown with wild jasmine and lantana creepers cover the hillsides, suspending the bungalow in jungle so dense I cannot see the town of Rudra, only nineteen kilometres away, where my clerk, Mr Chagla, lives.

Poor Mr Chagla must bicycle for over an hour to reach us, but as we are without a telephone his daily return to town is vital for organizing our supplies and attending to other business. Rudra has the nearest post office, as well as a doctor who presides over a small hospital and a branch police station with four constables.

Below Rudra, visible from our terrace at the bend of the river, sprawls the temple complex of Mahadeo. At sunset I often sit on the terrace with our bungalow guests to watch the distant figures of the pilgrims, silhouetted against the brilliant crimsons of the evening sky, descending the stone steps that lead from Mahadeo's many temples to the river's edge. With twilight, the water at Mahadeo starts flickering with tiny flames as if catching fire from the hundreds of clay lamps being floated downstream for the evening devotions.

My day usually begins on this terrace. I have formed the habit of rising before dawn to sit here in the dark with my face turned towards the river's source, an underground spring that surfaces 400 kilometres to the east.

In the silence of the ebbing night I sometimes think I can hear the river's heartbeat pulsing under the ground before she reveals herself at last to the anchorites of Shiva deep in meditation around the holy tank at Amarkantak. I imagine the ascetics sitting in the darkness like myself, their naked bodies smeared in ash, their matted hair wound on top of their heads in imitation of their ascetic god, witnessing the river's birth as they chant:

'Shiva-o-ham, Shiva-o-ham,
I that am Shiva, Shiva am I.'

Then streaks of pale light send clouds of noisy birds into the sky, evoking crowds of pilgrims swarming through Amarkantak's temples for the morning worship.

By the time the red ball of the sun appears over the hills, the activity I have been imagining at the river's source becomes the reality of the rest house with the appearance of our gardeners, our sweepers, and the milkman.

After issuing instructions to the early staff, I leave the bungalow by the northern gate for my morning walk. Almost immediately I enter the jungle. Under the great trees glistening with dew—teak, peepul, silk cotton, mango, banyan—the mud path is still deserted, crossed only by bounding monkeys, leaping black buck, meandering wild boar, as if the animals are glorying in their brief possession of the jungle. On my return in two hours I will be greeted on this path by sturdy tribal women from the nearby village of Vano collecting fuel for their cooking fires.

Our bungalow guards are hired from Vano village and enjoy a reputation for fierceness as descendants of the tribal races that held the Aryan invasion of India at bay for centuries in these hills. Indeed, the Vano village deity is a stone image of a half-woman with the full breasts of a fertility symbol but the torso of a coiled snake, because the tribals believe they once ruled a great snake kingdom until they were defeated by the gods of the

Aryans. Saved from annihilation only by a divine personification of the Narmada River, the grateful tribals conferred on the river the gift of annulling the effects of snake-bite, and I have often heard pilgrims who have never met a tribal reciting the invocation

> Salutation in the morning and at night to
> Thee, O Narmada!
> *Defend me from the serpent's poison.*

The Vano villagers also believe their goddess cures madness, liberating those who are possessed.

Beyond the valley on the next range of hills is a Muslim village with a small mosque adjoining the tomb of Amir Rumi, a Sufi saint of the sixteenth century. My friend Tariq Mia is mullah of the village mosque, and most mornings I walk all the way to the village in order to chat with Tariq Mia, for the old man is the wisest of all my friends.

On my way to Tariq Mia I sometimes pause at the summit of our hill to enjoy the view. Between the eastern hills I can see foaming waterfalls where the river plummets through marble canyons into the valley below the rest house, and if I turn west I can watch the river broadening as it races toward the Arabian Sea to become seventeen kilometres wide at its delta.

A day seldom passes when I do not see white-robed pilgrims walking on the river banks far below me. Many are like myself, quite elderly persons who have completed the first stages of life prescribed by our Hindu scriptures—the infant, the student, the householder—and who have now entered the stage of the *vanaprasthi*, to seek personal enlightenment.

I am always astonished at their endurance, since I know the Narmada pilgrimage to be an arduous affair that takes nearly two years to complete. At the mouth of the river on the Arabian Sea, the pilgrims must don white clothing out of respect for Shiva's asceticism before walking 800 kilometres to the river's

source at Amarkantak. There they must cross to the opposite
bank of the river and walk all the way back to the ocean, pausing
only during the monsoon rains in some small temple town like
Mahadeo, which has accommodated the legions of devout who
have walked this route millennium upon millennium.

Then I remind myself that the purpose of the pilgrimage is
endurance. Through their endurance the pilgrims hope to
generate the heat, the *tapas*, that links men to the energy of the
universe, as the Narmada river is thought to link mankind to
the energy of Shiva.

It is said that Shiva, Creator and Destroyer of Worlds, was
in an ascetic trance so strenuous that rivulets of perspiration
began flowing from his body down the hills. The stream took
on the form of a woman—the most dangerous of her kind: a
beautiful virgin innocently tempting even ascetics to pursue her,
inflaming their lust by appearing at one moment as a lightly
dancing girl, at another as a romantic dreamer, at yet another
as a seductress loose-limbed with the lassitude of desire. Her
inventive variations so amused Shiva that he named her
Narmada, the Delightful One, blessing her with the words 'You
shall be forever holy, forever inexhaustible.' Then he gave her
in marriage to the ocean, Lord of rivers, most lustrous of all her
suitors.

Standing here on the escarpment of the hill, a light wind
cooling my body after its exertions, I can see the river flowing
to meet her bridegroom in all those variations that delighted the
Ascetic while on her banks the pilgrims move slowly towards
their destination. From this distance the white-robed men and
women seem the spume of the river's waves, and as I watch
them I wait to hear the sound of Tariq Mia's voice calling the
faithful to prayer.

AJIT BHATTACHARJEA

THE OLD MAN AND THE DAM

Every morning, Sundarlal Bahuguna clambers down the steep path from his tin-shed hut in Tehri to the huge rocks that keep the Bhagirathi river in check. There he dips his emaciated body in the ritual bath that he claims gives him strength, together with the honey and *bael* juice on which he has survived for the last few months. Springing from Gomukh above Gangotri, the sacred river passes through a deep cleft in the mountains nearby before winding through the lower Himalayan valleys to meet the Alaknanda at Devprayag where it becomes the Ganga.

Not a 100 metres from where Bahuguna bathes, the Bhagirathi foams into two diversion channels dug into the mountainside, to emerge below the cleft. It is in the space between that the foundations are being laid for the sixth-highest dam in the world. The roads scarring the mountains on both sides indicate the gigantic proportions of the proposed dam. It is designed to rise 260.5 metres above the present river-bed, creating a 42-sq-

AJIT KUMAR BHATTACHARJEA was born on 8 May 1924. He is a veteran journalist who has been an Editor with *Indian Express* and *Hindustan Times*. He was also the United Nations and US Correspondent for the *Hindustan Times*. He is the author of *Kashmir, the Wounded Valley; Countdown to Partition (of India), the Final Weeks* and *Jayaprakash Narayan, a Political Biography*. Currently he is the Director of the Press Institute of India and has been since 1995, and is also a member of the Governing Council of the Indian Institute of Mass Communication, New Delhi. 'The Old Man and the Dam' has been taken from *Outlook*, New Delhi, 26 June 1996.

km reservoir upstream in five years.

With his long grey beard and wasted body, Bahuguna looks his part, a prophet warning of disaster. He is pitting himself against the social and environmental callousness symbolized by the advancing juggernaut of the high dam. It seems a highly unequal contest; his makeshift cottage will be the first to be submerged if the waters rise. But he is supported by a wide range of groups concerned with the protection of the Himalayas and its people. Religious sentiment is also involved in a region traditionally known as the abode of the gods. Significantly, many of his workers are women.

Upstream of the cottage is Tehri, once the capital of the princely state of Tehri-Garhwal. The town accommodates 25,000 people and is studded with temples (it is on the pilgrim route to Gangotri), two mosques, schools, courts and other official buildings that recall its status in the glory days. The Maharaja's palace stands on a hilltop above the town; it, too, will be submerged if the dam is filled to capacity. Citizens are already being urged to leave; many have accepted compensation. Some were warned that they should move out this month because the lower areas may be submerged by a flood. Since even the coffer dam is yet to come up, the misinformation has estranged them further from the administration.

Further upstream is a 40-km-long valley which the reservoir will fill. Ranged on the mountainsides are the clean, low, whitewashed houses, with carved wooden lintels, that identify village Garhwal. They are comfortably spaced out on separate terraces; crime is rare. Twenty-two such villages will be entirely submerged in the reservoir; nearly 100 will be partially submerged. The staircase of green terraced fields, sculpted over the centuries, will disappear in the lower reaches. In a letter last year to Narasimha Rao, then prime minister, Bahuguna protested: 'To build my ancestral house and the fields, my mother carried earth and stones over her head. There can be no compensation for my mother's sweat.'

Bahuguna was then led to believe that Rao had agreed to appoint an independent review committee and called off his campaign. He describes his current *vrata* (fast) as an act of repentance for being taken in. He is now concentrating on securing a commitment that the government will appoint a committee, headed by Justice V.R. Krishna Iyer, to review the project in all its aspects—technical, economic, social, cultural, ecological and spiritual.

After the elections, both subsequent prime ministers wrote to Bahuguna. A.B. Vajpayee expressed his sympathy and H.D. Deve Gowda assured him that he would look into the issues he had raised 'with care and in detail soon'. Instructions have been issued to 'stay the shifting of the local population till a final decision is taken on rehabilitation'. In his reply, Bahuguna reiterated the demand for an independent review committee.

The most dramatic aspect of the Bahuguna campaign centres on the possibility of the dam collapsing in an earthquake. A placard plastered on his hut warns: 'If the Tehri dam bursts, a 260-metre high column of water would wash away Rishikesh in just sixty-three minutes; seventeen minutes later the water would reach Hardiwar.' Tehri lies in a quake-prone zone. Seismologists differ on whether the rock-fill dam structure can sustain a strong shock; many of them, including former Russian advisers, express confidence that there is no risk; others, including Vinod Gaur, former director of the National Geophysical Research Institute, fear there is.

While the earthquake threat has captured media attention. Bahuguna's concerns—as indicated in his list of subjects for review—are much wider. The mammoth project endangers the traditions, culture and social relations of the region. Individual consumerism will be encouraged at the cost of community spirit. The trees being felled and roads blasted raise serious environmental concerns. The loose, friable nature of the surface

soil is evident from numerous landslides; it is bound to increase
siltation in the reservoir. The Wadia Institute of Himalayan
Geology has warned that impounded water will further weaken
rock and soil structures.

But the official Tehri Hydro Development Corporation
quotes its own experts to counter such fears. Rs 1200 crore of
the estimated total cost of Rs 5500 crore has already been spent.
The project is designed to generate 2400 MW of badly-needed
power at a lower cost than could be generated by other means.
Delhi is tempted with the promise of additional power and 300
cusecs of water throughout the year.

However, experience has taught that such targets are seldom
attained. The upstream Maneri project, near Uttarkashi, is still
limping after twenty years. An examination of its problems,
and the real costs involved, might help in assessing the future of
Tehri.

The Tehri controversy dates back to the early 1960s, when
V.D. Saklani, a senior advocate, began the campaign against
the inundation of Tehri and eventually took the issue to the
Supreme Court. Until crippled by disease, he led the movement
against the dam. Then Bahuguna took up the cause. Saklani
remains the president of the Tehri Bandh Sangharsh Samiti.

Opinion in Tehri is divided. Many have accepted
compensation. There is an air of inevitability about the
construction of the dam that the Bahuguna campaign is trying
to counter in Gandhian style. The official forces ranged against
him are well-entrenched. Talk of corruption is widespread.

The gulf between officialdom and the people is symbolized
by New Tehri, the township constructed as part of the project.
Laid out on a range high above the valley, like the hill stations
created by the British, it is designed as a modern tourist and
official holiday resort. In publicity posters, it is described as
'the first planned mountain city of independent India'. It has
magnificent official buildings. Even the jail is fit for foreign

tourists. No money has been spared in creating a dream resort town, with a sprawling colony for officials and engineers on its slopes and the huge reservoir below, whereas the focus should have been on rehabilitation. The rows of colour-coded buildings owe nothing to local architecture or tradition. Except for a temple and clock tower, there is nothing to remind the locals of the old Tehri. They will be strangers there.

A fraction of the amount spent could have cleaned up old Tehri and made life easier in the surrounding villages. A project to pump drinking water up from the Bhagirathi to fifty villages near Pratapnagar has been dropped. It was not part of the Tehri project and did not fit its resort-style vision.

PART IV

HIGH CULTURE

KIRIN NARAYAN

WHITE-BEARERS: VIEWS OF THE DHAULADHAR

Before I ever saw the Himalayas, I knew them from my
grandmother's cupboards. In her home in Nasik where my family
visited from Bombay each vacation, Ba had two large
cupboards—a wooden one with a mirror on the front, and beside
it a grey steel Godrej safe. Neither contained her clothes, which
were always folded up in khaki-covered suitcases under her bed.
Instead, both cupboards were stocked with memorabilia from
her spiritual quests. Ba could not read, but she liked to boast
that in her cupboard she had locked up sacred texts: all four
Vedas, the Gita, several Puranas too! On the exciting occasions
that Ba brandished keys in the presence of grandchildren, her
cupboards swung open with a scent of camphor and saffron.
Inside there were indeed holy books, some covered in brown
wrapping paper. Also there were khaki cloth bags or silver *thalis*
containing packets of ashy *vibhooti*, red kumkum, dried flowers,
twisted roots, sugar balls, tiny tridents, rudraksha seeds of rare
shapes. There was bright cloth that had been offered in temples,
then returned: red and green with gold fringes, or gauzy yellow

KIRIN NARAYAN is professor of anthropology and languages and cultures at
the University of Wisconsin–Madison. She is the author of *Storytellers,
Saints and Scoundrels: Folk Narrative in Hindu Religious Teaching* (1989),
Mondays on the Dark Night of the Moon: Himalayan Foothill Folktales (in
collaboration with Urmila Devi Sood, 1997), and *Love, Stars and All That*
(a novel, 1994).

edged in silver. There were postcards and pamphlets, and framed pictures of different deities. The powers of pilgrimage places from Rameshwaram in South India, to Badrinath, Kedarnath, and Gangotri in the northern reaches of the mountains were lodged in these cupboards.

White sari pulled over white hair, slim strong arms extending in grand gestures, Ba told of different gods and goddesses she had sought out at these places and the blessings they had granted her. When she spoke of the Himalayas, she told of arduous hikes, ice *lingams*, glaciers feeding sacred rivers. All around her, as she spoke, were framed god-posters with strands of tiny electric lights looped around them. I recognized the Himalayas from Ba's cupboards immediately: behind Shiva Bhagavan! The goddesses Lakshmi and Saraswati, seated in their respective lotuses, had lakes and forests stretching around them; the goddess Durga rode her prancing tiger in what seemed to be the stainless sky. Blue-grey Shiva sat cross-legged, lost in meditation. A cobra was wrapped around his neck, a sickle moon beamed from his forehead, and ice-capped peaks rose around him.

In 1975, when I was fifteen years old, my American mother decided to take up a long-standing invitation from family friends who had a summer home in Kangra, Himachal Pradesh. My parents had separated the previous year, and all my elder siblings had gone off to college in America. My mother and I were rootless, having left our home in Bombay; we were glad for the temporary grounding of a summer invitation. We took the long train trip north in April heat. In Pathankot, we hired a cycle rickshaw to carry our luggage into a chaotic bus yard. The bus up to Kangra was jammed. The seats were hard and narrow, the windows so dusty that you had to peer through them to see out. The bus engine strained as we began our ascent, plains dust settling. The air thinned and cooled, green fields and forests opened out, and suddenly, like spectres that just might be unusually shaped clouds, there were mountains.

The Dhauladhar or 'white-bearing' range of the Western Himalayas rises at a northeastern angle above Kangra valley. The mountains are mostly about 15,000 feet, with the highest peaks at 21,000. The valley, lush and patched with fields, follows the base of the mountains for more than twenty miles at roughly 3,500 feet. Looking up from the valley, the mountains are a stunning presence of green slopes rising to granite and ice. In April, before the summer heat and rains, the mountains were still frosted white like a line-up of opulent birthday cakes.

The friends we had come across India to visit were Sardar Gurcharan Singh and his wife Chattar. They usually lived in Delhi, but for the summer they often lived in a Kangra village. They had a home here on account of Norah Richards, an Irish actress and Indian nationalist who had lived in this village for many decades, carving up her enormous estate into land for landless 'untouchables', for her old students from Lahore and for city artists to retreat to. Sardar Gurcharan Singh was one of the few artists who had actually built on the land he had received from Norah.

Like everyone else, my mother and I addressed the Singhs as 'Sardar Sahib' and 'Mummy.' They had known each other since they were teenagers, and even in their old age, they had a sparkle in each other's presence. Sardar Sahib and Mummy lived downstairs, and they gave us their upstairs room. The room had a low ceiling and shuttered windows that opened out over the fields towards the mountains. On the hedges between fields were wild roses, jasmine and honeysuckle.

Sardar Sahib had studied Japanese art pottery in the 1920s, then had established a pottery outlet in Delhi, and soon his 'Delhi Blue' pieces were sought after for upper-class Indian homes. In this village setting, we ate off plates with white and grey glazes, drank coffee or tea from distinctive mugs of different shapes, sizes and colours and were served water from a jug of the most vibrant deep blue. Our meals and tea breaks were invariably accompanied by Sardar Sahib's vigorous laugh as he told stories. He told stories of the great Kangra earthquake of 1905 that he had felt tremors from as a child in Lahore; miracles of the Sikh Gurus; the adventures of his grandchildren in England. Soon after we arrived, my mother and I were folded into his stories: attending a local feast, we were ushered into an inner room where women were crowded on a charpoi. My mother sat down too, and the bed crashed to the floor, taking all the women down with it. Sardar Sahib collapsed with laughter whenever he told this tale, throwing back his turbaned head, bristling long beard rising slightly off his chest. He regularly offered to bring my mother a sample of the milk-sweet purported to be so libidinally energising it is called *palang-tod*, 'bed-smasher'. Mummy Singh, who had perfect teeth and a naughty smile, giggled at his side.

I unpacked my books over a make-shift desk raised off the floor upstairs, and began studying each day for the school-leaving exams I would write that December. As the summer progressed, white clouds steamed up above the melting snow on the mountains. Fleshy white gardenias bloomed in the garden. During the day, we spread out our clothes to dry on the gardenia bushes. At night, Sardar Sahib walked back and forth on the pale ribbon of cement path, chanting in the darkness from the Guru Granth Sahib. On a full-moon night, his beard caught the white of the glaciers and the flowers. When there was no moon, the Milky Way clotted the sky, outlined darkly at one side with mountains. Mummy sometimes walked in the night too, chanting under her breath. She wore tight white churidars around her sturdy calves, and white netted dupattas over her shoulders. The irises of her kohl-rimmed eyes shone when they caught the light.

Sardar Sahib took us around to visit various friends, cautioning them all before they offered seats to my mother. Some were locals, like Masterji, a squat schoolteacher who worked long hours amid tin cans of rare flowers in his garden, and spoke English with a wheeze, or Shastriji, the lanky Sanskrit teacher who was renting rooms in Masterji's huge family house, and whose bed my mother had broken. Also, we visited local residents who originally had come from elsewhere.

Norah Richards, the key outsider in transforming the social life of this village, had died several years ago at a grand old age. Her house was still standing, though, a maze of adobe that echoed with stories of her giant hearing aid, her megaphone for summoning servants, her generosity, her politics, her dietary fads. Visiting the abandoned house, I felt a latecomer, shut out from a legendary era.

One of Sardar Sahib's good friends who often spoke of Norah was the painter from Punjab, Sardar Sobha Singh who lived across the village by the main road. 'GROW MORE GOOD' exhorted raised cement lettering on the outer wall of his house. Sobha Singh had flowing white locks, which he wore without a turban. He only wore white kurta-pyjama and white shoes, one of which was a platform shoe because of polio. All day he sat painting at an easel set beside his bed. The finished paintings were exhibited in the room beside him, and poster reproductions of a few favourites were sold to visitors or local people who aspired to middle-class sitting-room décor. The gallery included paintings of Sikh gurus, and scenes from Punjabi folklore, like Heer standing at the door before Ranjha, or Soni swooning beside Mehwal. A popular painting was of 'Her Majesty the Gaddin', a pretty pastoralist Gaddi woman wearing a headscarf with a lamb in her arms. There was also a painting of Norah Richards herself, looking out in a regal and mildly disapproving way at the bright acrylics featured on the walls around her. For me, her beaked nose and white ringlets conjured up Miss Havisham from the Dickens novel on my desk.

While fuzzy birds in uncannily acrylic colours hopped and twittered in the aviary outside, Sobha Singh beamed, urging us to 'take coffee' brought in on a tray with Milkmaid condensed milk. 'For toffee,' he said, pulling out a five-rupee note occasionally from the pocket of his kurta and handing it to me. Though I did not consider myself a child anymore, it overwhelmed me to be noticed.

Just down the road from Sobha Singh lived Mangat Ram. Mangat Ram also only wore white kurta-pyjama. His white hair was cropped close to his head, and he wore thick black-rimmed glasses over a kind face bleached with white patches of leukoderma. In his small house, he had many musical instruments—sitar, tablas, harmonium, tanpura, and he played them all. I sensed that unlike Sobha Singh, who had his own Ambassador car and was surrounded by soft luxury, Mangat Ram was struggling financially like my mother and me. He walked everywhere with a white *jhola* over his shoulder. He even walked to the shop one kilometre away to collect the daily paper. In his front room, Mangat Ram would chat with my mother and Sardar Sahib as I looked on restlessly, wishing there were more books on the shelf to eye. Starved for diversion, I was endlessly delighted when kind Mangat Ram once described a Quaker missionary my mother knew as a 'Quacker.' I repeated this so often that now when I see images of Donald Duck, I think of Quakers.

Everyone was waiting for the Sanyals to arrive from Delhi. They came later in the summer, and their house up the hill near Norah's was opened and aired. B.C. Sanyal was well known for his sculpture, his paintings, his drawings, and his association with the Lalit Kala Akademi for artists. He had fizzy black eyes, curling black brows, a mischievous punning wit, and a grey beard that he parted in the middle with the minute precision of George Bernard Shaw. Mrs Sanyal, who taught English at a prestigious Delhi school, chewed paan, exchanged Iris Murdoch novels with my mother, and made memorably exquisite dishes. Sanyal Sahib was usually upstairs, painting on an open-air porch that faced the mountains. It seemed a long time before we trooped up to see his oils, watercolours, and pastels of village women clustered together, ironic self-portraits, jewelled green rice fields and, inevitably, mountains.

For me, being fifteen amid so many old people was a challenge. They had all the dignity, gravity and sure humour of seasoned lives, while I was a self-conscious adolescent without a stable home, whose thin skin was continually, painfully erupting. Each morning, I methodically reviewed every subject I would be examined on. In the hot, still afternoons, I walked to the main settlement of the village to Shastriji for help with my Hindi grammar, which had been hopelessly tainted by a Bombay upbringing. Shastriji's daughter Vidhya, tall and lanky like him, with close-set dancing eyes, became my friend, the only friend my age. Some evenings we went to the stream to do laundry or sat at the deserted schoolhouse exchanging confidences. Otherwise, if I was bored with studying, I watched swallows swoop under the eaves. I read my way through all the novels on the shelves, including the Mills and Boons that were Mummy Singh's favourites. The shelves also had art books. I feasted my eyes on the reproductions of Kangra miniature paintings from the seventeenth and early eighteenth centuries, with their romantic scenes of beautiful women waiting for their lovers or setting off on a tryst with Krishna. The flowering trees, bushes, open pastures, curving streams, carved doorways, arched windows were uncannily familiar, echoing our surroundings. I found it odd, though, that the paintings never seemed to feature the Dhauladhar mountains. Sardar Sahib laughed, saying that Krishna had lived in Brindavan, where there were just hills.

'What is it like to live with such beautiful mountains?' I once asked Vidhya earnestly.

She looked up, looked back at me and laughed. 'They're just there,' she said. 'We go about all the work we have to do and we don't even notice them.'

I was startled by what Vidhya said, gathering up her family's

laundry by the stream. Was she joking or could she really mean
it? Staring out of the window from my desk, I learned how each
mountain in the Dhauladhar range had its own character, its
ridges and shades of white. I longed to know the stories of the
mountains, to imagine happenings on those high peaks. If
faraway Ba could tell stories of such mountains why couldn't
people up close do the same? Yet whenever I asked for stories or
names, nobody could answer me. The only mountain that seemed
to have its own distinctive personality to the people around me
was Parvati's peak. Parvati, from *parvat*, mountains: the daughter
of the mountains, and Shiva's wife. As the rains came and snow
melted, making new patterns of glaciers and rock, it sometimes
seemed to me, looking up from my desk, that Parvati's mountain
carried the features of a serene, smiling goddess.

In 1976, we returned for another summer and in 1978 my mother
arranged to rent a house up the hill from where Sardar Sahib
lived. By 1980, when I had encountered anthropology in college,
my curiosity about the lives of village people around us began
to jostle against my shyness. Vidhya had married, but luckily
only one village away, and she remained my emotional mainstay
for daily visits and cups of tea. I began to drop in on other
homes where my mother had ties, to sometimes write down the
songs that women sang. Partly because of my Kangra experience,
I became an anthropologist. A decade later as a young faculty
member, I returned for a year to work on women's songs and
stories.

The dialect spoken in Kangra is termed 'Pahari' or 'of the
mountains' by local people, though linguists would call it Kangri.
It is a sweet language full of 'u' sounds: 'here' is *ithu*, 'there' as
thithu, and 'a little cup for a child' a *kappu*. In the songs that
women sang, mountains very rarely appeared since the focus
was on goings-on in the joint family, rather than on scenery.

Yet wedding songs implored fathers not to give their daughters to the high and distant slopes, and ballads begged husbands not to leave wives alone in such desolate places. Here is one of the earliest songs I wrote down in a careful Devanagari script that could not quite capture the nuances of the dialect, from a young woman called Bubbly.

> *The splashing rain scares me*
> *On mountain slopes, pine trees reach out to scratch me.*
> *I don't want to be alone, take me with you,*
> *The splashing rain scares me.*
> *How can I cut fodder when insects bite me?*
> *When I go to fetch water, thorns scratch my feet.*
> *Just look at the ravine where I draw water, look at the blisters on my feet!*
> *Take me along with you, my darling.*
> *I don't want to be alone, take me with you.*
> *The splashing rain scares me.*
> *The lightning crackles, teasing me,*
> *The herdsmen on the mountains see me and laugh,*
> *Just look at the leaks in the roof, look at the dung I plaster with!*
> *Take me with you, my darling.*
> *I don't want to be alone, take me with you.*
> *The splashing rain scares me.*

Back in the Madison library, reading about Gaddi shepherds who travel with their flocks across the northern wall of the Dhauladhar between Kangra and the next valley of Chamba, I once came across another memorable song about mountains. Like the songs I had heard from Kangra village women, this wedding song also described a bride's longing for the home of her parents when she was married off to a man from a distant village.

O mother Dhauladhar,
Bend a little,
O bend a little,
On this side lies my mother-in-law's place,
On the other side lies my father's home,
Bend a little, O bend a little.
On the marriage day in a palanquin
My brother gave me a farewell
'Bathe in milk. Blossom in sons.'
My brother's wife blessed me,
My mother gave me tears,
Bend a little,
So that I may see
My parents' home.[1]

It was this song that vividly underlined to me that even as we looked north at the Dhauladhar from Kangra—mountains rising up as though at the edge of the world—surely there were also other valleys, like Chamba, where people looked south at the same range.

In 1994, my mother could no longer stand living in her rented house with dank foundations, no running water, and a hillside's icy shadow in the winter months. She moved to a sun-drenched space nearer the foot of the mountains, where her Austrian doctor friend runs a charitable clinic. In this village, we encountered new sorts of people: settlements of Nepalis who had settled there after the Gurkha invasion of 1805, and also Gaddis who no longer herded their huge flocks of sheep on annual migrations. One Gaddi Brahmin who had previously worked in the slate mine became my mother's head workman in the building of her

---

1   V. Verma, *Gaddis of Dhauladhar: A Transhumant Tribe of the Himalayas.* (New Delhi: Indus Publishing Company, 1996), p.97-98.

new adobe house. Pritam was a lanky, narrow-faced man in his early forties, with a gentle, courtly manner. He always wore a Kulu cap tight over his forehead, and he seemed to know everyone in the village.

Coming to visit my mother in her new home, I missed the mountains as I had known them. Seen up close, from their base, they were no longer familiar. I missed my friends from the old village, missed the solitude of the open pasture behind my mother's old house, where one looked out at a long flank of mountains across the horizon. At the same time, being realigned in relation to the mountains brought different angles of insight into people's lives.

From Pritam, I began to learn some of the lore of Gaddis, whose wanderings take them into steep pastures and over high passes. Of course, the hills and mountains had names, Pritam said, delighted by my question. We were driving in a van back from Chamba, and he began to point out peaks. In fact, didn't I know that the hill on which my mother's house was located was part of the domain of the serpent deity, Pakhalu Nag? Indru Nag, who controlled rain, was over on that other hill; Bhagsu Nag lived further up beyond Dharamshala, and his maternal uncle protected Dal Lake.

Pritam's family had originally lived in Brahmaur, in Chamba district, which lies across the Dhauladhar range to the north of Kangra. Pritam's forefathers were hereditary mediums for the serpent-god, Pakhalu Nag. When Pritam's great-grandfather migrated over the mountains from Chamba, he brought the deity's *sangal*, or iron rods associated with possession, with him. On route, he threw the heavy rods into a river: 'If you have energy (*shakti*), carry yourself!' he said. Later, when the family had arrived at their new home in Kangra, he shook his hand, and the iron chains came in.

At first, the temple for Pakhalu Nag was built higher up on a different hill, called Kabrutu. The family lived there and would only come down to live nearer their fields at harvest. Later, they moved down near their fields, and Pritam's father had a dream: 'No one looks after me,' the serpent-god said, 'bring me down.' Following this dream, Pritam's father took up a collection from the villagers, and a temple was built on the Toral hill. The stone image of the serpent-god with the features of a human being was made in the nearby army cantonment town.

Under Pritam's guidance, I once went to worship this serpent-god. We ordered new clothes—an orange shirt and a turban—to be stitched for him by the roadside tailor (who, Pritam assured us, knew the measurements of all the local gods). The silversmith down the road made a small silver snake that would be present at the puja and then go home with me. One monsoon morning as mists blew off the higher mountains, and the water in the ravine tumbled and foamed, I sat cross-legged in the company of a village Pandit and Pritam by a fire, making offerings to the snake-god inside, as a huddle of local children and a few fidgety goats looked on.

When Ma and I first visited Kangra, electricity was unreliable. In the monsoon, buses would pull up before fast-rushing streams, and one would have to wade across and walk the rest of the way to one's destination. There was one phone in the village. At night, satellites blinked their way across the star-clotted sky. Visiting from graduate school in the 1980s, it was hard to imagine this quiet valley connecting to the rush of freeways and the barrage of communication that framed the rest of my life.

As I write in 2001, my mother, in her new village, has just been hooked up to e-mail, and messages fly in from her most mornings. She has reliable electricity now, which can be a nuisance when neighbours across the way crank up their television as they boil morning tea. Old adobe houses are being abandoned and new cement ones, with satellite dishes like reclining umbrellas, spring up where there were once open fields. Everywhere there are tall stacks of bricks or of split river rocks that people intend to use for their flat-roofed pukka homes. With tourism having declined in Kashmir, there are more ostentatious hotels built across the valley; planes fly in to an airstrip each week, and Maruti taxi vans go honking their way along the winding roads. One tourist place advertises an 'Unavailable Bar', which my curious mother could not resist investigating: it turns out that the bar carried rare imported liquor. Some of the local people I have known for all these years like all these changes, saying that now more things are available; others lament that the wisdom from the past is being forgotten.

The old people have moved onward: Ba, Sardar Sahib, Mummy, Masterji, Sobha Singh, Mangat Ram, all gone as Norah had gone before them. I imagine them lifting up from the tops of their heads, leaving the pupa of old bodies behind to soar higher than the Dhauladhar and merge with sky. Sanyal remains an embodied inspiration: he just turned a hundred years old in March 2001, and he is still drawing.

On my wall in Madison, I have a precious watercolour of Sanyal's in which monsoon clouds rise over fields, partially obscuring the Dhauladhar. Just as Vidhya once observed that mountains merged into the background, I too often do not see the picture in the rush and scramble of my own routines. When I do stop and really notice this painting, the Himalayas rise up momentarily in Midwestern America. Rugged snow peaks with idiosyncratic characters; grand white-bearing people looking out over shifting horizons: both stand tall inside me.

JOSEPH S. ALTER

MOUNTAINS OF MILK

There is an image etched into my memory, a memory of
childhood and growing up. The memory is of the kitchen in our
family home, sometime around 1970, when my mother taught
English literature and my father was principal of Woodstock, a
Christian international school with a history firmly rooted in
colonial missionization, located on the eastern end of the Landour
community in Mussoorie. The image is of the man who delivered
our milk.

   Roughly the same time that thousands of other milkmen
from several hundred villages made their deliveries to homes,
hotels, restaurants, confectioners, tea shops and boarding schools
throughout Mussoorie, our milkman would arrive at the kitchen
door around 8.30 or 9.00 in the morning, having carried thirty
or forty litres up from his village about eight kilometres to the
north-east. Squatting on the floor—before heading off to share a
smoke, tea and some gossip with the cook and cook's helper—
he would pour out our contracted amount of milk into a pan.
The pan was then put on the stove to boil slowly for twenty
minutes before being put aside to cool. As it cooled, cream would
rise to the top. This cream signified a great deal. Most directly

JOSEPH S. ALTER teaches anthropology at the University of Pittsburgh. In
addition to conducting fieldwork in the Himalayas, he has studied Indian
wrestling, ayurveda and naturopathy. Currently, he is engaged in a
sociohistorical study of the relationship between yoga and biomedical science
in modern India. Sections of this essay are edited from Joseph S. Alter's book,
Knowing Dil Das: Stories of a Himalayan Hunter.

it revealed the quality of milk.

Our cook, along with thousands of other cooks—working for families, hoteliers, confectioners, restauranteurs and boarding school nutritionists—would often accuse the men who sell milk of 'cutting' it with water. 'What have you brought today,' he would ask, 'watery milk or milky water? Yesterday there was hardly any cream at all.' Our cook usually asked this question with a wry sense of humour. If the volume of cream dropped very low, however, my mother—along with other mothers, hotel owners, confectioners, restaurant owners and boarding school nutritionists—would ask more pointed and less enigmatically humorous questions: questions that became very serious demands for improved quality. These demands, if not met, would sometimes result in 'contract termination', particularly when the parties involved were large-volume dealers and large-contract consumers. The constant threat of contract termination produced what might be called a discourse of chronic distrust that characterized the economy of dairying, and it is this relationship of dependent distrust—with all the ambiguity that conjunction conveys—that bound together those who were relatively wealthy and those who were relatively poor; those who could afford a suite in the Savoy and pay tuition at Woodstock on the one hand and, on the other, those who went deeply into debt to buy buffaloes and invest more time and energy feeding and caring for them than they could afford.

Even though this discourse of chronic distrust often took the form of friendly banter, in terms of economics, politics and policing, dilution was very serious business. If you got caught, you could be fined and sent to prison. More often than not, however, dilution was not an exercise in profiteering deception. It was simply a practical necessity: water had to be secretly added to milk to make up for what could not be extracted from pure, unadulterated, peasant labour.

In 1980, I conducted an ethnographic study of dairying in a

village community near Mussoorie. My concern, at least in part, was to understand the economics of milk production. In conducting this study, I came to understand the extent to which the production of milk as a commodity is linked to a particular form of labour, and a strict—and highly restricted—allocation of time, material resources and energy. Milk is produced from buffaloes, and although buffaloes are expensive, the real investment is measured in terms of the hours and hours of time spent every day cutting fodder, carrying water, and delivering milk, among a host of other activities. Women and children do most of this work, and it is no exaggeration to say that the real value of the milk sold in Mussoorie—its undilutable quality—is the distillate of their collective labour on the one hand and the transubstantiation of whole forests of leaves and mountains of grass into a valued commodity on the other. Dairying is a family enterprise, but domestic modes of production and reproduction do not mix very well with the priorities of capitalism, at least at the labour end of the spectrum.

The life story of Dil Das, who sold milk to Woodstock where I went to school, illustrates this point. Dil Das's grandfather had migrated down from the high Himalayas to settle near Mussoorie in order to take advantage of the market in bamboo basket-weaving and floor coverings. His father, Gur Das, bought land on a ridge about six kilometres to the east of town and established a home called Pathreni. Gur Das was one of five brothers, and Dil Das, who was born around 1925, was the eldest of his five sons. Dil Das's father and uncles made, sold and traded bamboo baskets for storing grain, and then became increasingly involved in contract work with the Landour Cantonment Board, making refuse baskets for municipal sweepers and chattai mats for homes and offices. While weaving was their primary source of income, Gur Das and his brothers farmed relatively small plots of steep, rocky, unproductive land, producing some wheat, barley, lentils and vegetables. The family had a team of oxen to plough the fields, a few cows and several buffaloes that produced both milk and dung, the latter—when mixed in to 'dilute' the rocky ground and supplement the soil— being as valuable as the former.

During the 1930s and early 1940s, Gur Das began selling small amounts of milk. However, it was soon after Independence in 1947 that Dil Das, then a newly married young man in his early twenties, established the family business as dairying and became a large-volume contractor. For twenty years between 1955 and 1975, Dil Das sold milk to Wynberg Allen School and to Woodstock, delivering between forty and eighty litres a day. Throughout this time, he had a rotating stock of ten buffaloes, buying at least two fresh young highly productive ones each year by taking loans from each school—and also, at much higher rates of interest, from moneylenders and banks—secured against future income from sales. He was, as a result, in chronic debt.

Buffaloes are expensive, and investing in them is risky. First there is the question of breeding. The general consensus among dudh-walas is that the highest quality stock is available—if one can afford the price—from nomadic Gujjars who herd hundreds of buffaloes up into the high Himalayan pastures during the heat of the summer. A buffalo produces milk for only about five years and only intermittently throughout that period. Consequently, a dairy farmer must stagger the age and shifting productivity of his stock to ensure that a more or less standard volume of milk will be produced on a daily basis throughout the year. When a buffalo is past its prime and no longer produces milk, it becomes virtually useless. In other words, there is almost no return on the investment, other than the value of milk produced and, as a rough calculation, a single Gujjar buffalo costs about as much as the net earnings on that buffalo's yield— estimated at 6 litres a day at a price of Rs 11 a litre—over the course of ten months. Thus 'investing' in buffaloes is, in economic terms, something of a contradiction in terms since 'reproduction' is a slow and uncertain prospect—males being more or less useless in the mountains—and ageing and death exercises a form of natural control over the means of production. Buying a buffalo is the antithesis of buying and controlling land or property that will never depreciate below a basic use value level. Buying buffaloes—and doing everything that is required subsequently—is also the antithesis of selling your labour for a wage, which at least has the virtue of being linked to human energy rather than to the liquid assets and capricious productivity of a non-human animal that is difficult to control.

There is also the problem of risk. Buffaloes are very sturdy creatures, and no more or less susceptible to disease than other animals, but they are not very well suited to living in the Himalayas. In early May, when the trade in young buffaloes is at a peak in Mussoorie—as is the tourist season, and therefore the demand for milk—dudh-walas often use the road leading out from Mussoorie as a relatively safe route by means of which to bring home especially skittish young buffaloes and their new-born calves. Often these buffaloes are herded along the road well before dawn in the hope of avoiding trucks, buses and taxis. Mussoorie is located on a long, narrow ridge overlooking the Dehra Dun valley to the south and the high Himalayas to the north. There are several access roads leading into town, one coming up and out of the Jumuna valley to the west into the Library Bazaar near the Savoy Hotel, passing near several palatial estates belonging to various royal families. Another road, aside from the main highway that brings up busload after busload of tourists from the railhead at Dehra Dun, is the one that leads off to Tehri to the east. This road runs above the house where I lived and I distinctly remember waking up early to train for the annual cross-country race by running along it. Between six and eight o'clock in the morning I would run out above and beyond Pathreni, passing as many as fifty dudhwalas, some leading mules, all heavily laden with canisters of sloshing milk. For many years I lived in constant fear of running into these herds, having once watched an enormous female face off and then smash her horns into a car she had forced to stop. My fears were justified as I rounded a corner in the dark one morning and incurred the wrath of a demonic beast protecting her two-day-old calf, the only creature on earth entitled by birth to drink pure milk. With red eyes bulging and blazing and nostrils flared she charged at me as though somehow I had become the embodied object of her pure, unmitigated fury.

Perhaps it is on account of these beady red eyes and menacing horns that these wide, heavy, plodding creatures have earned a place in mythology as darkly demonic. In this and many other respects, buffaloes are the opposite of cows. In any case they are hard to control, and because they are prone to slip off narrow forest paths and fall down cliffs, in the mountains they are almost always kept securely tethered. This reduces risk but it introduces the problem of labour allocation and investment.

The maintenance of buffaloes requires cutting and hauling fodder and carrying water, two activities that figured highly in the list of daily chores performed by Dil Das's family. Although relatively nutritious, grass and oak leaves—the fodder of choice—are bulky and have a high fibre content. Consequently, buffaloes have to consume large quantities in order to get enough nutritional intake to maintain a high level of productivity— about forty kilograms of grass and leaves per day, or about four hundred kilograms for ten buffaloes. Water is absolutely essential for maintaining a regular yield of pure milk, and during the hot season from April through June, a buffalo needs to drink about forty litres per day. There is a spring located about a kilometre to the west of Pathreni, and at various times a makeshift pipe has brought water somewhat closer but it has almost always had to be transported part of the way in twenty-litre canisters. For many families, water is much further away and can entail a round trip of two kilometres climbing up and down several hundred feet in altitude.

In some ways, simple mathematics tells the story. You need the combined labour of five or six adults working four or five hours per day to provide a regular supply of fodder and water to maintain the productivity of ten buffaloes. During the 1950s and 1960s, Dil Das was able to employ the labour of his four younger brothers. In 1955, he was about thirty years old and married, with a two-year-old daughter; Ratnu was twenty-three and newly married, Sheri was about eighteen, Rukam twelve and Tara about seven or eight. At this time, Dil Das's uncles, who were only slightly older than him, were, along with their wives, also involved in caring for the buffaloes and working the fields. The family worked together as a single unit and all 'ate from the same hearth' even though they lived in different locations, some up in *chans*—hamlet cow-sheds—on the Pathreni-Donk ridge and others down in the Koldighat valley two kilometres further east.

Up until about 1970 things worked out fairly well but as they grew older Dil Das's brothers went their separate ways. Most significantly, none of them had a large enough family— which is simply to say enough children—to provide the labour necessary to produce milk on a scale that was profitable. After about 1975, Pathreni seemed to slip over the edge from a condition of endless labour to a situation in which there was little value in work. By 1985, when I recorded Dil Das's life story, there was a high degree of ambivalence in his narrative account; although extremely proud of the fact that he had been a successful, large-volume contractor, he had come to regard dairying as a kind of work that had consumed his family—each of his three wives had died in succession of the same disease, he had no sons and he had nothing of material value to pass on as inheritance. He had a tremendous amount of pride, courage and, above all, a heart and soul filled with the milk of human kindness that remained to the end—and despite material hardship—pure and uncontaminated.

While conducting research in the early 1980s, and then again while recording the life story of Dil Das—who, you might say, succumbed to the discourse of chronic distrust while struggling against his alienation from land and labour—I would often encounter young girls carrying bundles of fodder two or three times their own size along steep mountain paths. Gura, Dil Das's daughter, was never among these girls. She was only about five in 1975 when her father got rid of his last buffalo.

It was not until after I had finished researching the economy of dairying that I began to reflect on what might be called the politics of consumption. I began to ask myself not just what milk was worth in straightforward, practical terms, but what it meant to those who drank it and to those who sold it to be consumed. I began to reflect on the cultural implications of exchange, and on milk's moral value as calculated in terms that must be distilled out of the culture of post-colonial petty capitalism. In doing so, I began to reflect critically on my own place in the politics of milk consumption.

Boarding schools are such that diet is often regimented in order to accomplish the specific ideological goals that inform nutritional health. Milk, among other things, provides a crucial link in the transformation of physical well being into intellectual development. As an academic institution, one of the things Woodstock was particularly concerned with was the health of its student body. Aside from being a simple concern for basic health, various specific nutritional practices were also part of a discourse on physical, religious, and moral growth and development; an ideological compulsion to 'build the body and train the mind', as one of the school songs put it. To achieve this kind of growth and development, the boys and girls in boarding were each given a glass of warm milk every evening at nine o'clock just after an hour and a half of 'study hall', and just before the lights went out. I can clearly remember, around the time when I was ten or eleven, visiting friends in boarding and being amazed at the number of cups, and the sheer volume of steaming milk, as a hundred boys my age lined up to concoct Ovaltine, Bournvita and hot chocolate—and thereby disguise the lingering, aroma-enhanced flavour of buffalo—with their allotment of 'candy cupboard' rations sent from home.

As a young boy growing up in the relative privacy and privilege of the Principal's House, I never got—or was compelled, as many with delicate palates felt—to drink post-study hall milk. However, I was able to eat, with great gusto, various concoctions made from cream that was skimmed off the milk every morning before being whipped—with an old egg-beater whose staccato grinding rhythm I can still hear in my half dreams of waking—into a rich, thick, frothy paste; a paste which, over the years, and over apple pie, chocolate cake, brownies, pudding, and, every morning bar none, over hot porridge, and on chapatis with jam, found its way, as cholesterol, into the blood of my grandfather and older uncles who died of arterial sclerosis, and, I am sure, into the chambers and muscle walls of my own much younger heart. I was an athlete, you see: a basketball player, a soccer player, a cross-country runner and a track 'star', and the logic of the day, which often scoffed at the preaching of cautionary science, was that cream was good. In addition to tasting like heaven, it gave to those of us who ate it a kind a condensed, high energy.

If you were to walk through Mussoorie it would be simple to find any number of examples of similar nutritional practices revolving around the local consumption of milk in various forms. Halwais or confectioners, who produce scores of varieties of sweets, yoghurt and cheese, provide the best case in point. Many of the sweets are produced from milk solids which are derived when the fluid is boiled down to a pasty residue called ravari or meva. A large volume of milk produced in the villages around Mussoorie is delivered directly to these halwais where it is poured into vats and slowly boiled until most of the liquid—for milk is mostly water in any case—evaporates. There must be at least twenty confectioners on the short, half-kilometre stretch of the road through the old Landour bazaar, and in the late autumn, the steam from the vats wafts out into the street mixing with other smells, but retaining—at least for those who have lived and worked in village hamlets—a trace scent of buffalo.

Eating sweets, drinking milk, and consuming yoghurt is regarded by many as not only healthy, but also a sign of prosperity and success. In the leisure culture of Mussoorie, upwardly mobile tourists are perhaps more concerned with a public display of wealth than they are with individual health. In any case, catering to the taste of those whose status is linked to the richness of their publicly consumed diet allows many Mussoorie confectioners to thrive. Moreover, tourism creates an environment where basic needs are sacrificed to taste; where only cream and butter will satisfy the desire of those who, in striving to rise to the top, take their leisure and come up out of the heat and dust of the plains into the cool, clear, pure air of the hills.

Diwali, the late autumn festival of lights, is an occasion when themes of wealth, auspiciousness and taste are ritually woven together. It marks a key off-peak long weekend in what has come to called—by the dominant tourist industry of Mussoorie—the 'winter season'. Thousands of middle-class tourists converge on the town taking their leave from industry and government service jobs in Delhi, Meerut and Lucknow. In early November, we would walk into town from school and survey the shops along the Mall Road filled with hundreds of different kinds of brightly coloured fireworks—deep green, twine-wrapped 'A' bombs, red and gold sky rockets, black and silver roman candles, earthen fountains covered with golden paper, metre-long strings of deep red 'lady-fingers', and mountains of yellow, pink, blue and purple cherry bombs. Each stall was festooned with bright lights to enhance the display which often extended well out into the street. Usually, on the night of Diwali, my parents would take us into town to watch as the sky was filled with bursting lights and the streets seemed to shudder under the impact of huge explosions. Often, one of the stalls would catch fire when a renegade rocket went astray and before long we would all be marched off into the relative safety of a back road.

In addition to watching the fireworks and setting off a few of our own, one of the reasons for going into town was to see the fabulous displays of sweets. One of the gestures of auspiciousness and goodwill on Diwali is to give gifts of sweets to friends, colleagues and clients. To accommodate the demand, confectioners produce mountains of sweets that are put on display before being sold and wrapped up in kilogram and half-kilogram boxes. There is a degree of competition between the sweet-shop owners to see who can put on the most spectacular display.

In the late 1970s, the proprietor of Omi Sweet Shop, in Landour's Shivaji Market, would remove all the tables and chairs from the seating area in his shop, set up a floor-to-ceiling tiered construction, and fill it, top to bottom, with four or five kinds of laddoo, five or six varieties of creamy white barfi made with pistachio and almonds, rasgoolla, rasmalai, son halva, malai chop, gulab jamun, and any number of other confections arranged in gigantic, metre-high, gold- and silver-covered symmetrical mounds. Behind the tiered construction, he carefully placed full-length mirrors to give the impression that one was not looking into a sweet shop, but into an unending cavern of sparkling, precious jewels. One year, we were all invited down by the proprietor of Sindhi Sweet Shop—a place where my friends and I would spend our pocket money on a seemingly endless supply of puris, aloo sabzi and kaddu bhaji, before heading off to watch John Wayne, Sean Connery and Kirk Douglas at the Rialto Cinema or Picture Palace—to witness a breathtaking work of magical mass production: a veritable army of cooks, cooks' helpers, and other employees had cleared out all the tables, and transformed the top floor of the restaurant into a mountain of barfi: a mountain of boiled-down milk.

It is these images of Omi's opulent sweet shop and the mass production of mountains of barfi, along with a memory of nutritional lectures on the correlation of milk, strong bones, and bright, shining teeth, that keep coming to mind as I write and think about the economy of dairying and the politics of consuming milk. Milk has powerful significance, and rich nutritional value, because of being, all at once, a valuable commodity, a key symbol and a highly condensed substance. But somewhere in the mix of meaning, money and metabolism, relative value gets lost in translation. The micro-millimetre-thin gold and silver leaf that is pressed onto sweets, making richness in one domain stand for richness in another, seems to signify the way in which translation obscures and perverts value. In coming to represent health and wealth among those who consume it, milk, for those who produce and sell it, has become a fluid channel through which resources are being drained away. The commodification of dairying has meant, ironically, that very little milk is consumed by the children of those who produce it, while their labour directly contributes to the girthy status of middle-class tourists and the physical fitness of missionary youth. Disparities of wealth are, of course, depressingly common, but given the multiplex significance of milk as a vital fluid in the gastro-politics of post-colonial India, it seems that what might simply be characterized as an economic injustice is also, and more significantly, embodied as a hierarchy of health, within the core and periphery of Mussoorie's milk shed—a fact encoded in low birth weights, child mortality and the brown-haired, big-bellied somaticity of malnutrition; and brought home, with brutal simplicity, in the abject, embarrassed apologies made to me on many occasions when tea, prepared by those who produce milk, had to be served black; for we are not talking here simply about poverty, but about a hydraulics of parasitic power. Looking at Omi's mountain of milk-based sweets, or, in the Woodstock kitchen, at the trays of coloured plastic cups full of warm milk, one must inevitably conclude that there is something fundamentally wrong with the distribution of not just wealth, but also of health and a meaningful sense of self.

There is an image I have in mind, an image that has taken its rightful place in my memory next to the milkman dispensing his 'milky water' into a pan on our kitchen floor. It is an image of a ten-year-old boy cutting oak leaves with a sickle while standing on the end of a branch extending over a cliff. He is wearing a ragged, grey-brown, threadbare shirt and shorts. He is singing at the top of his lungs, laughing and joking with friends on the ground. You may make of the image what you will. But what the image is made of is what makes pure milk. It would be too simplistic and imprecise to say that this is exploitation. Perhaps it is a form of diluted, impure, adulterated labour: an enigmatic, unhealthy mix of childhood and productivity.

RAVINA AGGARWAL

LEARNING FROM MOUNTAINS

'You are a mountain, not iron, after all. I am a human, not butter, after all,' I chant to myself, staggering along the endless Fort Road that stretches from the Zorawar Fort in Leh to the main market uphill. A friend, Geshe Lobsang, taught these words to me once. He used to recite them in Lakadhi on his strenuous journeys to Shigatse, where he studied with the wise monks of Tashilhumpo monastery before the Chinese occupied Tibet. Now his mantra comes to my rescue as I rush to meet my old teacher, Aba, who is waiting for me at the Cultural Academy. The morning's chill has given way to relentless afternoon sun. I am melting like butter.

I pass by the Penguin German Bakery and peer into the Gypsy's World office that is teeming with foreign travellers who have queued inside to try their luck at the telephone lottery. Dodging stray dogs and schoolchildren with Softie cones, I turn into an area nicknamed 'Bangladesh' where stalls and shops owned by Tibetans display their various objects of desire— Chinese crockery, Japanese batteries, imported cosmetics,

RAVINA AGGARWAL teaches anthropology at Smith College, in Massachusetts. She first went to Ladakh in 1989 and her research has focused on this mountainous region ever since. Her writings deal with border politics, literature, performance, feminism and community mobilization. She is the author of a recently completed book, *Beyond Lines of Control: Performance and Politics on the Borders of Ladakh* and has translated and edited *Forsaking Paradise*, an anthology of short stories from Ladakh.

second-hand sweaters, and pirated cassettes. The insistent honking
of a diesel-powered truck drowns out other noises in the bazaar;
a zooming motorcycle almost knocks me over. 'Ladakh is
changing so rapidly,' people often say. 'Telephones, tourists,
traffic! What next?'

I reach the garish yellow archway that leads to the courtyard
of the Academy. Groups of teenaged girls and boys have gathered
there, their eyes desperately scanning a list of roll numbers on
the wall posted by the Jammu and Kashmir State Board of
Education, hoping against hope that they are among the few
who have passed the eleventh standard exams.

Pushing past these students, I run into an older man but
when I start to apologize, I stop in surprise. It is Kaga-ley, whose
house I lived in for more than three months when I was writing
my dissertation in a village I shall call Riyul. He has come all
the way to Leh to find out about his oldest son's exam result.
The education department informed him that the report was
mailed but for a year they have received no news.

Spotting the boy in blue trousers hanging back shyly by
Kaga's side, I cry out, 'Aziz! Is it really you? How tall you have
grown!'

'Say Juley, Aziz, pay your respects,' orders his father.

'Salaam, Achey Ravina,' Aziz mutters dutifully.

How formal he sounds. In my memory, he is frozen as the
child with inquisitive and cheeky eyes, posing before my camera
in the grassy patch of their garden. Najma, his older sister and
accomplice, is in the picture too, gazing intently from under her
green veil. When I was first introduced to Najma and Aziz,
fourth and fifth of Kaga's six children, they had just returned
from school. Their father, who was also their schoolteacher,
had tried to infuse a love for Urdu calligraphy in them. He had
taught them that the first principle of being a good student is
aspiring to write with beauty. 'Shall we show you how well we
can spell?' they had asked me and then proceeded to display

their skills by spelling, in perfectly formed English letters, words for body parts they were forbidden from using in polite company.

Seeing Aziz in Leh, Riyul flashes before me, especially the room in their cement and adobe house that I shared with Kaga's daughter-in-law, Amina, where a son was born to her after a long, hard night of labour. Soon after the birth, female relatives had streamed in, bearing arrows of victory in cans filled with barley grain and ibex effigies carved from dough so that the new-born would grow strong and brave. They had purified the child with smouldering twigs of pencil cedar and water hidden from the stars and skies. Elders had whispered Allah's name into his ear and brought him talismans blessed by the akhon. But neither prayers nor medicines had been able to save him and he was buried after a few months, hidden from the stars forever.

'Amina's brother—how is he?' I try to redirect my thoughts to light-hearted family stories that we shared in those days. 'Remember how obnoxious he was, riding the goats, frightening the chickens, and shooting the birds with his slingshot! And how we told him that my rucksack had bombs in it whenever he tried to touch it and . . .'

'Kids grow older and calmer,' Kaga laughs. 'He too has reformed. Some things are new, some things the same. When are you returning to Riyul? It is the mulberry season. Najma will climb the trees and gather them for you.'

'Soon, soon, inshallah.' I start to leave and then turn back to yell, 'Come for breakfast tomorrow. And bring Aziz with you.'

Aba never asks me when I am returning. He knows I will fly in with the fair weather. If not to Riyul, I will make it to Leh at least. Like Kaga, Aba is a schoolteacher and it is his family that largely bears the burden of hosting me in Riyul. I send him a message every summer when I arrive and he takes a few days off to visit me, work with me, translate for me, help me however I need to be helped. Once, I sent a note scribbled on a paper napkin with a bunch of Italian tourists from Uletokpo where my friend, Angchug, runs a magical campsite by the Indus. I sent it to the high pastures, a five-hour walk from the road, where Aba was assigned for that year. The napkin reached him somehow.

'Aba, I am here,' I had written in Ladakhi. 'Chris is with me as well. I will stay in Leh for a month. Please come.'

Four days later, Aba knocked on my door, immaculate in his goncha and woollen hat, holding a bag of delicious, dried apricot seeds he had brought for me. These seeds were from the very same trees outside his house that blossomed with white flowers every spring. I remember how the existence of those trees had astounded me the first time I entered the village. Not just the trees, but the terraced fields, the rundown medical dispensary and musical prayer wheels, the uniformed schoolchildren with slates and chalk sitting in neat rows in the schoolyard, the whitewashed monastery with the eleven-headed and thousand-armed Avalokitesvara and the mural of the goddess, Apchi, to whom the neighbourbood was dedicated. A living village amidst the mountains, virtually invisible from the road.

I am no mountain goat even though I was born under the sign of Capricorn. Unaccustomed as I was to climbing, it had taken me thirty minutes and some help to reach the flag at the entrance of the village. The villagers were also not used to strange Indians from the plains showing up in this Inner Line area. They had interrogated me thoroughly and checked my permit to make sure I was not a spy.

I had moved into Aba's house, which, like most other old houses in his neighbourhood, was connected, physically and socially, to a labyrinth of other residences. Aba was the headmaster of the secondary school in Riyul then, a scholar through and through, with a stiff, tall, bespectacled frame that could appear formidable to those who did not know him. Initially, I too thought of him as staid and exacting but gradually came to admire his sense of humour and compassion. Aba came from an unusual family. His eldest brother, with whom he shared the house, was an accomplished astrologer. A second brother had renounced the temptations of worldly life and adopted the life of a hermit before his death. His youngest brother was a well-known monk who had travelled to Europe and America. He passed on to Aba gifts such as a Polaroid camera and tape-recorder that visitors to Ladakh had sent him in return for the guidance he had provided them.

In that house, high up in the middle of the mountains, Aba had designed for himself a little study where treasures of all kinds were stored. There were periodicals, magazines, dictionaries and other written gems with pages well-thumbed and blackened from use. Aba would sit late at night in that shadowy room lit by a stone lamp, devouring dates and data from all kinds of sources. His knowledge of Ladakhi history never failed to amaze me. Besides revising and expanding the chapters of his manuscript on Ladakhi history, Aba recorded performances, copied songs from rare old books, and visited Leh once a month for a radio programme or to submit an article to *Shes-rab-zom*, the Journal of the J&K Cultural Academy. In his capacity as a schoolteacher, Aba had wandered from village to village, on foot, on horseback, and in buses, crossing the frozen Indus to reach a school in Zangskar and travelling in tents of yak wool to teach nomad children in the Chang Thang plateau. He was intimately aware of almost every mountain pass, rock inscription, and lineage in these regions of Ladakh. Even though he had not ventured beyond Srinagar at that time, his knowledge of local geography grounded him and instilled in him a deep curiosity and imaginative understanding of other places he had seen in maps and pictures.

Aba was both insider and outsider in Riyul. He cooked and cleaned, fixed his house and built new extensions to it, assisted in the fields occasionally, and made his way to school day after day, teaching social studies and Ladakhi. Yet he also looked upon the village and its inhabitants with the gaze of a detached bystander, fascinated by the spectacle of their rituals and customs, which he rendered into abstract cultural frameworks. In turn, his fellow villagers perceived Aba with a mixture of respect and condescension. When we visited other places around Riyul, he was greeted with honour and more often than not, seated at the highest rung of the visitors' line and requested to lead the dance. In one's own village, Aba would say with a sigh, nobody is valued.

Ama, Aba's wife, was his companion and his antagonist. Whereas he was a man of letters, she had received no formal education. Although her natal village was in the region of Zangskar, she coped comfortably with the culture of Riyul. While Aba usually refrained from drinking alcohol or casually dropping in to visit neighbours, Ama was always willing to exchange a cup of *chang* with friends. While Aba found gossip hard to sustain and talk of the here and now tiresome, Ama kept detailed notes on kith and kin. For the most part, Aba and I conversed in Urdu. He taught me through literary techniques, pointing to dictionaries, helping me translate, and interpreting what I did not comprehend. Ama forced me to learn Ladakhi as she spoke no Urdu. When Aba would exhibit me to his guests and boast of my ability to speak Ladakhi, Ama would shrug her shoulders and mutter that it did not seem that remarkable to her, for he spoke my language, did he not? She taught by setting an example, by demonstrating and indicating with her body when verbal communication failed. It was with her that I ventured into the fields, into the valleys and pasture grounds. And while Aba would adjust his schedule to fit mine, in Ama's case it was I who had to follow the rhythm of her movements. She tolerated my intrusion into her household with much tenderness and some exasperation, having to bear most of the burden of the chores created by the addition of an extra mouth to feed.

Noticing my paranoia of snakes, Aba would reassure me that they emerged from hibernation only in August and stayed for just one month. Ama would reprimand him for these half truths, saying that his cover-up could only frighten me further and that I should know that snakes lingered around for almost four months and that they sometimes crawled into rooms to look for birds' eggs if you left the windows open. Awareness of things as they are will make you drags-po, morally upright and strong, she would say, holding her thumb erect to indicate courage and fortitude. She reminded me of the female oracles I had observed who would force you to face the darkness in your soul in all its frightening nakedness. Aba, on the other hand, was like a Mahayana teacher, assuring a fatigued devotee that the monastery was just around the corner of the mountain, taking the demerits of lying upon himself if it would persuade the climber to fulfil her spiritual mission and reach the pinnacle. With his attitude of gentle persuasion, I overcame many hurdles.

I decided to help Aba cope with the high rate of teacher absenteeism by teaching English in the middle school. This school served both the Muslim and Buddhist segments of the village. There were five teachers for fifty students. My teaching assignment was to cover the textbooks of the seventh and eighth standards. I found that students were experts when it came to skirting craggy rocks in the high mountains, or identifying the household to which a stray sheep or goat belonged, or distinguishing hundreds of varieties of weeds from regular saplings in the field. But the system of schooling demanded a different kind of knowledge. One day, we read an excerpt from *Gulliver's Travels* that started with a shipwreck, leading to Gulliver's encounter with the Lilliputians. I went over the lesson several times but when I posed some questions about the reading, blank faces stared back at me. Finally, a student asked what a ship was. What is the ocean like, inquired another.

The region in which Riyul is located is surrounded by mountains and the Indus flows through the narrow gorge between them. Lakadhis who have travelled to the plains and visited places on the ocean often marvel at how limitless the horizon seems. The waters of the Indus in Ladakh are not navigable; it made sense that most of my students could not imagine what a ship was. So we left the books behind and went to the irrigation canals that are engineering wonders built by villagers to bring the waters of glacial streams into the fields. We tore precious sheets out of notebooks and made odd-shaped paper boats. We sailed them in the stream and with thundering sounds and swaying hands, we divined up a storm. So rapt were we in our lessons that we did not notice the presence of an irate elder until he shouted at us for polluting the canal. Upstream water is sacred; it is to be preserved for drinking. Washing or bathing in it can upset the cosmic balance and unleash the anger of the serpentine deities that inhabit the underworld, resulting in crop failures, sores, leprosy, and other such afflictions. I realized that experimental instruction was all very well but first I had a lot to learn about local philosophy.

I continued with the English lessons for a while but even though it was I who was attempting to teach the children English, I felt that it in the end it was they who helped me learn Ladakhi. So strong was their influence on me that once, when I sang a wedding song that Najma had taught me, Ali, a friend from Kargil, started laughing uncontrollably. 'You're singing just like a child,' he observed. Anthropologists, learning the rudiments of culture and language, are often compared with children but I was embarrassed and stopped singing, whereupon Ali told me a story about 'baby-talk'. During the Partition upheaval, the story went, a man was taken prisoner by the other side. For years he implored his captors to release him so that he could return to his homeland. When he was granted his wish after twenty years, he refused to go back. All through his time in captivity, he had yearned to return to hear his child's baby-talk but now his freedom meant little to him for he had lost that opportunity forever. 'That's how sweet the talk of children is,' Ali consoled me.

Tolerance and appreciation of children was a feature of Ladakhi society that stood out in virtually all aspects of life. Aba believed that a good teacher must gently coax with words, not slaps or scoldings. He delighted in my efforts to teach with field trips around the village but some of the teachers worried. What if the Block Development Officer hauled them up for not reading the book from cover to cover? I tried to conform to their concerns but soon my interest wore off. Used to teaching at the college-level, I grew impatient when my students came unprepared for their lessons. Time and temperament not being suitable, I ended my stint as a schoolteacher after a few months. Nevertheless, I am still thrilled when I run into students from that class and they remind me of the songs I had taught them to sharpen their English vocabulary—only they have hung on to the melodies and forgotten the words!

Of the students I used to teach, one or two have gone on to study in Jammu and Delhi. Some have been recruited in police, army and government jobs; others have opted for lives as farmers. For every student who has matriculated, there are two or three who never passed the tenth standard. As the high-altitude district of Ladakh grapples with modernity, education is its biggest concern. How can it be, Ladakhis want to know, that the annual passing rates are as low as 5 per cent, the lowest in the country, when the federal government spends the highest amount here per child per capita? Everyone is pointing fingers. Parents blame teachers for not meeting standards and for not attending school regularly. Teachers accuse parents of valuing education only for material reasons and students for lacking the ability and dedication to learn. Students complain that they are left completely befuddled when the medium of instruction switches from Ladakhi at home or in primary schools to Urdu and eventually English. Not speaking English, older teachers like Aba, so revered at one time, are increasingly becoming marginalized.

In the mid-nineteenth century, invading armies led by the Dogra chief, Zorawar Singh, drastically changed the monastic and feudal roots of Ladakhi life. The conquerors were soon followed by civil administrators, British officials and well-meaning missionaries who pushed their own ideas of literacy, hygiene and morality upon the natives. Like their colonial predecessors, the development policies of the Indian government and the armed forces continue to operate under the assumption that education and knowledge from urban centres will erase the backwardness of tribal and peasant societies in border areas.

In the 1950s, when Aba and Kaga were students, schools were few and access to them was difficult. Today, school buildings have been built in most villages. Repairing and maintaining them, however, is still a concern and ensuring the participation of the community yet another. In one neighbourhood of Riyul, for instance, a school was constructed at a considerable expense. But because it bordered the cremation area, most of the pupils and teachers were afraid to approach it and it remained abandoned for a long time. 'Why do you build in areas that no one will use?' I asked an engineer. 'It's not our fault,' he replied. 'This land was worthless for cultivation so it was the only area that villagers were willing to surrender.'

Unable to find meaning in the education system, farming villages often view it as an alien imposition or an external responsibility. The academic calendar only adds to this disassociation. The exam schedules of hill schools are different from schools in the plains but winter holidays in the hills are intended for the benefit of outsiders studying in private boarding schools. For locals, extended winter vacations mean that students have little to do during the icy cold months. And during the summer, when it is time to reap the harvest or find jobs as trekking guides, school becomes a low priority.

Exasperated by the ineffective performance of government schools, parents are investing heavily in private ones. But even though they admit members from all communities, private schools are fashioned along distinct religious lines. They are located away from the villages and only a small number of wealthy families can afford them. Government schools are the ones that have the potential to be truly integrative and transforming on a mass scale, if their curriculum and functioning are managed properly. This is a position also taken by some disaffected youth who are now working for education reform through non-government organizations. 'We cannot romanticize the past as if Ladakh were a museum. Nor can we blindly follow the culture of outsiders and forget our own,' I am told over and over again in the course of my interviews with groups such as LERN (Ladakh Education Research Network), SECMOL (Students Education and Cultural Movement of Ladakh) and RDY (Rural Development and You).

It is an absorbing discussion on the future of education with the founder of LERN that has kept me from being on time for my meeting with Aba. By the time I get to the Cultural Academy, Aba is passionately engaged in a conversation with some playwrights and poets. Not wanting to interrupt, I inquire about the possibility of obtaining essays on literature and education written by Ladakhi scholars. A clerk points me in the direction of an office with red carpeting and glass-panelled windows. Sitting against a backdrop of blue skies and mountains, the Academy's director and his attendants obligingly shuffle around to make a seat for me. The director is patient as usual. The

librarian is out for lunch and hasn't returned, he says. No one
has the keys to the library. Will I have a cup of tea instead?

After tea, Aba and I head off for an appointment with a
dedicated official from the State Archives who is working for
improving education and employment opportunities and for
ending social prejudice against caste-musicians who once
wandered the Himalayas on foot for their livelihood. Aba is not
one to care for caste taboos. He has many friends in the
musician's settlement and is an enthusiastic supporter of its
culture.

My day has been intense and I am not looking forward to
trekking across the Sahara for the meeting. The 'Sahara', known
to others as Leh's Polo Ground, is a route that is as frustrating
as it is breathtaking, especially on a hot summer's day. People
who traverse it end up dry, dusty and deluded, imagining they
will find relief when they see the oasis of government buildings
on the other side, only to find that it is a mirage and there is
merely more waiting in their destiny when they arrive. But as I
deliberate with Aba on whether or not we should make the trip,
another one of Geshe-la's precious sayings comes to mind. I
imagine a young Geshe in his red monk robes, hiking for the
sake of knowledge all the way to Tibet. I think of him beseeching
Dolkar, goddess of journeys, over and over again, 'Please make
my strides much longer and the mountain paths much shorter.'
Looking up at the path before me, I take a long step forward.

MONISHA AHMED

THE GOAT IN THE SHAWL

For the grass that you have just eaten, oh goat,
Give us some good pashmina.
For the water that you have just drunk, oh goat,
Give us some good pashmina.
Sit down on the grass and be still, oh goat,
So that we can take out your pashmina.

It was an evening in late June and Targyas sang this song while
he was busy combing pashmina out of one of his goats. It was
getting dark but Targyas combed slowly, careful not to hurt the
animal. He knew that a sudden harsh yank could injure the
goat, pulling at its flesh and drawing blood. Last week his
daughter, Dechen, had tugged on the comb so hard that she had
severed a goat's leg. Targyas had been unable to stop the bleeding
and eventually the animal succumbed to the injury. In a land
devoid of agriculture, pashmina goats were precious
commodities for the nomads; their fibre was a major cash crop.
Targyas could not risk that happening again.

MONISHA AHMED received her doctoral degree in anthropology from Oxford
University in 1996. The subject of her dissertation was the weaving traditions
of the nomadic pastoralists of Rupshu in Eastern Ladakh. This work is being
published as *Living Fabric: Weaving in Ladakh Himalaya*. At present she is
working on a project to document the textile arts of Ladakh. She is co-
founder of the Ladakh Arts and Multi-cultural Outreach Trust that works
with local performance artists and women's weaving organizations in Ladakh.

As he combed, Targyas wondered to whom he would sell his pashmina this year and at what price. He would like to sell to his old friend Asgar. Although Asgar did not always offer the best price, there were other advantages to doing business with him. He usually gave loans to Targyas at no interest and would help him transport his goods from Leh if he had a vehicle coming to Rupshu. Sometimes, Targyas would even stay in his house in . Choglamsar, a town near Leh. But Asgar had aged and it was likely that he might not be able to make the long and arduous journey to Rupshu. His sons did not have quite the same disposition as him and so Targyas was unsure whether or not he would trade with them.

Gathering the pashmina he had combed, Targyas twisted it tightly into a bundle and put it in his saddlebag. It was a clear night and the moon was rising behind the mountains. He stretched and gazed out at the arid landscape of the vast undulating plains of Changthang. It was here that the nomads of Rupshu lived, often camping at altitudes ranging from 12,000 to 15,000 feet, in an extreme environment where temperatures drop as low as —50°C in winter.

The nomads were camped at Norchen, and even in the dark he could discern the outline of their brown yak-hair tents as the fires burned inside and smoke gradually snaked out of the smoke-hole in the roof. Stooping at the door, Targyas entered his tent. Inside, his wife and younger brother were arguing. 'I want to eat meat,' she said, looking towards Targyas despondently. 'One of the goats is ill so let's kill it.'

'No,' replied Sonam adamantly. 'It is a young male goat and can bring us much pashmina. Pashmina brings more money than wool and we need all the money we can get.'

'But the children want to eat meat,' Tashi Dolma replied, knowing she was losing her argument.

'There is a doctor from the Animal Husbandry Department in Leh here. I will go and bring him right now. Only if he says

he can't help the animal will I kill it,' Sonam said and went off
to fetch the man.

Goats are cherished amongst the nomads of Rupshu and
though meat is central to their diet, decisions regarding their
slaughter are taken with some trepidation. A short while later
Sonam returned with the doctor, but the man reeked so strongly
of alcohol that Tashi Dolma doubted he would be capable of
giving any treatment. The doctor gave the goat an injection
and left, assuring Sonam that it would recover. Sonam decided
to wait and see what happened. The next day the goat was
feeling better; Sonam remarked that it was moving around and
eating grass. 'No meat then,' I said to Tashi Dolma and she
laughed.

Soon after Targyas finished reciting his morning prayers
and offering incense to the gods in his tent and the livestock
outside, he walked over to the chief's tent where a meeting was
being held. The men were discussing the year's prices for
pashmina and wool, as well as making arrangements for the
approaching prayer ceremony. This is an annual event in Rupshu
and usually lasts for ten days. Targyas mentioned that the Wool
Board had already announced its price for pashmina for the
current year. He had heard it on the radio. But the headman
paid no attention to his words. The Wool Board's price was of
little consequence to the nomads as the government bought less
than 10 per cent of their produce. And anyway, the headman
reminded Targyas, the word on prices is out much before the
Wool Board's announcement even reaches the radio station.
News travels via the road—up from Kashmir or Himachal.
Rupshu, unlike Kharnak and Korzok (the other two nomadic
communities in Ladakh), lies along the Leh-Manali road and
they are generally the first to hear the current year's prices.
Shrewd businessmen, they are occasionally known to take
advantage of the situation. Tashi Dechen, Targyas's neighbour,
would repeatedly boast about the time he went to Korzok when

news came in that the new rate was Rs 750 a kilo. The unsuspecting Korzokpa sold him their pashmina at a little over last year's price of Rs 325. Tashi brought the pashmina back to Rupshu and later sold it for double the price.

At the meeting, the headman fixed minimum and maximum rates for pashmina and wool, but told the men that they could decide on actual prices individually with the trader who purchased their fibre. The rule is that the sale of fibre is not allowed before the conclusion of the prayer ceremony, but in fact it does occur. Only the deals are struck, however; the fibre does not leave the camp. Luckily, Targyas did not have to bid for prices with the traders before the combing season unlike his brother in-law, Tsering Samphel, who, unwilling to wait out the uncertainty, had already struck a deal with Abdul at a little over last year's price, even before combing the fibre off the goat's back.

It had been difficult the previous year, what with the social and economic boycott that existed between Buddhists and Muslims. The nomads had always sold their pashmina to Muslim traders from Leh, who had then sold it to their Kashmiri counterparts, who took the raw material to Srinagar where it was woven into exquisite shawls. The new Buddhist traders who had emerged, encouraged by the Ladakh Buddhist Association, did not comprehend the workings of the trade. Also, they had taken advantage of the situation and forced the nomads to sell at low prices. Yet, despite the adversities of the boycott, Targyas had still managed to trade with Asgar. They had met clandestinely at night in the high passes or narrow valleys, sending messages through Tibetan friends. Of course, because of the poor visibility there had been a little cheating, even between friends. Asgar tilted the scales in his favour or Targyas mixed some dirt in his pashmina.

But now the nomads were facing new threats and unlike the boycott, these were harder to circumvent. Pashmina was entering

Ladakh from across the Tibetan border and this was affecting their price, forcing them to lower it. Traders in Leh and Kashmir claimed that this pashmina was exceptionally fine quality and wondered if it had something to do with the quality of grass in Tibet. But government officials in the Wool Board in Leh doubted its authenticity and were convinced it was mixed with other fibres.

Ironically, just as the trading season was opening, news had come to Rupshu that two trucks loaded with Tibetan pashmina had crossed into Ladakh. Unable to confirm the report, some nomads felt it was a ruse to bring down the price of pashmina just when they were negotiating a rate as high as Rs 2500 per kilogram. But what was there to grumble about! It had always been this way. As far back as Targyas's uncle, Meme Sonam, could recall, their pashmina was always considered inferior to that from western Tibet. In fact, when he was young, their pashmina was worth even less than wool. Traders from Leh wouldn't even consider buying it. They dismissed the region of Rupshu as being too close to Leh and alleged that as a result, its pashmina could not possibly be good. All this changed some forty years ago, when the border between Ladakh and Tibet closed. Now the traders were constrained to buy from them. Though Sonam was astounded by the escalating price of their pashmina, he remained sceptical as well, wondering how long this windfall would last. There was talk about the government opening the Indo-Tibetan border at Demchok, as this place had marked the territory between the two countries before 1962. If that happened, the nomads feared it would be a return to the old trade routes and, once again, their pashmina would have very little value in the Indian market.

In the past, Meme Sonam had also kept far fewer goats than his sons did today. It wasn't because he didn't like the animals. After all, they did give more milk than sheep. It was a simple case of arithmetic—wool guaranteed grain and pashmina had little value then. And besides, no one wanted to keep goats in those days because they were considered to be inauspicious animals. Shepherds had never liked them for they were difficult to tend, forcing them to walk fast in the mountainous terrain. Whenever the villagers needed to sacrifice an animal at the village shrine to their gods, it had always been a goat, never a sheep. The monastery at Korzok still offered an old goatskin at the conclusion of its prayer ceremony, though it was rumoured that in the past a goat had been sacrificed there as well. But none of the lamas living there would confirm this. Goats frequently appeared in verbal insults and the nomads abused each other saying, 'may your goat fall sick' or 'may all your goats die'.

When the prayer ceremony ended, the headman officially declared Rupshu's trading season open. Targyas and his brothers were sitting outside their tent, busy making plans about where to sell their wool and pashmina. 'Look, now the world is getting ready to get out there and sell!' Sonam commented, referring to all the activity in the camp where men were busy gathering their saddlebags and filling them with pashmina and wool, each preparing for their trading journey. Sonam was also preoccupied with collecting his saddlebags and repairing holes in them, or emptying any that were full from previous trips. Targyas then loaded them with the fibres and stitched the bags across the top, sealing them tightly. Many of the bags hadn't been used since last October, when the brothers had gone to the lake at Tsho Kar to collect salt. By evening, the brothers were ready. Their saddlebags were packed and piled, each one bearing Targyas's mark of identification—the sheep's eye. This was a pattern that Targyas had inherited from his father; he wove it into all his saddlebags. In fact, all the men had such a pattern but while the eldest son retained his father's, the other sons made marginal changes to the same pattern. These designs were particularly useful when the men travelled together on their trading journeys when as many as several thousand saddlebags may be strewn around a campsite. The pattern enabled them to easily distinguish their bags from others.

It was decided that while Targyas waited in Rupshu for Asgar to come and buy their pashmina, Sonam would set off for Thiksey with the family's wool and Nawang and Dorje would accompany Sonam for part of the way. But the younger brothers had plans of their own as well. They had decided to carry their wool as well as pashmina, and first stop in Gya, a village on the other side of the Taglang La pass. Here they would exchange their wool for barley with relatives and friends. Once that was done, they would leave the grain with a cousin in Gya and proceed to Leh with their pashmina. Finding a buyer in Leh would be a little more tedious but they commented that it could be done in the following manner: 'We'll wear our Changpa clothes, then take some goat hair and rub it all over ourselves. Then, we'll walk through the bazaar in Leh and just you watch! All the Kashmiris will come running after us and ask if we have pashmina to sell!'

As the men departed on their trading journeys, the camp was quiet and appeared deserted. There was no trace of the groups of men that usually sat around playing cards or *cho-lo* (dice) loudly, hollering as they gambled their money away. Tashi Dolma, stretching her backstrap loom out in the pen, decided it was a good time to teach her only daughter, Dechen, how to weave. After all, the girl was almost sixteen years old now and would have to get married soon. Weaving was a prerequisite for this. Look at how Namgyal Lhamo had been sent back from Kharnak by her husband after only two months of being married. What a disgrace to her family it had been! Namgyal's husband had complained bitterly, saying that she was lazy, she could not cook and, most of all, she could not weave. What use was she to him? Skilful weavers were always highly commended by others and much sought after as brides. In spite of being a mediocre weaver herself, Tashi Dolma had been lucky. She had still managed to marry two brothers. But now things were different, what with all the commercial dyes and coloured wool available in the market and the new designs that the Tibetan refugee women were so proficient in displaying! The demands on young women's weaving had increased; they were expected to display a deftness for weaving designs into carpets and blankets and an artistry for combining colours.

Dechen took her seat on the small rug in front of the loom, excited yet apprehensive, pulling her stomach in as her mother tightly fastened the belt around her waist. 'Keep your legs stretched out in front of you. That's how you maintain the tension in the warp,' Tashi Dolma said. 'And your feet must touch those stones supporting the heddle rods.'

Straining her young body, Dechen obliged her mother. The warp on the loom was for weaving *snam-bu*, the woollen fabric used in all clothing. Dechen's first attempts were clumsy and the threads would keep breaking. Tashi Dolma, who was not known for her patience, grew irritated and Dechen was relieved to see her grandmother, Abi Dolma, approaching. The old woman was more tolerant and Dechen felt it would be better to learn from her. Abi Dolma took over from her daughter-in-law who, growing increasingly restless, quickly retreated as soon as she heard her youngest son wailing.

Dechen managed to weave a few inches and then stopped to stretch her legs, relieved to hear her mother calling her for lunch. The next few days continued in much the same way for Dechen—her mother would set the loom up in the morning and then leave her fumbling at her weaving. Her grandmother would then come and help. Dechen looked longingly at Phunsog, her younger brother, as he departed with the livestock each morning. Later, she confided that she envied Phunsog going with the sheep and goats, 'I miss going herding. I long for the open space, and the freedom of doing whatever I wanted when herding. I was happy then. Here I have to sit cramped all day. My legs hurt, my back hurts. But they all say that I must learn to do this. Wait till Phunsog has to learn to weave!'

Little did she know then that he would never have to learn to weave—two years later Phunsog became a lama and lamas are prohibited from weaving.

One evening, when Phunsog returned from a long day spent herding the livestock, he had a newborn kid tucked into the front of his robe. The small goat was yelping pathetically and Phunsog explained that this was because it was hungry, 'He was born this morning, along the way, around nine. The mother took off without feeding him.' Tashi Dolma and Phunsog made desperate attempts to search out the mother and force her to feed her child, fearing the kid would die without milk. They succeeded, but while this goat survived, a few days later, another died. The family mourned her loss because she was still young and gave a lot of pashmina, in addition to milk. 'Our mother fed her old *mchod-pa* (religious offerings made from barley flour, butter and water),' Sonam said bitterly. 'We told our mother not to give it to her but she didn't listen. The goat ate too much and it was bad for her stomach. Now that she's dead, what can we do?'

A few weeks passed and Dechen's weaving was showing signs of improving, all thanks to her grandmother. But Abi Dolma's weaving was old-fashioned. She knew none of the new designs or patterns or how to weave with the new wool and cotton threads available in the market. How was Dechen to learn these? In desperation, she appealed to her aunt, Angmo, who was a highly accomplished weaver. How Dechen envied the ease with which her aunt wove, while she struggled, the threads getting entangled in her hands.

Admonishing her, Angmo retorted, 'Always keep the warp

taut and straight. Otherwise, you will give birth to an abnormal child.'

Dechen looked at her aunt, confused.

'Hasn't your mother told you about why we women weave, hasn't she told you about the importance of a woman's weaving?' Angmo asked softly. Gently patting her stomach, she continued, 'It is so that you are more desirable as a bride, so that you give birth to many children. Your weaving is a sign of your fertility. Your weaving will attract men to you. They will come to your father bearing pots of *chang* (barley beer), asking for your hand in marriage. Soon your parents will give you your *pad-rag* (turquoise-studded head-dress), to declare you are of marriageable age. You must be a reasonably accomplished weaver by then.'

'But who will teach me, my mother is not a good weaver!' Dechen exclaimed, growing anxious. 'You teach me, Aunt Angmo, you are a much better weaver than my mother. Look how fast you weave your blankets and rugs, look at the beautiful designs you weave. She can't do any of that.'

And so began Dechen's lessons with Angmo—each morning as Phunsog departed with the sheep and goats, Dechen would go to her aunt's tent. She discovered how women look at things around them, such as flowers, pieces of jewellery, and religious symbols, to draw inspiration for their designs. She learnt the difference between good and bad wool, how to discard wool that was heavy with grease, how to always choose wool with a long fibre length and plenty of curls. She learnt how to card wool, lay the warp and size it before laying it on the loom. She leant the difference between weaving fabric for a man and for a woman, the former was always thicker and made from softer wool. She learnt all the intricacies of wool and that women never wove with pashmina, despite herding the renowned pashmina goat.

Asgar had still not come and Targyas was getting anxious. Meanwhile, Sonam had returned from Thiksey where he had bartered the wool for barley with the village headman. The exchange had been at the rate of one kilo of wool for fourteen kilos of grain. Since the harvesting was still to be done, the headman had only given him a quarter of the grain from last year's stocks, promising the rest later. This made Targyas even more anxious and he reproached Sonam for not returning with all the grain or its equivalent in cash. The last time they had traded their wool with Thiksey's headman, unprecedented rains had destroyed most of his crop and he had not been able to meet his dues in grain. Instead, he had given Targyas the equivalent in money. Targyas had had to go all the way to Leh to buy grain. Grumbling about the extra effort he had been compelled to put in and the high cost of transport he had incurred, Targyas admitted, 'The best would be if someone came here with a truck full of grain and we could exchange it with our wool and be saved the trouble of taking our wool out.'

This is why Rupshu looks forward to the annual visit of Nawang Tsering, a trader from Lahaul whose forefathers have been coming here for generations. In one year, he purchases approximately 5000 kilograms of wool. In an area devoid of shops, Nawang's mobile one is a veritable delight for Rupshu. He generally spends three months there during the summer, and brings everything: tea, rice, flour, lentils, potatoes, sugar, spices, onions, velvet dresses, cotton cloth, woollen and nylon socks, dyes, playing cards, and prayer flags. In addition, Nawang also receives requests for specific articles, a silver butter lamp for someone's altar or a piece of brocade for a forthcoming wedding. He always tries to bring what he can. His makeshift tent-shop is the centre of activity: men gather there to hear the latest news and play cards, women visit to see what new fashions he has brought and ask if they can try them on, and children come with their small bundles of pashmina and wool to exchange for sweets.

Ghulam Mohammed, another trader from Leh whose father had been a former palace trader, arrived and Targyas considered selling his pashmina to him. After all, how long could he wait for Asgar? It would get difficult to store the pashmina when they moved camp and if it rained, his pashmina would get spoilt. He also needed the money to pay his share towards the construction of the new monastery at Thukje and he had to buy turquoise stones for Dechen's *pad-rag*. There was also the issue of Phunsog, who was considering becoming a lama, for which Targyas would have to give a small donation to the monastery at Dubbock to get his son admitted. But he could always delay Phunsog's entry. Usman was also giving a good price, at least double that of last year. Would Asgar give the same? The uncertainty was making Targyas anxious. Many men were selling to Usman. If he waited longer the price of pashmina might fall, then he would be doomed. He found it hard to believe when I told him about the high prices that pashmina shawls were sold for. The pictures I showed them of elegant shawls made it hard to imagine that they were woven from the same fibre that came from the backs of their goats. When they sold the pashmina, it was dirty and mixed with goat droppings, and smelt heavily of urine. Now here it was as a shawl, draped around a beautiful woman, being advertised in a glossy fashion magazine. When I lived in their camp, I had a shawl with me and Tashi Dolma marvelled at the softness of its weave and the fine embroidered pattern on the border.

It was unfair that they did not benefit from the high prices that shawls sold for, even though they got more money for their pashmina now as compared to the past. The government in Leh was proposing to set up a Pashmina Cooperative for the nomads, but traders in Leh and Kashmir had already said that they would boycott it. It was futile all around. But still there were nomads living on the Changthang, and even some families that had migrated to Leh returned because they could not cope with life there. And now that goats were the basis of a new affluence for the nomads, it was more lucrative to live the life of a nomad.

Phunsog spotted a blue Gypsy in the distance. Wasn't that Asgar's? He ran to tell his father. Quickly Tashi Dolma put a fresh pot of tea on the stove and swept the dirt off their best carpet. Relieved at last, Targyas went to receive the elderly man. Exhausted, Asgar muttered that this would probably be his last trip to Rupshu. He was getting too old to make the journey. He stayed the night in Targyas's tent, leaving early the next morning after giving a 50 per cent advance for the pashmina he had bought. The price had been fixed and soon a truck would come to take the pashmina to Leh.

Targyas was content and glad he had waited. Although it was not as much money as he had thought he would get, it was still marginally higher than what Usman had offered. Now he would be able to buy turquoise stones for Dechen. Asgar had also promised to loan him the money for Phunsog to enter the monastery at Dubbock. Targyas hadn't had much pashmina this year compared with the amount of wool, so he was pleased with the money he got. He smiled and said to me, 'If pashmina came out like wool we would all be rich'

Pleased with himself, Targyas wandered over to Nawang Tsering's tent. He would see if Nawang had any vegetables to sell. Now that he had a little money, he felt like treating his family. It was evening by the time he returned to his own tent. Nawang offered him tea and they chatted about the old days when Nawang's father had been the largest purchaser of pashmina from Rupshu but had been edged out of the business by traders from Leh who had offered the nomads higher prices.

A chilly wind blew as he walked back clutching his bag.

The mountains surrounding the campsite were washed in a golden hue from the light of the setting sun. He walked quickly, knowing his wife would be anxious and the children hungry. Clouds were gathering in the distance. A dog barked and Targyas bent to pick up a stone. A lone shepherd was returning with his flocks, probably delayed because his animals had strayed too far off in search of pasture. In a few days, it would be time to move camp; it was evident that the grass on the high pastures was decreasing as the colour of the mountaintops changed from green to brown. But in this light, it was difficult to discern.

PART V

FRONTIER DREAMS

HARISH KAPADIA

THE SAGA OF SIACHEN

Whatever the hardships,
Whatever the difficulties, let me,
Oh Allah, return there again.

—A BALTI SAYING

For every mountaineer, some areas are more attractive than others. For me, the lure of the East Karakoram worked like a magnet. I had not visited any trans-Himalayan areas until 1980. But once I found a trail there, the grey and barren valleys of the East Karakoram became my main areas of travel and climbing. What differentiated these areas from others was their rich history. Caravans had passed through for centuries; Dogra generals had conquered them and the 'Great Game' was played within their confines. Visiting this region was almost as much an intellectual pleasure as a physical achievement. Amongst all these ranges, the Siachen Glacier with its long history, high mountains and

---

HARISH KAPADIA began climbing and trekking in the range around Bombay, the Western Ghats, and first visited the Himalayas almost forty years ago. He has explored areas around the war-torn Siachen Glacier and Karakoram Pass, one of the few persons allowed to climb there. He has published twelve books based on his Himalayan experiences and has been the editor of the prestigious *Himalayan Journal* for the last twenty-five years. He was Vice-President of the Indian Mountaineering Foundation from 1997-1999 and was awarded the IMF Gold Medal by the Indian Mountaineering Foundation in 1993. 'The Saga of Siachen' has been taken from the *Himalayan Journal*, Vol. 55, 1999.

the present-day war scenario became a major attraction.

I had crossed the snout of the Siachen in 1985 for the first time, explored the Terong valley, climbed peaks and played a small part in its history. I nursed a desire to return there to reach the head of this long glacier. After a great deal of correspondence with several government departments, I got permission to trek there in 1996. We first climbed in a side valley, Terong. When we returned to enter the main glacier we received the incredible, devastating news that our permits had been withdrawn by a senior commander in the army. Reason and compromise did not work. He wouldn't budge. We protested and, following our return to Leh, the army relented. I was asked if we would go back. I refused, stating that we were civilian mountaineers for whom time and mood mattered. We could not go back to the area like soldiers under orders. A critical report followed and I spoke at different gatherings, narrating my bitter experience. I was like a hurt child. I had great respect for the Indian army and felt betrayed.

So when I applied to visit the glacier again in 1998, I was apprehensive about obtaining the clearance. There was discussion within the army about whether or not to allow us, mainly because of my criticism of the army in the past. But now there was a different general in charge. He listened to the protests and then asked two questions. 'Are we a democratic army ? And if an Indian citizen is wronged by us, does he have the right to criticize us?' He added further, 'In 1996, we were wrong in stopping the expedition when they had been given full clearance in advance.' Without pausing, he added, 'My order is not only to let them go, but give them all the support required.'

With my faith in the democratic Indian army restored, I returned to the Siachen Glacier.

For me, it was the start of another saga related to this great glacier. During the 1996 expedition, my younger son, Nawang Kapadia, accompanied me, as he had on several expeditions in the past. He had a chance to see the army in action first hand and talked to many officers, both juniors and commanders. The army life, as he saw it then, excited him enough to make up his mind to join their cadre. After going though the procedures and training, he was soon commissioned as a Gorkha officer, Lt. Nawang Kapadia. While rushing to the rescue of an injured jawan, however, he was shot and killed in Kashmir. Thus the Siachen and the Kashmir war became a tragic part of my life.

Two questions are often asked when I mention the Siachen Glacier where a war has been raging between the Indian and Pakistani armies since 1984. Firstly, if there are no human settlements there nor is any productive use being made of this area, why is the glacier so important to both countries? And secondly, what are mountaineers doing in a place where artillery shells are regularly exchanged? The answers to both questions lie in the geography and history of this glacier. It is said that a nation that does not know its geography is condemned by history. So it is imperative that issues related to this glacier are better understood.

The 72-km-long Siachen Glacier in the East Karakoram is one of the longest glaciers in the Himalayas. It has a number of peaks, side valleys and at its head lies the Indira Col, the divide between South and Central Asia. The Nubra river drains the glacier and ultimately joins the Shyok river near Khalsar. To the west lies the West Karakoram (now under Pakistani control) and towards the east is the Shyok basin, bordering China. The northern slopes of the Indira Ridge lead to the Shaksgam valley.

It is commonly believed that before the conflict started in 1984, the Siachen Glacier had been lying in quiet isolation. Given the inhospitable climate of this region, such a belief is understandable, but not true. The glacier has had visitors for a long time, both local and foreign.

In the valleys to the west of the glacier live the Baltis, who have an interesting story to tell about the Glacier, which they call Saichar Ghainri (*ghainri* is 'glacier' in Balti). They say there used to be a small Yarkandi village at the entrance of the Teram Shehr Glacier, where the Yarkandis would meet the Baltis for trade. It so happened that once some Yarkandis descended the Ghyari nala and abducted a Balti woman. Wanting to take revenge, the Baltis sought the help of a famous mullah. He gave them a *tawiz*—a talisman whose power, he said, would punish the Yarkandis. He instructed them to place it on the Bilafond La (pass) and return via a different route, through the Nubra valley. The Balti villagers disregarded the mullah's instructions and returned the way they had gone. Soon a great storm hit the Siachen Glacier and caused immense destruction. It is believed that the storm would have destroyed everything in the glacier had the mullah's directions been followed completely.

As it was, the destruction was not total and the wild roses that grew aplenty near the snout of the glacier and in the lower valleys were spared. It is these roses that give the Siachen Glacier its name: Siachen means the Place of Roses (in the Balti language, *sia* is 'rose' and *chen* is 'place of').

From the time of William Moorcroft, who passed near the glacier's snout in 1821, the existence, length and location of the Siachen Glacier had been a matter of much speculation among Western explorers. In 1848, Henry Starchy became the first Westerner to discover Saichar Ghainri; he ascended it for two miles from its snout in the Nubra valley. E.C. Ryall of the Survey of India sketched the lower part of the glacier in 1861 and ascribed to it a length of sixteen miles.

During his famous second Karakoram journey in 1889, Sir Francis Younghusband (then Colonel Younghusband) approached the area from the Urdok valley. He was seeking a crossing into the Indian subcontinent from Central Asia. Following a side valley of the Urdok Glacier, he reached the foot of the Turkestan La. He felt this pass, and not Bilafond La, as it was then believed, was the main axis of the Karakoram. In other words,

Younghusband thought that the axis along the Turkestan La (along with the nearby Indira Col) was what separated South Asia from Central Asia. Defining the actual axis thus meant that several square kilometres of territory would be added to British India at the expense of Chinese Turkestan (now Xinjiang province). Younghusband's explorer instincts were correct but since this was still uncharted terrain he could not be sure.

Younghusband's belief was confirmed in 1909 by T.G. Longstaff who, along with Arthur Névé and Lieutenant Slingsby, was the first to traverse this great glacier. They crossed over Bilafond La (or, Saltoro Pass, as Longstaff called it then) and named the glacier in the east, Teram Shehr ('Destroyed City'), in keeping with the legend of the mullah that was narrated to them by their Balti porters. The peaks there were named the Teram Kangri group. They then retreated by the same route and went down the valley and approached the Siachen Glacier via the Nubra valley. Longstaff climbed up from the Siachen snout in the south and observed the same peaks as he had identified from the Bilafond La. This was conclusive proof of the length of the Siachen Glacier and the actual location of the Turkestan La—an important discovery as it established the true dimensions of the Karakoram. What he wrote in his book *This My Voyage* is quoted often:

> 'Younghusband was a true prophet. Col. Burrand of the Survey had suspected the truth. The avalanche-swept pass, whose foot Younghusband had reached twenty years before, was on the main axis of the Karakoram range which thus lay miles farther north than had been believed. We had stolen some 500 square miles from the Yarkand river systems of Chinese Turkestan, and joined it to the waters of the Indus and the Kingdom of Kashmir.'

The next important explorers to visit the Siachen Glacier were the famous Workman couple. Fanny Bullock-Workman and William Hunter Workman were Americans who had a special interest in the exploration of the Karakoram and they focused their attention on the Siachen Glacier in the years 1911 and 1912. Entering via the Bilafond La, the Workmans camped on the glacier with a large entourage of porters and two Alpine guides. This group spent more than two months on the glacier and they climbed many peaks and visited almost all the corners of the upper Siachen. Grant Peterkin, a surveyor attached to this expedition, surveyed the glacier thoroughly and named a few peaks, including Teram Kangri, Apsarasas and Ghent. Names like Sia La, Junction Peak, Hawk, Tawiz and several others were given by this expedition. It was the Workman expedition that visited and named Indira Col after the Hindu goddess, Laxmi, one of whose many names is Indira. The general supposition that this col was christened after Indira Gandhi, who was the Prime Minister when the Indian troops captured it in 1984, is erroneous.

In 1929, Dr P.C. Visser of the Netherlands, on his fourth trip to the Karakoram, explored the two Terong Glaciers and the Shelkar Chorten Glacier, all unknown until then. In his group were Rudolf Wyss and Khan Sahib Afraz Gul of the Survey of India, who stayed in the Terong valley and completed surveying and naming the main peaks in the lower part of this great glacier. In the same year, the Italian Duke of Spoleto expedition crossed the Karakoram by the Muztagh pass and reached the Turkestan La from the north. They descended from the Turkestan La after discovering the Staghar and Singhi Glaciers.

The survey and exploration of the Siachen was completed a year later by another Italian, Giotto Dainelli. Recounting his journey up to the Teram Shehr glacier junction through the Nubra valley in the *Himalayan Journal*, Dainelli wrote:

> ...thus reaching the Siachen tongue with all my baggage, a caravan of seventy coolies and six and a half tons of food for the men, carried by an additional caravan of ponies and supplementary coolies. On the 9th of June—exactly two months after my departure from Florence—I was heading for my first depot up the glacier. I hope my English colleagues will

appreciate this rapidity of execution, which I consider a record!

(Compare this with present timings—one can reach the glacier's snout within three days from Delhi without taking a single step.)

Dainelli, with a Miss Kalau as his only companion, stayed at the Teram Shehr junction and carried out various geological surveys. He could not return by the same route owing to the flooding of the Nubra valley in the lower reaches. So he crossed over to the Rimo Glacier in the east by a 6200-metre pass which he named Col Italia.

World War II and the turmoil of Indian Independence put an end to all activities in this area for a few decades. After the Indo-China War of 1962, the entire area became 'restricted', even for Indian climbers, although it is known that some parties from Indian security agencies did visit Bilafond La.

The ambiguity about the exact delineation of the border is the cause of today's conflict. The 1949 Indo-Pakistan agreement demarcated the cease-fire line. It extended up to the point known as NJ 9842 near the Shyok River, after which the line moved 'thence north to the glaciers', leaving the boundary vague.

The one opportunity to do away with this uncertainty came during the 1972 Shimla talks. It can safely be said that there may not have been any fighting on the Siachen if, during those talks, Indira Gandhi had pressured the Pakistani Prime Minister Zulfikar Ali Bhutto to agree to demarcate the borders along the Saltoro Ridge. A desperate Bhutto had pleaded with the Indian Prime Minister that he be trusted to do this at a later date, as he did not want to antagonize his generals. '*Aap mujhpe bharosa kijiye*,' he is reported to have said.

Even as the ambiguity about the Line of Control remained, between 1972 and 1983 Pakistan promoted and permitted many foreign expeditions on the Siachen Glacier. These expeditions, accompanied by Pakistani army liaison officers, generally crossed over the Gyong La, Bilafond La or Sia La to enter the glacier, and climbed many peaks on the glacier. These climbs are the grounds on which Pakistan laid claim to the glacier. It has to be noted here that, apart from the 'political statement' these expeditions made, the teams were able to do explorations and climbs of the highest order. Peaks like Teram Kangri, Singhi Kangri and others have been climbed in the area.

During this period, the Indian army also sent three expeditions to the glacier. Two of these were led by the well-known climber, Col N. Kumar. They reached Indira Col and climbed several other peaks, including Saltoro Kangri and Teram Kangri. The fact that these expeditions (1978, 1980 and 1981) took place was made public only in 1983. The Indian government made an attempt to pass them off as mountaineering ventures but their actual intentions were pretty obvious.

Maps soon began to be published in Europe showing the extended Line of Control joining the Karakoram Pass in the east, following the Pakistani claim. These maps conceded the entire Siachen Glacier to Pakistan, and showed Pakistan and China sharing a long common border to the east of Siachen.

In 1984, Pakistan gave permission to a Japanese expedition to attempt Rimo, a peak located in a side valley east of the Siachen and overlooking parts of Aksai Chin. Such an expedition would have linked Pakistan-controlled Kashmir with China, along the historic trade route that leads to Chinese Turkestan over the Karakoram Pass. The Indian army decided to take action to prevent the expedition from proceeding, and thus began the Siachen imbroglio.

Soon after India occupied positions on the glacier, the first Indian mountaineering expedition arrived in the Siachen to counter the policy adopted by Pakistan in the past. The following year, in 1985, an Indo-British expedition (led by this writer with Dave Wilkinson) was given permission to climb Rimo peak, by approaching it from the Nubra valley in India. Our success and the international publicity generated created awareness that the area was controlled by India. In 1986, an American team reached the Indira Col.

There was one more chance for peace over the Siachen Glacier when General Zia-ul Haq and Rajiv Gandhi agreed to a ceasefire. Tensions on the glacier eased but not domestic political tensions, particularly in Pakistan. Benazir Bhutto, then in the opposition, marched in the streets with bangles on a plate for Pakistani generals. 'Wear these bangles if you cannot fight on the Siachen,' she taunted them. Unfortunately for peace in Siachen, General Zia was killed in a plane crash in 1988, Benazir came to power the next year and hostilities resumed on the glacier. One of her first official acts was to visit the Pakistani side near the Siachen Glacier.

Mountaineering on the main glacier ceased until 1996, when my team from Bombay arrived on the glacier with full clearance from the Indian government but was turned back. After protests and a critical report, however, the situation was rectified within a year and it was decided to allow Indian mountaineers on the glacier. In 1997, an Indian women's team (led by Bachendri Pal, the first Indian woman to climb Everest) traversed the glacier and stood on India Saddle, a point some seconds north of Indira Col.

It was in this situation that we returned to the glacier to complete our unfinished venture.

On 30 June, we moved to an army base camp after proper acclimatization in the lower Nubra valley. The army agreed to shift some rations and kerosene by helicopter to the middle of the glacier and to provide food at intermediate camps. By 3 July, we were ready to move up the glacier with eight Sherpas as support.

Soon we were treading on historical ground. It was a great feeling moving up the glacier once again. We passed the entrance to the familiar Terong valley in the east. We had explored it thoroughly in 1985 and again in 1996. We stayed at the northerly turn of the glacier. Several peaks rose in the south and east while to the west we saw the Gyong La valley that led to the famous pass of the same name. Many expeditions had come up to Siachen by this pass. In the next seven days, we gradually built up our supplies, moving the equipment and specialized food up the glacier over three camps. As the snow had melted, we set these camps on moraine. We were camping on rocky ground everywhere. After the third day, we saw several groups of peaks rising in the northeast. We saw the massive Singhi Kangri (7751 m), justifying its name (*Singhi*—'difficult'). In the same group was Afraj ('one who leads others') at a height of 6815 metres. We named this central peak of the glacier after Khan Sahib Afraj Gul, the Indian surveyor who visited the area in 1935 with the Visser expedition and named several peaks.

The view from the middle of the glacier was stupendous. In one sweep, we could see the upper Siachen Glacier leading to India Saddle and the Indira Col. In the east rose the gentle Teram Shehr Glacier with Junction Peak rising from the only green meadow on the edge of the glacier. To our immediate east rose the peaks at the edge of the Teram Shehr plateau. Bullock-Workman had named one of the peaks 'Laxmi'. As Lord Vishnu is the Hindu god of preservation, we chose to name some of the peaks after him: like Padmanabh (7030 m), the highest peak on the Teram Shehr Plateau. We hoped that Vishnu would protect and prevent further destruction there.

Apart from traversing the entire glacier, our expedition had two other aims. One was to reach Col Italia at the head of the Teram Shehr glacier and attempt the highest peak on the Teram Shehr plateau, Padmanabh (7030 m). A good route to approach the Teram Shehr Glacier was opposite the famous 'Kumar Camp'. A wide gully flowed down from the Teram Shehr onto the Siachen Glacier. On the right of the gully were the gentle slopes, the only green slopes in the area. These could possibly have been the site of the settlements mentioned by the Workmans.

The best way to approach the Teram Shehr Glacier was via this gully, which would have saved us the long turn-about approach. But the two-and-a-half-kilometres across the Siachen Glacier were not considered safe and we had to cross under cover of darkness to avoid the risk of being caught in the shelling from across the border.

So it was decided that with some support, Divyesh and Cyrus would attempt the peaks on the Teram Shehr plateau directly across Camp 3, which lay below. They were to follow the ridgeline of Bhujang (6560 m) that was at the edge of the Teram Shehr plateau, and then make their way to the base of Padmanabh (7030 m). Any thought of reaching Col Italia had to be given up. Throughout our stay we were always aware of being in a war-zone. There was daily artillery firing across and above our route, helicopters were flying and we met soldiers on their way down, tired and haggard. This is a very different playground for mountaineering.

In the meantime, the main team moved up the glacier, which was completely snow-bound even through the summer months. Almost thirty to forty feet of snow covers the entire glacier in winter and the temperature plunges to below minus 40 degrees C. We were visiting the glacier during the best time of the year and were in the easiest part of the glacier. Yet the cold was harsh and the hardships ahead evident. The glacier flattens out ahead of its centre. We passed a side-entrance leading to Bilafond La ('butterfly shaped glacier') in the west. This was the Lolofond Glacier (named after Dr Tom Longstaff). It was small and flat and joined the Siachen after a small expanse. The historic peak of Tawiz (6400 m) dominated the sky. To the northwest, another historic peak, Hawk (6754 m), raised its head. Thence it guided us throughout till the head of the glacier. The sight of the Saltoro Kangri peaks (7742 and 7705 m) rising above the Peak 36 glacier was unforgettable. Its sheer size and the difficulties of the rock walls on its slopes make it a challenging objective. Today,

Saltoro Kangri II (7705 m) is one of the highest unclimbed peaks in the world.

After four more camps, we were nearing the head of the glacier. There were not many serious obstacles except for a few crevasses. We walked in short marches in excellent weather. A little later, we passed another valley in the west, leading to Sia La and Convey Saddle. The Siachen Glacier was now broad and on its eastern edge rose two shapely pinnacles (Staghar Towers I and II). There was a deep notch to its south. This was Staghar Pass through which the Japanese expedition had crossed to the east to make the first ascent of Singhi Kangri. Soon we neared our goals, Sia Kangri I (7422 m) and II (7092 m), formerly known as Hardinge. Their walls were gigantic and we were under the threat of avalanches. We placed all our camps at a careful distance from them. Our last camp on the glacier was a little above the 1912 'Ridge Camp' of Bullock-Workman.

We decided to reach Turkestan La (5810 m) that lay on the head of an eastern valley. On 20 July 1998, four of us with our Liaison Officer and a Sherpa left by 6.30 a.m. Winding our way through a crevasse and going up a gentle valley, we were at the La in two hours, overlooking the Staghar Glacier. We could clearly see the eastern slopes leading down gently to the glacier and the ice-penitents of the Staghar Glacier. The view to the south included several peaks around the Singhi Kangri ridge, with Staghar Pass clearly visible. I admired the tenacity of the Japanese team that had crossed the Bilafond La and Staghar Pass in 1976, ultimately to climb the steep and sharp ridge of Singhi Kangri.

The ridge on which we were standing rose gently towards the north and a deep notch could be seen on it. This was the Turkestan La (North) which Col. Francis Younghusband wanted to reach in 1889. It is sometimes called 'Colonel's Col'. The Indira ridge leading from the foot of Sia Kangri to 'Colonel's Col' and turning south to Turkestan La (East) is the northernmost ridge of India at present and it forms a major divide between South and Central Asia. The main Indira Col (west) is located at the foot of the eastern ridge descending from Sia Kangri. It is at this exact spot that the heads of the Siachen and Urdok Glaciers meet. Records show that Col. N. Kumar's team reached this Col in 1981 and the Americans reached it in 1986. On the same ridge, a point of 6000 m is erroneously marked on the present map as 'Indira Col'. It is a steep saddle and by no stretch of the imagination can be called a 'col' (a col is the lowest point on a ridge). We proposed to call this point 'India Saddle'.

On 22 July 1998, we started at 6.30 a.m. and walked northwards over crisp snow and a gently rising glacier. After turning around the 6150-metre peak, Faiz ('one who is at the top'), we saw a wide bowl opened in front of us. Facing us was the Indira Ridge and a panoramic view. To the north was the Indira Col (West), the main Indira Col. I decided to reach this Col with Sherpa Pemba Tsering. We reached the pass after a walk of two hours. At the pass, we made a safe anchor and walked upon the northern cornices to look down at the Urdok Glacier. This beautiful flat glacier led northwards to join the Shaksgam river. Several peaks were visible but unfortunately Gasherbrum I was obscured by clouds. To the north was Chinese Turkestan where trekkers in recent years had roamed freely. Apart from this political division, we were standing on a major geographical divide too. The waters from this col drained southwards into the Siachen Glacier and the Nubra, Shyok and Indus rivers to merge with the warm waters of the Arabian Sea. Waters to the north drained into the Urdok Glacier and the Shaksgam, Yarkand, Tarim and Qyurug rivers to merge with the Lop Nor lake.

The other members of our team, Vijay Kothari, Kaivan Mistry, Vineeta Muni and Capt. Suhag, climbed towards the India Saddle. After a steep slope, where they had to use crampons, they stood on the northernmost point of India and enjoyed similar historic moments as we did. All of us gathered at the camp by afternoon. It had taken us a walk of ninety-eight kilometres on the ground and twelve days to reach the Indira Col (twenty days in all, including days for ferrying loads and resting). The glacier rose from 3550 metres to 5840 metres, a mean rise of one to twenty-six, over a distance of seventy-six kilometres (the geographical length of the glacier). Indian climbers had finally arrived on the glacier.

For the past seventeen years, soldiers of the Indian Army have been in the Siachen. The army lives on the glacier under a severe resource crunch. Supplies are taken up by helicopter but there is always a shortage of air transport, sometimes even to evacuate the injured. Under such circumstances, it is hardly surprising that the glacier is under severe environmental strain. Much of the garbage is put into crevasses or dumped on rocks and snow. In winter, all this is covered under a thick layer of snow and the entire area appears like a beautiful white sheet. But come summer, all the cans, drums and human waste come to the surface and litter is seen everywhere. The army cannot burn the garbage on the glacier; nor can it destroy it there, much less bring it down.

Some serious thinking about the ecological conditions on the Siachen Glacier needs to be done. The war has taken a heavy toll of men and material on both sides. It is an impasse in which no side seems to be gaining. The only solution to save this great wilderness is to stop the war. This is a matter for the governments of India and Pakistan to consider. As a mountaineer and lover of this glacier, I can only pray that some steps are taken to conclude this never-ending war and save the glacier from destruction. I hope that the powers-that-be will listen to the anguish of the glacier and the soldiers serving on it.

In the Balti tale, the mullah, whose tawiz had destroyed the glacier, had made another prediction: if, due to human folly, the storm did not cause total destruction of the glacier, another 'storm' may visit the glacier in a century to complete the job. This war seems to be fulfilling his prediction.

As I spent my last evening on Siachen, lovely moonlight covered the snow and the next day a blue sky extended beyond the frontiers—frontiers of people who share a similar culture, language and ethos. I could remember couplets written by poets of Pakistan and sung by artists of India. But soon enough, under the same sky, artillery shells were shooting across. Hopefully, some day soon, there will be peace on the Siachen glacier. Roses *(sia)* will grow wild, ibexes will roam and mountaineers will explore and climb freely.

SANJOY HAZARIKA

THE MIZOS, MAUTHAM AND ST. FRANCIS

Every fifty years, there comes to the Mizo Hills a beautiful but
deadly season—the flowering of its sprawling bamboo forests.
The flowering of the bamboo is *mautham*, signalling a vast
upsurge in the rat population when armies of the creatures appear,
like an evil stream out of the Old Testament, destroying crops
and food and creating near-starvation conditions. During
mautham, rats flourish and breed extensively, attracted by the
tender bamboo shoots and flowers. They feast on the bamboo
forests, on standing and stored crops and grain, stripping bare
farmlands on the hillsides.

The Mizo Hills are tough terrain. They lie at the tri-junction
of three nations: India, Burma (Myanmar) and Bangladesh. They
run in great parallel strips from north to south into Burma, their
jagged edges and crowns a dark blue in the shade of the shadows
cast by the evening sun. In the mornings, the valleys cradle

SANJOY HAZARIKA, who studied in Shillong, in London and at Harvard
University, reported for *The New York Times* out of South Asia between
1981-1996. He is an acknowledged specialist on North-East India and its
neighbourhood, makes documentary films on the region and is the author of
five books, including *Bhopal, the Lessons of a Tragedy; Strangers of the
Mist,* and *Rites of Passage* (Penguin India 2001). He was a member of
India's first National Security Advisory Council and a member of the Advisory
Panel on Decentralization for the National Commission to Review the
Working of the Constitution. He is associated with the Centre for Policy
Research, an independent think-tank in New Delhi, and runs the newly
formed Centre for North-East Studies and Policy Research.

lakes of mist, which climb their way lazily up the hillsides as the sun rises.

For centuries, the hills have done the work of sentinels, ensuring the safety of the Mizos from more powerful foes, enabling their inhabitants to see a potential enemy from a great distance. The mountain passes along the current India-Burma border also helped establish traditional trade and travel routes, with intermarriage between the Mizos and their brethren, the Chins, in what is now Burma, sharing common traditions such as language, song and dances. Few Mizos liked to travel to the hot and sticky plains (they still don't) where they had to deal with avaricious merchants and traders.

The hills also ensured that the Mizos, hunter-gatherers in earlier times, remained fit and nimble. They had to walk to get anywhere—to the nearest market, to their fields, to tend to livestock, to fetch water, to hunt. They were natural fighters, and their terrain was wonderfully suited to guerrilla campaigns, as they showed during the 1966–1986 insurgency. During the bush war with Indian troops, the guerrillas used the hills as their ally while the bamboo forest was their best cloak; they vanished into the jungles after an ambush, leaving behind a frustrated enemy, which usually vented its anger on the innocent.

The Mizos are people with a great sense of community and common sense, practical not flamboyant. They are a small group, barely seven lakhs, in a nation over a billion strong—less than one-thousandth of the Indian population. Mizoram is located in India's north-east, which is home to seven states, some 350 ethnic groups, and many insurgencies. It is part of a great tropical rainforest that plunges south-eastwards from the eastern edge of the Himalayas to the tip of the Malaysian peninsula and the Gulf of Tonkin. Seething with unrest, anger and violence, and marked also by the extraordinary beauty and simplicity of their people and landscape, these jungles sweep across six other nations: Myanmar and Thailand, Laos and Kampuchea,

Malaysia and Vietnam, and touch the fringe of a seventh, Bangladesh. Damaged by freebooters, timber contractors, marauding politicians and militants, the forests still hold within them the stories of life and death, tragedy and hope, of power, bitterness, healing and compassion. These forest communities span international borders with ease, sharing affinity even though they belong to different nationalities, bound by a social kinship that is more vital than their links with the perceived mainland— New Delhi or Dhaka, Yangon or Bangkok.

The jungles protect their own and their secrets. And one of India's most challenging insurgencies sprang from the remarkable mautham phenomenon in the jungles of the Mizo Hills, a phenomenon that is as unique as it is feared. In 1959, the mautham was particularly bad, creating near-famine conditions and desperate calls for assistance from the stricken communities. At the time, the Mizo Hills were known as the Lushai Hills and were part of the larger state of Assam, which has since fragmented into smaller provinces. Relief convoys took time to get there, battling the terrain, the jungles and muddy narrow tracks with hairpin bends, before they could reach succour to the Mizos.

It was the mautham of 1959 and the Assam government's failure to respond in time which fuelled the anger and then the alienation among the Mizos. This bitterness was channelized by a young bank clerk named Laldenga, who dreamed of a free and vibrant nation of Mizos, on the very eastern fringe of India, independent of Delhi, with Myanmar to their east and Bangladesh on their west. The near-famine lasted two years, giving Laldenga time to mobilize the bitterness among his people and form the nucleus of an insurgent movement.

When the Mizo National Front proclaimed independence in February 1966 and captured the major towns of the Mizo Hills, the Indian government, at first stunned by disbelief, reacted with an awesome display of its anger and firepower. Towns were strafed from the air, helicopters ferried troops across the rugged terrain, and villagers who had lived in their homes for generations were given a few hours to bundle their possessions together, forced into trucks and relocated elsewhere.

Many people suffered during this traumatic experience, when communities were herded together in what were called 'Regrouped Villages' or RVs. Joseph Zokunga, one of my Mizo friends, says that these were little better than prison camps, with barbed-wire fences and passes for residents and visitors. There were searchlights and soldiers on watchtowers. It was a sad and shameful chapter in India's history; but more such chapters have been written with group after group as a result of Delhi's unfailing blundering responses to their concerns.

But Joseph, of whom I just spoke, was not a friend when I first met him. His story is similar to that of many other Mizos of the time although I knew little of it. Indeed, today's young Mizos, living in what is now one of the most peaceful states of India, know too little of the harm that their people suffered at the time or the trauma visited upon earlier generations.

In the 1960s and 1970s, even at the peak of the Mizo insurgency, the militants followed a code of not harming civilians; even the families of Indian police and military officials were safe when travelling through militant-controlled land. The same was not true of their opponents and stories of torture and rape, destruction of property and illegal detentions of Mizos abounded.

I confronted that bitterness when I met Joseph. At the time, in 1970, he led one of the best-known pop groups in Shillong, then the joint capital of both Assam and Meghalaya. They were in great demand at school music and dance 'socials', the high point of the social calendar for senior classes (when teenage groups would get a chance to mingle 'officially'), fetes and major musical events. This little man with a beautiful baritone, who wore high-heeled shoes and seemed to trot rather than walk, had the girls screaming and the men beating time when he came on stage.

One day that summer, we sat next to each other in a bus bound for Guwahati, in the plains of Assam. It's a journey that I have done thousands of times over these past decades but this particular visit is imprinted in my memory. We were to catch a train from Guwahati to Bombay, en route to a student conference. We talked of general things, making conversation and assessing each other; I was in some awe of him—Joseph was older and a well-known figure in town, and I had heard him at the socials as well as pop shows in town. I knew nothing of him otherwise.

The conversation veered to his family. Until that moment, Joseph spoke in short, gruff sentences, sticking to the very basics. He came across as a brooding presence, intense and sullen. He seemed to resent speaking and even my presence. I was uneasy. But when the subject of his family came up, the words flowed in a torrent and I listened in growing horror and shame.

His father had a small radio repair shop and, like many other Mizos, was uninvolved in the politics of the time. When the revolt erupted in 1966, Joseph's father was detained along with thousands of others. He insisted that he was innocent, that he wanted to go back to his family and would they please release him. He said he knew nothing of the underground. His captors were not convinced.

Joseph was expressionless all through the telling of the story. He continued, without a flicker of anger or grief touching his countenance. 'They pushed him to the floor and then they stamped on him with their boots, they kept kicking and stamping for a long time, and he kept screaming for help.' They methodically broke his fingers, those tools used to mend transistors and radios; they damaged his ribs and his legs. They sent the old man back to his family, broken and crippled.

I am still surprised that Joseph did not join the 'underground'. God knows—he had enough reasons. Apart from the barbarity inflicted on his father, his family was among those who were regrouped and tossed into settlements surrounded by barbed-wire fences and guards. But I think that he was aware of his responsibilities as a young man and the need to support his family.

Joseph's father died some years ago, without recovering from the physical or mental trauma of those days. There was no Amnesty International accessible to them in those days, no Asia Watch; no South Asia Human Rights Forum, no South Asia Human Rights Documentation Centre. There was no National Human Rights Commission in India. So to whom could they appeal? To those who were guilty of the abuse itself? Thousands of stories about people like Joseph were never heard; the perpetrators remain unpunished.

Yet men like Joseph have overcome their hatred. That was nothing short of a spiritual rebirth for him and experiences such as these have provided a strong foundation for the state. These days, he is an assistant director at a state government-aided music academy in Aizawl, capital of Mizoram, using his magnificent voice and musical skills to develop a love of song among new generations of Mizos. He does not merely sit in classrooms in Aizawl but goes to villages to seek new talent. The Mizos are born musicians and singers. They are also deeply religious, and everything shuts down on Sundays when, Bible in hand and dressed in their best suits and dresses, men, women and children step to their community churches.

Examples of their devotion are heard and seen every evening in Aizawl and elsewhere, when church bells peal, congregations gather and sing, men and women go into religious trances to proclaim their faith. The hottest event of the year is the young faith-healer who can make the crippled walk again.

I don't know if Joseph goes to such gatherings but he is a man of deep beliefs. He's older and a bit thicker round the waist now, he drives a scooter but his walk is brisk and confident.

And I have found few experiences as exalting or touching as
listening to Joseph singing— .

> Lord, I pray thee
> Make of me
> An instrument
> Of thy perfect peace.
> Where there is hatred,
> May I bring love.
> Where there is despair,
> May I bring hope.
> Where there is darkness,
> May I bring light.
> Where there is death,
> May I bring light eternal.

Men like him have gone through trauma and tragedy. To
hear them singing of love and conquering hate is a humbling
and even troubling experience: for they have tapped a secret
which many seek but few find—the power of forgiveness. It arms
them with a unique weapon that enables them to forgive, if not
to forget what they have faced. It equips them to better understand
the world around them, share the pain of others in the region
and move forward, instead of being stuck in self-pity and trapped
by chains of hate and revenge.

It is in the telling of Joseph's story today and in my retelling
of it, that I remember my reaction to it: the horrified, shamed
silence of an ignorant teenager. Yet it is from these stories of
change that hope grows, strong and true, for they provide the
surest evidence that deep within ordinary people lies the power
to transform this venal, malignant world—or what they know
of it. For without hope can there be life?

AGHA SHAHID ALI

POEMS FROM 'THE COUNTRY WITHOUT A POST OFFICE'

1. SON ET LUMIÈRE AT SHALIMAR GARDEN

Brahma's voice is torn water:

It runs down

the slopes of Zabarvan
and Kashmir is a lake

till a mountain to its west
is pierced with a trident

and the valley drained to reveal
the One Born of Water,

AGHA SHAHID ALI was born in New Delhi on 4 February 1949. He was educated at the University of Kashmir, Srinagar and the University of Delhi. He earned a Ph.D. in English from Pennsylvania State University in 1984, and an M.F.A. from the University of Arizona in 1985. Agha Shahid received several fellowships and was awarded the Pushcart Prize. His many volumes of poetry include *Rooms Are Never Finished* (2001), *The Country without a Post Office* (1997) and *The Half-Inch Himalayas* (1987). Agha Shahid Ali died on 8 December 2001. A posthumous collection titled *Call Me Ishmael Tonight* will be published in 2003. These poems have been excerpted from *The Country without a Post Office*, W.W. Norton & Company, Inc., New York, 1997.

now easily slain.

Who was that demon
of dessicated water?

No one knows
in the drying land

where a rattle of cones
is thatching

the roofs of kingdoms.

We watch the wind.
And unhealed,

the centuries pass:

Slaves plane the mountains
with roots they carried

in trunks from Isfahan:

Spotlights lash their backs
as Shalimar blooms into

the Moghuls' thirst for
terracing the seasons

into symmetry.
In the marble summer palace,

a nautch-girl pours wine
into the Emperor's glass,

splintering the future
into wars of succession,

the leaves scattered
as the wind blows

    an era into

another dynasty's bloody arms.

2. A HISTORY OF PAISLEY

Their footsteps formed the paisley when Parvati, angry after a
quarrel, ran away from Shiva. He eventually caught up with her.
To commemorate their reunion, he carved the Jhelum river, as it
moves through the Vale of Kashmir, in the shape of paisley.

You who will find the dark fossils of paisleys
one afternoon on the peaks of Zabarvan—
Trader from an ancient market of the future,
alibi of chronology, that vain
collaborator of time—won't know that these

are her footprints from the day the world began
when land rushed, from the ocean, toward Kashmir.
And above the rising Himalayas? The air
chainstitched itself till the sky hung its bluest
tapestry. But already—as she ran

away—refugee from her Lord—the ruins
of the sea froze, in glaciers, cast in amber.
And there, in the valley below, the river
beguiled its banks into petrified longing:
(O see, it is still the day the world begins:

and the city rises, holding its remains,
its wooden beams already their own fire's prophets.)
And you, now touching sky, deaf to her anklets
still echoing in the valley, deaf to men
fleeing from soldiers into dead-end lanes

(Look! Their feet bleed, they leave footprints on the street
which will give up its fabric, at dusk, a carpet)—
you have found—you'll think—the first teardrop, gem
that was enticed for a Moghul diadem
into design. For you, blind to all defeat

up there in pure sunlight, your gauze of cloud thrown
off your shoulders over the Vale, do not hear
bullets drowning out the bells of her anklets.
This is her relic, but for you the first teardrop that you hold as you descend past flowstone,

past dried springs, on the first day of the world.
The street is rolled up, ready for southern ports.
Your ships wait there. What other cargo is yours?
What cables have you sent to tomorrow's bazaars?
What does that past await: the future unfurled

like flags? news from the last day of the world?
You descend quickly, to a garden-café:
At a table by a bed of tzigane
roses, three men are discussing, between
sips of tea, undiscovered routes on emerald

seas, ships with almonds, with shawls bound for Egypt.
It is dusk. The gauze is torn. A weaver kneels,
gathers falling threads. Soon he will stitch the air.
But what has made you turn? Do you hear her bells?
O, alibi of chronology, in what script

in your ledger will this narrative be lost?
In that café, where they discuss the promise
of the world, her cry returns from its abyss
where it hides, by the river. They don't hear it.

The city burns, the dusk has darkened to rust

by the roses. They don't see it. O Trader,
what news will you bring to your ancient market?
I saw her. A city was razed. In its debris
her bells echoed. I turned. They didn't see me
turn to see her—on the peaks—in rapid flight forever.

(*for Anuradha Dingwaney*)

3. I SEE KASHMIR FROM NEW DELHI AT MIDNIGHT

Now and in time to be,
Wherever green is worn, . . .
A terrible beauty is born.

                  —W.B. Yeats

1

One must wear jewelled ice in dry plains
to will the distance mountains to glass.
The city from where no news can come
is now so visible in its curfewed night
that the worst is precise:

                From Zero Bridge
a shadow chased by searchlights is running
away to find its body. On the edge
of the Cantonment, where Gupkar Road ends,
it shrinks almost into nothing, is

nothing by Interrogation gates
so it can slip, unseen, into the cells:
Drippings from a suspended burning tyre
are falling on the back of a prisoner,
the naked boy screaming, 'I know nothing.'

2

The shadow slips out, beckons *Console Me*,
and somehow there, across five hundred miles,
I'm sheened in moonlight, in emptied Srinagar,
but without any assurance for him.

On Residency Road, by Mir Pan House,
unheard we speak: 'I know those words by heart
(you once said them by chance): In autumn
when the wind blows sheer ice, the *chinar* leaves
fall in clusters—

　　　　　　　　one by one, otherwise.'
'Rizwan, it's you, Rizwan, it's you,' I cry out
as he steps closer, the sleeves of his *phiren* torn.
'Each night put Kashmir in your dreams,' he says,
then touches me, his hands crusted with snow,
whispers, 'I have been cold a long, long time.'

3

'Don't tell my father I have died,' he says,
and I follow him through blood on the road
and hundreds of pairs of shoes the mourners
left behind, as they ran from the funeral,
victims of the firing. From windows we hear
grieving mothers, and snow begins to fall
on us, like ash. Black on edges of flames,
it cannot extinguish the neighbourhoods,
the homes set ablaze by midnight soldiers.
Kashmir is burning:

　　　　　　　　By that dazzling light
we see men removing statues from temples.
We beg them, 'Who will protect us if you leave?'
They don't answer, they just disappear
on the road to the plains, clutching the gods.

4

I won't tell your father you have died, Rizwan,
but where has your shadow fallen, like cloth

on the tomb of which saint, or the body
of which unburied boy in the mountains,
bullet-torn, like you, his blood sheer rubies
on Himalayan snow?

                I've tied a knot
with green thread at Shah Hamdan, to be
untied only when the atrocities
are stunned by your jewelled return, but no news
escapes the curfew, nothing of your shadow,
and I'm back, five hundred miles, taking off
my ice, the mountains granite again as I see
men coming from those Abodes of Snow
with gods asleep like children in their arms.

                (for Molvi Abdul Hai)

ABDUL GHANI SHEIKH

THE WIND

We climbed halfway up the mountain and stopped to rest by a big boulder. Dawn broke and the morning light draped itself around us. I looked at my village, at the monastery on the mountain, the ruins of the old fort, the dilapidated school building where I had studied until the fifth standard, green terraced fields, rocky pastures, and narrow paths on which we had spent so many days of joy and sorrow.

My gaze came to rest on our house, hidden behind the willows and poplars. Bundles of grass and cakes of dung were arranged neatly on the roof. Our cow was at the manger, eating grass. Our horse was tethered to a peg near the garden.

My eyes skipped to the small graveyard where my ancestors were buried. Tears filled my eyes.

'Aba,' I thought, 'we are leaving you behind and going away from this village. Not with pleasure but in helplessness.'

I bade farewell in my heart, as though I was looking at my village for the last time. My wife's and daughter's eyes were

ABDUL GHANI SHEIKH is a Ladakhi historian and fiction-writer. Among his books are two collections of short stories, *Zojila ke Aar Paar* and *Do Raha*, a historical novel, *Woh Zamana*, and a romantic novel, *Di hi to Hai*, which won the Jammu and Kashmir Cultural Academy's Best Book award. His non-fiction writings include *Ladakh ki Kahani* and *Kitaabon ki Duniya*.

Translated by Ravina Aggarwal. Taken from *Forsaking Paradise: Stories from Ladakh*, Katha Press, New Delhi, 2001.

moist with tears too.

We rested for a while and started walking again. Sonam's words were echoing in our minds. I remembered him knocking softly on our door two or three hours ago, and entering the house furtively.

He looked subdued. Squatting on the bare floor, he whispered, 'Siddiq, I have bad news for you.'

We stared at his face in alarm.

'All of you must leave this house and go,' my close friend whispered.

'Don't joke like this now,' I said apprehensively.

'It's not a joke. I'm serious. Now. At this moment. Leave!'

'Why?' I shouted.

'I don't have an answer for this "Why" at this time, Siddiq.' A teardrop rolled down his cheek.

My wife and daughter began wailing. 'What have we done wrong? What crime have we committed?'

'The fault is not yours or ours. This wind has blown in from the town.'

'Who told you so?'

'Tashi did. Dorje told Tashi. Tshering told Dorje. Tashi was saying that I should not disclose this to anyone else or these people will burn his house down.'

'These people?'

'Yes. These people who have come from the town say that you must surrender one or the other. Your village or your religion! Siddiq, only humans bring such winds.'

Sonam was behaving very mysteriously. We were astonished at the sudden turn of events. The villagers had always been kind to us, so what had changed? We had lived here for three generations. Far from any harassment, it was love that we had received from everyone. They had shared our joys and sorrows with such sincerity!

'I don't believe my ears, Sonam.'

'If only it could be that way.'

Then Sonam addressed my wife, '*Achey*, this is not the time to cry. Prepare to leave now.' After a few moments, he said again, 'Leave through the mountains, Siddiq, and make for the town.'

'How shall we cross the mountains in this darkness?'

'It is dangerous to take the road,' he warned us.

Sonam rose and disappeared behind the door. He had come in like a thief and vanished like one.

We made three bundles of our clothes, useful wares, my wife's jewellery, and packed some dry bread as well. We filled the manger with hay and fodder and tied the horse to a peg near the patch of grass in the garden. We put some grass in the pen for our sheep and goats and then, crossing the stream, made for the mountains.

The yellow rays of the sun quivered over the peaks before the sun itself appeared from behind a mountain. We were only about a hundred and fifty steps away from the top when we heard the beat of drums and a sound like the buzzing of flies. Our feet were rooted to the spot. In a few moments, a crowd emerged from the grove in front of us. We managed to hide behind a boulder as the crowd marched forward. The sound of slogans reverberated in the air. I felt as though strong gusts of wind were attacking us from all four directions. Sonam was right when he said that it was only humans who brought such winds.

Five decades ago, a gale had swept in from the town, bearing the smallpox epidemic. Several lives had been lost. Many houses had been destroyed. My *abhi*, achey, and *nono* had been consumed by this gale.

Then the cool, easterly breeze had come with the message of Independence. Pleasant winds drifted into our land, spreading the light of education and offering us electricity and irrigation

water. But *this* new current was entirely different. Poisonous,
malignant wind! Never had such a wind blown into our village.
It was even more menacing and toxic than the air that carried
smallpox. That wind had taken the lives of people but had not
separated humans from humans.

From the summit we could see the crowd gradually moving
towards our house. Most of the people were strangers to me.
Then, suddenly, I saw Dorje, my neighbour, in the crowd.

'Dorje!' I called out instinctively.

'Aba, look,' my daughter shrieked. 'Azhang Sonam is also
in the procession.'

'It can't be true. Sonam would never come.'

'Look closely, Aba. The man who holds the flag, who else
is that if not Azhang Sonam?'

It was true. The man holding the flag was her Uncle Sonam.

'Look Aba,' my daughter cried out again. 'Azhang Tshering
and Azhang Tashi are also there.'

'Speak softly, Fatima,' my wife admonished.

My heart sank at the sight of my close friends marching
with the crowd.

They stopped in front of my house and their provocative
chants echoed in the mountains, creating a sinister atmosphere.
I could see Sonam, Dorje, Tshering and Tashi raising their fists
in response to every call.

Most of the people in the procession probably thought that
my family and I were hiding in the house. Many of them broke
into it when no one came out in response to the calls. Among
the intruders were Sonam, Dorje, Tshering and Tashi.

After some time, when these people stepped outside, they
were carrying things looted from my home. Sonam had taken
the gas cylinder and stove. Tashi was hauling the big copper
pot that the villagers used to borrow from me for all big feasts
and celebrations. Dorje carried something under his arm. It
looked like a carpet. Tshering cut the rope that tied the cow to

the peg and drew it away. A man took hold of the horse. Two men released the sheep and goats from the shed and led them aside. One man stumbled along under the weight of our tent, another keeled over from the burden of a trunk.

I could not believe my eyes. My wife and daughter were watching this spectacle with riveted eyes from their hiding place behind a boulder.

Had Sonam cried crocodile tears in front of us yesterday? Had Tshering, Tashi and Dorje played a trick to make me homeless? The world is full of betrayal and friends so disloyal, I thought in my heart.

I was searching for answers when I saw smoke rising from a window in my house. Within a blink of the eye, the whole house was consumed in flames. Tongues of fire touched the skies. Darkness swam before my eyes. My wife screamed.

'*Khuda ka shukr hai, Khadija*, our lives have been spared,' I uttered tonelessly.

Gradually, as the crowd dispersed, we left our hiding place and moved stealthily until we reached the summit. Sorrow had driven away all feelings of fatigue or hunger.

We finally reached the town the next day and saw several refugees like ourselves. We had no further news of the state of our fields, gardens, grain, or cattle. All links with our village were totally shattered.

Two months passed in this manner. One day, in the town, I saw Sonam approaching me. Hatred swelled in my heart and blood rushed to my eyes.

'What else have you come to take, Sonam?' I turned my face away as he came up to me.

'Siddiq, I regret that we could not save your house and all your possessions. We tried very hard to stop those people from setting your house on fire but our efforts were to no avail. But your gas cylinder and stove are with me. Tashi has your pot. Dorje has saved two of your carpets. Tshering is looking after your cow. That night, we went back quietly to your half-burned house. We recovered some pots and pans and two bags of grain, which we have kept safely. All these things with us are your possessions. We are waiting for the day when you will return to the village, my friend. My Angmo and Dorje's wife, Dolma, say that the village seems desolate without Fatima and Khadija.'

Was it the morning wind or the fragrant evening breeze? After a long time, I felt the clear air surround me.

ACKNOWLEDGEMENTS

Grateful acknowledgement is made to the following for permission to reprint copyright material:

HarperCollins Publishers for the extract from *Touching My Father's Soul: A Sherpa's Journey to the Top of Everest* by Jamling Tenzing Norgay;

Oxford University Press for the extract from *Cheetal Walk: Living in the Wilderness* by E.R.C. Davidar;

IndiaInk and Gillon Aitken Associates for the extract from *The Everest Hotel* by I. Allan Sealy;

Penguin Books India for the extract from *Rain in the Mountains: Notes from the Himalayas* by Ruskin Bond;

Outlook for the extract 'The Old Man and the Dam' by Ajit Bhattacharjea;

W.W. Norton & Company, Inc. and Ravi Dayal Publishers for the poems from *The Country without a Post Office* by Agha Shahid Ali;

Rogers, Coleridge & White Ltd and Penguin Books India for the extract from *A River Sutra* by Gita Mehta;

Penguin Books India for the extract from *The Book of Shadows* by Namita Gokhale;

Katha Press for the extract from *Forsaking Paradise: Stories from Ladakh* translated by Ravina Aggarwal;

The Himalayan Journal, Vol. 55 for the piece 'The Saga of Siachen' by Harish Kapadia.